THE GOSPEL OF ADAM

David L Bishop

ISBN: 0692314431
ISBN 13: 9780692314432

In Memory of my father

Neil E Bishop

PROLOGUE

I had warned him. I had even begged him to trust me and to simply stay home. Of all the moments I wish I could do again in my life, that night will always rank in my top five. If only he had listened to me that night and stayed home, then I know the world would be a better place for everybody today.

I remember that April night very well. I had left his office with an uneasy feeling in my gut. I wanted to believe he would heed my advice and things would continue as planned for days and weeks to come. Despite my desire to trust him I kept running through his parting words as I had bid him good night. He had not told me he was staying home, as he knew I wanted to hear. In fact, he had gone out of his way to avoid saying anything close to those words. Still, I wanted everything to work out so he would be safe. In the years before that fateful night, he had always surprised and impressed me with his ability to find the right path. Yes, he had often listened to my advice; but when he flat-out ignored me, he still found his way to a good result. Knowing of his abilities helped to fuel my hope that everything would actually be fine the next day. Ironically, had I just gone back to my own home that night, I would have drifted off to sleep with that expectation.

Instead of heading straight home to sleep, that uneasy feeling led me to stop for a drink. Even after a few shots of whiskey, I immediately recognized some of the voices coming from the table in the corner. I rounded the bar, and my stomach dropped. Sitting at the table, quite drunk, was the majority of the security team for upper level government leaders. At that moment, emotion overtook me. I grabbed the shirt collar of the man closest to me, a man whose name I sadly never did learn, and demanded to know why they were not on duty. I don't know if it was their level of intoxication or my rarely seen outburst of emotion that had them all so flustered, but no answers came for what seemed like hours. In reality only a matter of seconds passed; but after the whispers I had heard concerning an upcoming plot, every second they wasted felt like hours to me. Finally they told me that they had been preparing for security duty that night when they received orders giving them the night off instead. They were simply using the change in plans to enjoy some drinks and relax.

As soon as I heard this, I went numb. I wanted to scream at them for being so stupid as to abandon their posts, but I knew it wasn't actually their fault. They were simply following orders and probably assumed that other security arrangements had been made for the night. Even though they had done nothing wrong, they could see by my face that something bad was going on, at least in part due to their actions. Before they could begin to make excuses, I dropped the man I was still holding and turned to run out of the bar, hoping I still had time to prevent a disaster.

I bumped into several men as I ran out of the bar. To be honest, it was more like running over them, but I didn't have time to care about being polite. I simply knew that I had to hurry if I was going to save him. I knew for certain, after seeing the security team at the bar, he hadn't stayed home like I had begged him to do. If he had, there would have been no reason for the orders cancelling all of the security detail. The fact that the men were not all on the same watch left me no doubt that this was part of a sinister plan.

I had felt certain just a day earlier that everything was on the verge of helping me achieve my goal and find my true reward. As I ran through the streets that night, dodging horses, my mind was filled with thoughts of what was at stake—not just for him, but also for all of humanity. I ran as fast as I could, hoping to get there in time to save him and preserve all of the plans that had been made for the future. I noticed all of the other people out that night were behaving in a calm and normal manner, so I knew that I still had time. Surely if I was already too late, panic and frenzy would be filling the streets of the city.

My hopes once again began to grow as I saw the theater building up ahead of me. I felt a sense of relief come over me, as I was nearly there and would be able to save him after all. Then, just as soon as I had thought things would work out, I slipped in a puddle of some kind. It could have been water or horse urine. It simply didn't matter what it was. The only important thing was that I lost my footing and went tumbling into the path of a carriage heading the other direction. I had to quickly roll out of the way to avoid being trampled by the pair of horses. From that point things only got worse, as the man driving the carriage had stopped and was trying to make sure I was not hurt. Normally I would have appreciated his gesture to help me and used it to hold out faith that humans could actually be good. But at that moment I knew I needed to keep moving and get to the theater immediately.

After I was able to get away from the carriage driver, I quickly made my way to the theater. Saying a quick prayer of thanks that everything was still quiet, I opened the back door and started up the stairs. I quickly realized that I had not escaped the incident with the carriage as unscathed as I had believed. A sharp pain in my knee was the only warning before I found myself stumbling on the steps. Looking down, I saw that I had rolled over a piece of sharp metal lying on the ground. I quickly pulled the shard out of my leg and tossed it aside; my injury was only minor and would be forgotten soon.

Knowing I had once again lost precious seconds, I started back up the stairs. I thought that if I had made it here and everything was still calm, maybe I truly was ahead of any plot against him. It was even possible that something had happened to change the plotters' plans. I knew it was quite easy to disrupt even the best of schemes, so maybe I had no reason to panic.

Then I heard it. A single gunshot echoed down the stairway, and my heart dropped. I flew up the final few steps, hoping for some kind of miracle. Instead I saw the dark, glassy eyes of a man totally shocked to see me coming through the door to the balcony. I was blocking his path down the stairs, so the man went over the balcony and down to the stage below. I learned later that he had broken his leg when he landed on the stage, which ultimately helped lead to his capture. None of that was important to me. I looked down and saw all of my hopes fading. The desires we had for putting things on a proper path were now lost. There on the floor of the balcony, dying, was President Abraham Lincoln.

I have thought about that conversation with the security officers in the bar that night many times in the years following. The fact that orders were delivered to give them the night off proved to me that it was an orchestrated move to remove the security from the targets that night. Even though they didn't remember the name on the orders for certain, I am sure I know who sent that note. I know the history books often cover the plot to assassinate President Lincoln, Vice President Johnson, and Secretary of State Seward. I know the conspirators were captured and killed for their crimes. Still, I also know that there was more to it than what is in the history books. I know that it was my place to prevent the tragedy and thereby ensure that the United States would be able to rebuild and grow smoothly from the ashes of the Civil War—avoiding the major issues that have continued to plague the powerful nation. I know that, as in so many other moments over the course of history, arrogance and pride served to drive me, and humanity, off the proper path. I know this was as much a part of my story as it was the history of the United States. There are many more things that I know and hope to share with you.

SECTION 1 CHAPTER 1
MY APOLOGY

B eing human is a pain in the ass.
I am not telling you anything new. I am sure you have thought this many times before; after all, you are human. You have been hurt. You have suffered, cried, and felt lost. And you have been forced to endure any number of other painful aspects of this human condition. Now, after reading this obvious statement, you are doing one of two things. You are either now obsessing about all of the bad things and pain you have experienced during your lifetime, or you are one of the rare people filled with thoughts and memories of happy times and accomplishments.

Now, welcome to the next stage, where you try to rationalize and defend yourself as not truly being one or the other, but a good combination of the two. You understand that there are both good and bad things in this world. You do not see the world through one myopic point of view. You are better than that. In all honesty, I don't really care. That is not the point. No matter what you try to tell yourself, somewhere inside your mind you know that being human requires you to feel pain and to suffer. That is the point I want you to remember as we move forward with my story. I will tell you the truth about being human and why you are so familiar with pain. My story, which you think you know, gives insight into the human condition in its entirety. The good and the bad—I know it all far too well, and I am here to finally tell the truth.

I had hoped my story would be easier for me to tell; but then again, why should this be easy? I can't remember the last time I was able to talk openly and honestly about who I am. As I tell you my story, you will better understand your own existence and the nature of humanity. Being human is a chaotic mixture of feelings, lessons, and experiences. I have already acknowledged that there are some good and amazing experiences in life. By all means, enjoy those moments for all that they are. But when you are honest, you know that life as a human is shaped by your experiences with pain, suffering, and death. From the very moment you are born, you are exposed to stimuli designed to cause a reaction. Leaving the safety of the womb, which was created to provide for you and protect you from the dangers of the world, suddenly bright lights and loud sounds bombard you and you are welcomed into a world of strangers. These strangers poke and prod you looking for signs that you are alive and well. Strange, isn't it? Show us you are alive and well by responding to pain and annoying stimuli. Talk about an honest welcome to the world of suffering. Then, as you continue to grow and age, things only get worse. No matter what you do or where you go, somebody is pushing and prodding you to get a reaction. Every decision you have ever made is the result of outside stimuli. Yes, I know, you are thinking not all experiences are bad, and you have made some good choices based on pleasant stimuli. So, yes, you are right. I won't deny that there are good things in life. I only ask that you be honest with yourself. Have you made more decisions seeking the good things or looking to avoid the pain?

I simply want you to think about the pain you have felt as a human being. Why is that important? Well, if you are not truly aware of how unpleasant being human is, then what I have to say next will have no meaning. After all these years I am finally going to say what I have always wanted to say to every single person I have ever met. For all of your pain and suffering as a human—I am sorry. I apologize for every scrape and bruise, every hurt feeling and misunderstanding, and every failure or unfulfilled dream you have endured in your lifetime or will experience in your future. No, I am not speaking out of sympathy or empathy, or even in metaphorical or philosophical terms. I am offering you a sincere and heartfelt apology based on responsibility, guilt, and a full acceptance of blame. Yes, I mean that exactly how I said it. For everything that has ever gone wrong in your life, you can blame me. It is entirely my fault that being human is the painful experience you know rather than the beautiful paradise that was intended. Because of me, life is not glorious, amazing, peaceful, and perfect. I denied you that life, and I apologize.

Maybe I should take this moment to step back and introduce myself. I have different names in different cultures and religions, as well as the countless identities and aliases that I have used through the years. But when it is all said and done, I am just me—the same person with many names. No, don't go jumping ahead of me. I am not the Devil, Satan, or Lucifer. I know I kind of set you up to think that, but he is a different character in the story of humanity. No, I am another person you think you know. The name I am most comfortable using is Adam. Yes, *that* Adam. I am the Adam from the creation story. I am the first human. So, you see, I do have every need to apologize for your life's problems. I know that many people blame Satan, Eve, or even God Himself for allowing the perfect Garden of Eden to be turned into the world of pain we know today. Yes, God could have started over and remade the world in perfection. Yes, of course Satan tempted Eve to eat the forbidden fruit, leading her to bring sin into the world. I fully understand those points of view and the natural desire to spread the blame around. Still, there is just cause for me to be the one to apologize to you. I hope to clarify why that is as well as tell you my story. I can promise that you do not know anything of my true part in the story of humanity. What I have to tell you will amaze you and make you think. It will horrify you and hopefully lead you to a better understanding of what it means to be human.

CHAPTER 2

IN THE BEGINNING...

I assume that you are familiar with the general story of my origin, or at least some version of the creation story. You know, there was nothing, then suddenly...BANG...creation started and the path to life began. I just have to say that I have gotten many laughs listening to all religion and science arguing over every tiny detail. All the hate makes each group blind to the fact that they are both telling the same story. Seriously, stop being so arrogant and narrow-minded. Open your eyes and see the possibilities; you might just find that you have more common ground to stand together than what divides you. I have little doubt that you get my point, but for now, back to my story.

Yes, I am Adam. I was the first human to walk, think, speak, breathe, and exist in this world. I was not alone for long, though. Now aren't you all smart, sitting there thinking about Eve. I had lived alone and always enjoyed the quiet, peaceful nature, as it was all I had ever known. I was comfortable and...well, to be honest, had no need or desire to have anybody else around. At least, that was what I thought at the time. I had never known anybody else, so how could I possibly feel alone or have any notion of what I was missing? Still, though I didn't know it, it had been decided that I was not going to be alone any longer.

I will never forget the day that my solitary life ended. As I was finishing up a relaxing swim in the river, I noticed a strange animal standing on the shore. I had never seen anything like it in my long existence in the Garden. As I got closer, I began to realize that this animal looked a lot like me, and it was actually was another human. There were two legs and two arms, feet and hands, toes and fingers, and a face that had two eyes, a nose, a mouth, and ears. Still, this human was not exactly like me; there were distinct and obvious differences. The hair was longer and looked to be much softer. The skin looked smooth and silken compared to my rougher, hair-covered skin. There were also differences in the body, which was shapely and had more curves than mine. I have to say that this first time seeing her standing in front of me did have an interesting impact on my own body. Of course, I clearly now know that this other human was a female and that nature was taking hold of my body. Just remember, this was the first time a man had ever seen a woman—especially such a beautiful, naked woman as Eve. I had no idea what was possible or what all the differences and natural urges meant, but it sure was amazing to make those discoveries. Now, get your mind out of the gutter. I am not going to turn this story into some trashy work of pornography. Besides, as good as the physical aspects were, everything else is what truly holds the key to my story.

As you know, Eve was literally made for me. We fit together in every way you can imagine. Throughout all of human history there has never been a better or more complete match. I know that there have been some legendary couples, real as well as fictional, but they all pale in comparison to my relationship with my beloved Eve. Our days were spent exploring the lush and plentiful land surrounding us, constantly finding new plants and animals. Life was amazing. In fact, I don't hesitate to say that it was perfect. This truly was the perfection that God had intended for humanity on earth in His Garden of Eden. How quickly that would all change.

One day, while walking through the garden, we found a tree that neither of us had ever seen before. As we approached this new tree, we began our usual bantering of back-and-forth questions. What would the fruit taste like? Would the tree be comfortable to sleep under? What name would we give this new tree? This had been our standard practice every time we found something new in our own personal paradise. My suggestions for names were always more descriptive of the taste, color, texture, or how it grew. Eve, on the other hand, simply liked to be creative in her ideas, making them much better options than my own. I mean, be honest, do you want to enjoy a kiwi or a small, brown-outside, green-inside fruit? Do you want to see an elephant or a long-nosed gray beast? So, yes, Eve was much better at naming things than I was. Still, after all these years, I think about that last tree. I am sure Eve would have come up with an amazing name for the tree and its fruit. Now you know it as the Tree of Knowledge and the forbidden fruit. As for me, the name I pick now is simply *death*.

We were about to reach the tree when we both suddenly came to a halt. A voice inside my head commanded me to stop. I didn't need to ask Eve if she had heard it as well, because the look on her face told me all that I needed to know. In the blink of an eye and a flash of light, there was a man standing in front of the tree. This man was obviously no simple human like me—and definitely not like you. No, this man was clearly the Architect, the Creator, God, who had put everything here in this place. Even without any introductions, this man, God, began to tell us how He had created everything, including Eve and me. Just remember that the details don't really matter for your faith. What you know or don't know of the specifics isn't nearly as important as your belief and understanding of the general and overriding story.

Choice has always been essential in God's creation. My choice was to accept the perfect world in which I lived and take care of all I had been given. Because this was my choice, Eve could not simply make the same choice; she had to be given her own. So this tree was created, and Eve came into my life. Naturally, Eve and I were still a bit confused. Following some further explanations, we finally understood everything. Through the creation of this tree and the instructions to not eat anything from it, there suddenly existed a choice. The choice for how to live and what to believe, which was also created for all humanity at that moment, gave Eve free will and allowed her to survive.

God explained that as long as we each lived up to our choices, all would be well. In time, each new life in the Garden would have its own choices to make. We were now free to live happily together in this utopia. We walked away from the tree knowing that we had an eternity of joy ahead of us. It would be no problem to not eat from the tree in exchange for all we were given in paradise. How stupid it seems now. We truly were naïve and unprepared for what was about to come. Only later would I fully comprehend what it meant to be the custodian of the Garden of Eden.

CHAPTER 3

LIFE IN THE GARDEN

Life was very good for a long time. I have no idea how long by any calendar system; we simply had no concept of time. Eve and I continued to enjoy everything paradise had to offer. Of course, at the time, we didn't think of it as paradise; it simply was the world. We knew nothing of suffering or longing, and we believed that this life we were living was all there was or ever would be.

There was a constant supply of fresh water from the many different natural springs, creeks, and rivers. This was well before pollution entered the picture, so the water from all of the numerous sources was always crystal clear and fresh. Now, you might think that I am crazy, but as Eve and I would drink from the different water sources, they each seemed to have their own flavors. I don't mean subtle differences like you can find in today's water from town to town, but I mean actual flavor. I am not talking about the fake, modern-world flavors that you can find on the shelves of every grocery store soda aisle, but simply a hint of real fruit flavor to the water. I found myself enjoying the more subtle tastes, and I sometimes even had to take several drinks from the water before I was truly able to place the flavor of that water. Eve, on the other hand, was always the bolder and daring one of the two of us. She wanted water that almost exploded with flavor from the first drop. She would search high and low throughout the land, looking for the strongest flavors; and then she would combine them to create her own mixtures. Eve always wanted more.

Perhaps if I had been more observant, I might have noticed this hint of daring and reckless behavior in my Eve. Looking back, it has been relatively easy to pick out those traits, but at the time I only loved her more for her spirit and passion. Still, I wonder if I could have prevented what was to come and protected the rest of the world had I simply done a better job looking out for Eve. It is really not surprising that I missed the slight hints concerning Eve's thrill-seeking. After all, we had the whole world, as well as each other, to explore.

It truly was an amazing life, and we wanted for nothing. There seemed to be an endless selection of fruits and vegetables for us to enjoy. As we spent our time exploring, we would always find a plentiful grouping of fruit trees or some vegetables growing just off the path. With all of the sources we found for food, it was quite easy to enjoy a diverse selection and avoid exhausting any particular supply. Rarely when we did become hooked on a specific kind of fruit or vegetable, and we would eat the whole supply we didn't have to worry, because shortly after we finished one source, we'd find another.

Since folks always seem curious about one matter, I will simply tell you that our diet did not consist of only fruits and vegetables. With all of the animals around us, we had an amazing selection of meat to enjoy. We were so well provided for in this paradise that we did not even have to actively hunt the animals for their meat. When our supply of meat would begin to diminish, we would find an animal of some kind already dead, waiting to be a source of food. The first time I saw one of these animals waiting for me, I didn't realize that it was meant to be a source of food. This thankfully occurred before Eve joined me, as she would have laughed for hours at my difficulty in figuring everything out, and she never would have let me forget about my confusion. The first time I saw a dead animal, I felt sad that something had died, and I quickly ran from that place, thinking it was not natural. Up to this point of living in the Garden, I had never seen anything dead. I wanted to know how something like this could happen. I thought maybe it was an admonition for something I had done wrong. Then I had the notion that the dead animal might actually be a warning not to me, but for me. Perhaps there was something in that clearing that God intended for me to avoid. Seeing as how I chose my food and water sources based upon what I saw the animals eat or drink, this dead animal would clearly serve as a good sign that something was wrong. With this thought in mind, I crept back to that same spot so I could once again see the perished animal. There before me was the dead animal, unmoved from where I had originally seen it, but around it were others. I saw a whole variety of animals come together to share the meal of this one dead animal. That is how I figured out that the meat of an animal could be eaten as well as the fruit from the trees and the vegetables from the ground.

The next day, I went out exploring again. I hadn't gone very far at all when I again came across a dead animal. I knew from what I had seen the day before that I should use this as a plentiful food supply. I also knew that if I left it here, other animals would come to partake of the meat for themselves. I quickly grabbed the leg and began to pull the animal back to my home camp. The whole way back, I wondered about how I was going to eat this animal. The skin looked to be incredibly thick and tough, as it was not showing marks from me dragging it along the ground. There was no way I would be able to bite through with just my teeth as I had seen the other animals do. Even before I was able to make it back to my camp, the answer was provided for me. My path took me right past the place where I had found the previous dead animal. Changing my mind about returning to camp as quickly as possible, I decided to stop and take a look at what was left. I hoped I could scavenge some meat there and buy some time to consider how to get through the skin of the fresher animal.

I saw quickly that there was nothing left for me, but I wanted to look closer anyway. After all, this was the first dead anything I had ever seen. What I found was actually better than any leftover meat would have been. I found a solution to my problem. There in the messy heap of remains, I actually saw several solutions: a full tooth broken off from one of the animals responsible for consuming all of the flesh, as well as several broken bones with sharp, jagged edges from the dead animal itself. With the sharp point of the tooth to puncture the skin and the jagged edges of the bones to cut with, I had every confidence that I would soon be enjoying my first taste of meat.

When I eventually made it back to camp, I realized that I needed to find a rock or small log in order to hammer the tooth through the thick skin of the animal. I put the animal down next to the fire, hoping to keep it safe from the other animals and protect it for me. When I finally found a rock that would work, I headed back to camp. Then I noticed the aroma. I didn't know what it was yet; but it was coming from my camp, and it smelled good. As I got back, I knew instantly what it was: the animal. I didn't understand what the smell meant until I used the rock and tooth to puncture the skin allowing me to use the broken bone to cut into the flesh. Then I saw that the side close to the fire was a different color; it was not slimy with blood and other liquids inside, as the side away from the fire was. I cut myself a piece from the section facing away from the fire; after all, the animals had simply eaten the flesh from the carcass. The taste was not something I would say I enjoyed. I kept it down, but it was a fight. I looked at the section by the fire. It smelled so good. I knew that fire was a blessing for light and warmth, but my instincts had always kept me from getting too close. I fought with myself for a while on this dilemma before my hunger and the smell won out. I cut a piece of flesh from the portion that was closest to the fire. It was amazing!!! Yes, I know now that all I had done was cook the meat; but remember that this was all new to the world. I had just invented cooking, and it was obvious to me that cooked meat was much better than raw. I now knew that animals could be a source of nourishment as well as the companionship and entertainment that I had been enjoying.

I never did tell Eve about that first experience of learning to cook and eat meat. When Eve came into my life, I simply allowed her to believe that it was a natural thing to know how to do. As we lived in our world, we never had to want for meat. Just as the fruits and vegetables were there for us to find, so too was the meat. When we were out of meat at home, one of us would stumble upon a dead animal just waiting for us. There was never more than one, but it was always one big enough to feed us for several days without any trouble. Also, like the fruits and vegetables, the kind of animal would change so that we could enjoy the different flavors and textures. This was even true of fish. One day when Eve was sitting by the water, she saw some fish that had somehow gotten trapped on land following a change in the tide. Being the more daring one of us, she cooked the fish on the fire. and we discovered that fish too made an excellent meal.

There was no doubt that God was taking care of us and providing all of this bounty for us, which moved us to show our thanks daily. How can you not be thankful for such an existence? As grateful as both Eve and I were then, only in the many years since have I been able to fully appreciate the magnitude and understand the perfection that was lost.

CHAPTER 4

THE END OF PARADISE

The day began like any other in my life to that point. I woke up to the smell of fresh food being prepared by Eve. She was the early riser of the two of us, so breakfast had become her responsibility. I was always amazed at how creative this beautiful wife of mine could be in discovering new combinations and methods to prepare food. When I would cook, it was always very basic and simple. If Eve was lucky, I would add some fresh berries, but often I would simply put the meat over the fire and call it a good meal. Eve soon grew tired of eating my rudimentary cooking and claimed that duty solely for herself. She said that she couldn't dream of being forced to survive on my cooking. Naturally, I was more than happy to allow her to assume all control over our meals. I guess I could have worked harder to learn to be a better cook, but honestly, why should I? After all, Eve seemed to have the natural ability to create amazing meals from the same basic ingredients I used, which simply confused me.

On the other hand, whenever it came to working with the countless animals in our Garden, it fell to me. In the realm of all other living beasts, I had a natural ability that Eve lacked. We quickly found that we were both talented at some things, but other times one of us seemed to simply be much better. This division of labor according to our skills allowed us to maximize our efforts for the benefit of each other and maintain a harmonious life together.

Yes, everything started out like normal on that day with me waking up to the smell of food cooking. I remember smelling a combination of meat and sweet fruit. As I awoke I looked around for Eve, eager to start the day together. When at first I did not see her, I saw no need to worry or be concerned. We were living in paradise, so there was never any reason to be worried that something might have happened to her. Besides, Eve often enjoyed a nice walk toward the river in the morning after getting breakfast started; she called this her private exploration time. Once I was fully awake and ready to face the day, I began to dish up the food so it would be ready when Eve returned. As usual, I didn't have to wait long. I actually felt her before I saw her. I know that it might seem crazy, but it was common for us living together in the Garden. It wasn't like I could read her mind or anything like that; because of our perfect connection, each of us always knew that the other one was nearby

I lifted my eyes just as she was coming into sight through the tree line. I will simply say this: no woman has ever been more beautiful than my Eve. I know that many opinions exist on beauty. Trust me, the claims regarding Helen, Nefertiti, and all of the beautiful women through history that you are now thinking of are well-deserved. Still, none of them could hold a candle to my Eve. She was perfection. It was amazing that I got any work done when my wife was near me, but somehow nothing was ever neglected. Watching her walk toward me was enough to make me understand that this truly was paradise. By the time she reached the fire, I had finished dividing the food so we were able to just sit back and enjoy all that paradise had to offer.

Mealtime with Eve was always an adventure. As beautiful as she was physically, her mind, heart, and spirit made her the perfect beauty. We would discuss the schedule for the day and any new discoveries either of us had made. We also often wondered together about the meaning of us being there in that Garden. God had made it clear to us that He had created this world, and that we were provided for was beyond question. There was just so much more to know and so many questions left unanswered. Still, we always came to the same ending of that conversation—it was not our place to understand everything all at once. As we learned and discovered things, it seemed obvious that this was how God intended life to be for humans. The whole of God's creation was there for us to know and understand—all we had to do was learn and grow together.

Breakfast that fateful morning began the same as so many others before it. I had no idea that it was going to be the last and final time everything would feel right. About halfway through breakfast that day, Eve dropped a huge bombshell on me. During her morning walk, she had not gone over by the river. Instead she had walked toward the middle of the Garden, where the forbidden tree was located. She paused after telling me this, waiting for me to react, but no words came to my lips. Once she continued her story, I realized that I was holding my breath. She reassured me that she had only looked at it from a distance, and I finally felt myself slowly exhale and begin to breathe again. I asked her why she would even go near that tree, knowing that it was the key to her existence here in paradise with me.

After a bit of stalling, she answered that my question was also her answer. I had been made in conjunction with the entire world to serve as protector and custodian over all of creation. I was connected to everything. Eve, on the other hand, was made for me later, and her life was tied directly to the choice brought into the world by the existence of the forbidden tree. I had never thought of it before, especially not in those terms. She saw me as an integral part of this world, as I was created alongside everything, while she felt that she was only tied to something that was labeled as forbidden. I finally understood that she would have many more questions about her place in the world than I did. Sadly I didn't have any real answers for her other than to tell her that I loved her as my wife and that this Garden might have been perfect, but it wasn't paradise until she entered my life.

I walked around the fire to take her in my arms. I held her and kissed her, telling her that she was made by the same God who had made me, and she was every bit as perfect. She belonged here in this Garden with me. That was the true perfection of her, that she was able to improve what was already heaven on earth. After a brief silence, I told her to look around at all that was here for us to enjoy. We were living in perfection, and the price for this gift was simple: take care of each other and not eat from one single tree. For all that we had been given, I would gladly refrain from eating the forbidden fruit. Eve simply smiled and let the topic drop at that, if only to finish eating before shaking my world yet again.

As soon as the last bite of food was swallowed, Eve jumped straight back into talking about her visit to the tree. I guess I should have known that Eve would not truly let the conversation end until she had finished telling me what she wanted to say. She never was one to let something fully drop until she was satisfied that all details had been covered and no point of view had been left unexamined. In this case, it would be more accurate to say that she only paused the conversation so we could finish eating before she told me the most important part of her story. While she had been exploring by the forbidden tree, she had made a new discovery. There in the tree was a new kind of animal she had never been seen before. As she described this new creature, I got chills running up and down my spine. This new animal just seemed wrong in every way to me. Of course the big concern I had was that it was in the forbidden tree, but the physical description made it seem much more ominous. The creature had wings and no legs of any kind and yet was able to live and move around on land. Up to this point, the only animals we had seen that didn't have legs lived in the water. Even the birds of the sky had legs to use when they returned to the solid ground. I was torn between my curiosity about something so different and my fear of why it was so different and living in the forbidden tree. Eve tried to explain to me that when it was flying, it hovered rather than soaring as the birds did. Then when it returned to the ground, it moved in a graceful motion, using its entire body to propel itself forward. The more that she described it, the more convinced I became that something was not right about this creature. Then again, who was I to question the design of any creation of the same God who had brought me this paradise and my precious Eve? There were plenty of animals that seemed different or strange. Surely this was just something new. I was very curious and quite nervous to see this creature for myself; but we were out of meat, and I had planned on bringing in a fresh supply today. Eve's opinion was quite clear, as she thought that the new animal was much more important than worrying about a brief break in our meat supply. We finally reached a compromise that if she would wait while I brought in the meat, then we would go investigate her discovery before doing anything else. She reluctantly agreed, and I set out to find what blessing God had provided for us that day.

I started out walking along one of my favorite paths in the Garden, trying to relax and enjoy the perfection surrounding me. Normally this was a very easy task to accomplish, but today relaxation was eluding me. My mind kept going back to the conversation with Eve over breakfast concerning the new animal. It really bothered me that Eve had been so reckless as to wander near that tree by herself again. After hearing her explain her desire to understand her place in this world, I could see her curiosity. But at the same time, I simply could not grasp how she could risk everything in this paradise like that. Still, there was more bothering me than just her being around the tree; it was the animal. Yes, it was crazy to think of this animal that could fly and then move around on land without any legs, but my real concern was the impact it so clearly had on Eve. The tone of voice she used when describing the animal was one I had not heard before. Her normal sweet voice was gone and replaced by something almost ominous. I wasn't sure what was going on, but it was giving me a strange feeling. I felt like there was some missing piece that would pull everything together and allow me to protect Eve and our life together in this Garden. Having that kind of thought was by itself unsettling to me. At no time while living in the Garden had I ever felt any need for protection. Even when I sensed Eve watching me, I had felt only an anxious need to find the source rather than any notion of fear as I felt now.

I was just about to give up on collecting the food so that I could go back to camp and continue the conversation with Eve; I also thought of possibly even going to look at the creature myself. Then it started. In that moment, the world I knew and the world you know began to collide. As I stood there with some berries in my hands, just a short walk from my camp, I knew that everything was changing. In that instant, I knew that I had failed and that everything was my fault. The normal feelings of peace, love, comfort, and joy were gone in a flash. The rush of new feelings was physically crippling. I know that these emotions are part of the human experience. You have dealt with them on a daily basis for your entire life, as I have since that moment. Still, in that instant, they were entirely new to me, and I was completely overwhelmed. In my head, I simply knew that the reason for this was Eve being at the forbidden tree. I could see it clearly in my mind. My perfect Eve was standing under the tree and had picked a piece of fruit from one of the branches. I hoped that she would realize what she had done and simply drop it and walk away. Maybe then we could pray for forgiveness and God would take away these horrible emotions that were flooding through me.

I pulled myself together—well, somewhat—and I started running as fast as I could toward the tree. I hoped that I would be able to get there before anything else went wrong. I willed myself to run faster by telling myself that when I got there I would be able to fix this and I could still protect Eve. I am not sure what I thought I could do. It wasn't like I would be able to put the fruit back on the tree. Eve had already broken the rule by touching the fruit and picking it from the tree. I just kept hoping God would allow us a second chance, and most importantly, not take my Eve from me. Despite being created in the Garden alone, I could no longer imagine another day in paradise without her. These thoughts encouraged me to run faster than any human has ever run since. As I got closer, I was formulating what I was going to say to Eve, and more importantly, to God. I had just about convinced myself that I truly could fix everything. I was starting to believe that all would be fine. I had a growing faith that I was going to be able to save the situation and protect my Eve. In one blinding flash of light and pain, I realized that I was too late.

In that instant, pain entered the world and has been a constant in human life ever since. In my many years on earth, I have felt many pains of extreme degree, both physical and mental. None of that comes close to what I felt at that moment as I experienced the very first incarnation of pain for humanity. It was a pure pain with no built-up resistance to soften the intensity. Every single nerve in my body seemed to explode in pain at once. My vision went white—blindingly painful white—with no color registering through the intense agony. My ears burst with a shrill screaming, causing them to bleed. I knew that I had fallen. I remember hitting the ground and tumbling for several yards from the speed I had been running. If I had broken all of my bones in the fall, I am not sure I would have even noticed over the pain I was already feeling. As I was rolling, I felt like every single fiber of my body was on fire, being ripped apart, or exploding. This pain was pure and perfect. There is simply no other way to describe it. No pain since then has been so extreme or so fully encompassing of the entire body in a single instant.

I am not sure how long the pain lasted. It could have been mere seconds, or it could have been hours; time simply had no meaning. Still, like all things in life, it eventually subsided, and my body finally began to relax. As the pain lessened, I became aware that something was different. It is hard to explain what it felt like for me to go from being a perfect creation to being a human being as you understand it, but it was obvious that something had changed in a very significant way. Everything felt just a little different. I could now feel little annoyances in every part of my body. I sensed things I had never noticed before, such as the rough, uneven surface of the ground where I was still lying and the small scratches on my skin starting to itch. My joints no longer moved as freely as they once had, and they now met with some resistance when I tried to stand up. Once I was standing, I looked around to regain my bearing, and I noticed that my vision was no longer as crisp and clear as it had been. The same could be said for my hearing. These changes all combined to make me feel as if I was no longer connected to the Garden, which fed into the biggest change I was now very aware of—fear. I realized that danger could be anywhere. All of these plants and animals, as well as the rest of creation, had the potential to be dangerous to me. As soon as I realized this danger, my thoughts quickly jumped back to Eve. I had to get to the tree and check on Eve. It was obvious to me that the horrible ordeal I had just endured was a result of her eating the forbidden fruit. I was filled with dread. If her eating the fruit had done all of this to me, what had it done to her?

The free will choice to not eat the fruit was what had allowed Eve to live. I could only assume then that she had died when she had made the choice to disobey. *Dead.* That word suddenly had meaning to me, where before it had none. Yes, I had been eating dead animals for a long time, but their death had always been a part of God's plan to provide for us in the Garden. This death was not part of the plan. It was wrong. It was painful. My perfect Eve was dead because I had not looked out for her. I had left her alone, knowing that she was tempted. I should have done better for her. My head was pounding from these thoughts, and my body was screaming to simply curl up in a ball and cry for hours. Still, before I could give in to those desires, I had to see her. I was convinced that she was dead, but I had to see it for myself and hold her one last time. I slowly finished the trip to the tree, which I now thought of as death. I wasn't sure what I would find when I got there. I knew the pain that I had suffered, and I hoped and prayed that God had been merciful to Eve and simply taken her life as He did with the animals. When I finally got there, I was at least partially relieved to see her body on the ground and showing no signs of the pain I had suffered. She simply looked to be sleeping. With tears running down my face—something entirely new to me yet at the same time something I fully understood—I pulled her body close to mine as I sat down under the tree. I held her tight and wiped the leaves from her skin and hair. I knew that she was gone, but I just couldn't let go. My precious Eve was all that I wanted. I begged and prayed for God to help me. I am not positive what all I offered, but I am sure that I made every promise I could in hopes for my love to come back to me.

CHAPTER 5

A DEAL IS MADE

There was a sudden flash of light in front of me. Even before I could open my eyes again, I knew from past experiences that God would be standing there with me. He told me to open my eyes, and sure enough, there was the same physical form of God who had visited with me many times during my life in the Garden. The only difference was that this time He had a sad look on His face to replace the smile that had been there during every other visit. He told me to leave Eve there under the tree and to follow Him so we could talk. Part of me wanted to scream in protest that leaving Eve there seemed wrong to me and I would not leave her body unprotected. I knew that I had lost her, but the mere thought of something happening to her body filled me with dread. Still, I knew that God could have simply abandoned me as a punishment for all of my failures, yet He had come to talk with me instead. I clung to the hope that God's presence there was a positive sign. I wanted to believe that somehow things could still be returned to the perfection that had vanished with my inability to prevent Eve's sin. With that hope, I placed Eve's head upon the ground and rose to follow my God and Creator.

We walked for quite a distance in total silence. Several times I started to say something. I wanted to know what I could do to save Eve, or at the very least, I wanted to understand. I wanted to scream and beg for answers. The silence of our walk was only making things so much worse in my head. Just about the time when I couldn't handle it anymore and was going to break the silence, I saw something I had never seen before. There in front of us was a gate at the edge of the Garden. Now, I knew for sure that I had walked much farther than this before and had never come across any gate, wall, or any other type of boundary to the Garden. I had always assumed that our paradise was truly never-ending and went on forever in all directions. Knowing what I was thinking, God finally spoke. He explained to me that indeed the Garden of Eden had been created without any borders. The entirety of the planet had been there for me to explore and enjoy in perfection. The key words I noticed were "had been," as in past tense. Everything had changed when Eve picked the fruit, and the changes had cemented when she ate from it.

I immediately began to defend Eve and her actions. I begged God not to blame Eve. I fully accepted responsibility for everything. It had been my job to care for and protect everything within the Garden, and I had failed by allowing her to be tempted. God listened very patiently as I listed every excuse I could think of as to why it was my fault and what I should have done differently to protect Eve from this transgression. Finally, God told me that He knew my mind and my heart, but Eve alone was responsible for her actions. She had been given her own free will, just as I had been. Yes, it was my role to protect the Garden, but Eve was not a lower animal or a plant. She was a human and therefore in charge of her own choice. When she was created, God had taken great care to explain to her that the key to her survival in the Garden was her use of her free will to choose that life. The tree had been a necessary component of providing her with that choice to live. Her free will had led her to make the choice to eat of the tree, and I was not responsible for that. I understood what God was saying, and it was obviously true; but I loved Eve, and I wanted nothing more than to have her back, alive and well.

Suddenly the gate was open, and for the first time ever, I was looking at a world other than the paradise of the Garden of Eden. I won't lie to you. This truly was looking into a different world. The first unavoidable difference to hit me was that the vibrant greens of the grass and trees were absent outside of the gate. As far as I could see, the predominant color was brown. Sand covered many areas of the ground; and where there was grass, it looked to be a harder textured brown. The blue sky decorated with clouds that I had always known became a clear sky with little cloud cover to shield the heat of the sun. It didn't take long for that difference to be very noticeable. Simply standing near the gate I could feel the heat radiating through from the desolate-looking world. That world clearly was a stark contrast to the Garden I had always known. I could not even bring myself to admit to the reality of why God was showing me that horrible place. I knew in my heart that I was seeing my punishment. While Eve had sinned and brought death into the world, I had allowed perfection to be tarnished. Looking through that gate was a visual depiction of what I had done to Paradise.

Before I could ask any questions about this strange and horrible new world, God again began to talk. With one simple statement, everything was forgotten and joy filled my heart again. As soon as God told me that Eve was not actually dead, I fell to my knees, thanking Him for His mercy and promising to do a better job from now on to repay Him for His generosity. I swore to do anything to make up for my failure. After a few moments of this, God continued. It was not as simple as Him just forgiving and forgetting what Eve had done. No, she was not dead at this point, but merely held in place, allowing time for our conversation. Eve had broken the one rule she had been given, and there was no way that life in the Garden could continue for her. It was God's plan to send Eve out into the new world on the other side of the gate. In that world she would live, suffer, and eventually die as a mortal human being. I would be allowed to remain in the Garden as I knew it, with the addition of the gate so I could see the painful life Eve would be living because of her failure. This would always serve as a reminder to me to know that my choices had consequences, and in time I could use that visual to help my future wife understand as well. Yes, I was to remain in the Garden, where the pain would once again be gone. I would have this life just as soon as Eve left the Garden, and eventually God would provide for me to move on with a new female. God promised me that the new woman would be every bit as perfect as Eve had been. The only real difference was that since Eve had sinned and been expelled from the Garden, there would be no need for such a specific rule regarding choice for the new woman. The choice would simply be to believe, love, and trust in God, allowing us to remain in the Garden, or to live outside of God's love and expectations in the world beyond the gate.

I knew in my head that God did not have to be so kind to me; that He could very easily just wipe out our existence and start over with a whole new Garden and new people. Still, my heart knew what it wanted, and my soul hurt at the thought of losing Eve. No matter how perfect the new woman was going to be, she would not be my Eve. I begged again for Eve to get a second chance. I promised to watch out for her better and to never let her out of my sight. Not only would I watch over her, but I would also do my best to teach her how to understand God as I did so that she would not be so tempted again. I like to pretend that my pleas for Eve made some impact on God, but deep down I believe that He always intended to do things exactly how He did them.

God told me that Eve simply must leave the Garden, but that my free will could not be ignored. I was still clean and free to remain in paradise without sin, pain, or suffering for as long as I continued to exist in that state. If I chose to do so, I could look through the gate from the Garden to see Eve at any point that I wished, but she would not be able to see in from the other side. Still, I could use my free will to eat from the tree and place myself in the same sinful condition as Eve. At that point, we both would be expelled from the Garden of Eden. Outside of the gate, we would experience pain and suffering. We no longer would have a food supply provided for us, but we would have to hunt and find it on our own. God also told me that there would be other people in that world. Some of them would be good, kind, and helpful, while others would tempt us and try to do us harm. Those other people would also serve as a reminder that we were no longer the perfect pair living in paradise, but were now two of many living in the wilderness. At this point I was very scared of what living outside of the gate would mean, but the thought of losing Eve forever was equally painful. I found myself looking out the gate at the wasteland and then back into the Garden to see paradise. Could I be happy in the Garden without Eve or could I be happy with Eve outside of paradise? Then God made an offer to me that I was quick to jump on.

If I chose to live outside with Eve, He would not abandon us, but He would allow me the opportunity to continue choosing Him over the world of sin. Eve and I would still know God and live by His desires. To help demonstrate our devotion to God, we should conceive and have children, raising this next generation to understand the story of God and to embrace His love for humanity. This task would be a key to allow us all to return to the Garden. I won't say that I thought it would be easy, but I simply did not see how Eve and I could fail, given our love for each other and our experiences to this point. Before I knew it, we were back at the tree where, sure enough, Eve was still right where I had left her. With the choice made in my mind, I thanked God and promised that I would never forget His love and mercy. He in turn promised me that He would always be watching over us, even outside of the Garden. I might not always see or feel His presence as I had up to this point, but He would never abandon us. With a quiet nod of understanding, I grabbed the same piece of fruit from the ground that Eve had taken a bite from and took a deep breath. Right before I ate the fruit, God vanished from my sight, but I still felt Him in my heart and soul. I remember thinking that feeling would be how I connected to God outside of the Garden rather than seeing Him face-to-face. While I knew that I would miss the interactions, I took comfort in knowing that I would at least always be able to feel His presence.

With a glance down at Eve, I brought the forbidden fruit to my own lips, just as she had done earlier. It was the sweetest taste I have ever known. There is no way to truly describe the flavor other than perfect, and I wanted more. I was about to take another bite of this divine fruit when the world began to spin, and I fell to the ground. Just as the world was going black, I reached out and took Eve's hand in mine. I knew that even if it meant living in that horrible world outside of the gate, when I woke up, we would be together again.

CHAPTER 6

LIFE OUTSIDE OF THE GARDEN

E ve and I woke up suddenly. Despite being a bit disoriented, it was very obvious that we were no longer under the forbidden tree of death upon the soft grass. Instead we were leaning against a hard rock in the hot sand. As my eyes came into focus, I saw the last dwindling image of the gate to my former Garden home fade into nothing but a desolate sea of sand. We truly had left paradise, and I was determined to return us safe and sound as quickly as possible. Having not been a part of the conversation with God about the consequences of eating the fruit, Eve was not able to adjust quite as quickly. Naturally she had many questions, especially considering her curious nature to begin with. Not wanting to hide anything from her, I began with reminding her about the role of choice in our creation. I described her connection to the tree, and I ended by telling her that since she ate the forbidden fruit, I had made the choice to join her outside of the Garden. As I am sure you can guess, at this point she simply stared at me and proceeded to tell me how stupid I was for giving up everything just for her. I understood why she felt that way, but it had been my choice, and even now I do not regret that decision. She was my perfection, and my love continues to this day to be pure and perfect, even after all of these years.

To be perfectly honest, I don't think she was truly upset at having me there with her. She simply was determined to put up the strong front and hold onto her pride. As I listened to her talk about her abilities to survive, I felt the hardness of the rock pushing into my back. Everything in this new world seemed to be so hard and grainy. As I felt that vast difference from the softness of the Garden, I reaffirmed my promise to God that I would do everything to return us safely to the Garden of Eden. With a deep breath, I took Eve's hand. We got up, brushed the sand from our bodies, and set off to begin our new life outside of the Garden: no longer humans living as perfection, but now perfectly human.

There is no true way to describe the shock to our systems caused by losing our place in the Garden. As we looked around the new world of ours, Eve and I were totally lost. Everything in the Garden had been so bright, clear, and colorful. Now we saw none of that. In every direction we were surrounded by dull and dark colors lacking the true intensity we had been used to in the Garden. Over the years, I have adapted and learned to see the differences as you do, but nothing in this world comes close to what I once knew. This immediate and shocking welcome to the outside human world was only the first of many realizations about our new lives. The air was no longer cool and refreshing on our skin, but was instead hot and dry. Between the heat and the pressure, it felt as if there was no way skin could hold out too long before simply being torn to shreds. I remember actually thinking that this was God's way of torturing us for failing Him. I questioned why He had not just killed us, rather than making us suffer like this. I am not proud of this time of doubt and fear; neither can I say that it was my last such moment of doubting God caused by my new human weakness. This is something I am sure you are quite familiar with yourself. Still, I had just been living in the Garden of Eden. There was no way I should be able to question what God had offered—well, offered before I had failed. Yes, God should have erased everything and simply started over after the fall of humanity. Rather than doing that, He had opted to offer a chance at redemption. How could I possibly have doubted God? I can still put myself back in that frame of mind to help me any time I start to question the ways of God. I had failed, and yet I still had a chance to fix everything. I set myself firmly to the task that I would not give up until the Garden was once again my home.

As I looked around the new world, I noticed some movement off in the distance. I remembered God talking of other people being in the world now. The question was: were these good people or bad people? The very notion that there now could be bad people was both confusing and greatly upsetting to me. Did they know God and reject Him, or were they unaware of God entirely? I had so many questions about everything. This fact was made even more bothersome by Eve asking many of the same questions that I had as well as some of her own that I had not yet considered. All I could do was tell her the painful truth that I simply did not know most of the answers. I wanted to be the source of strength for her and comfort her with answers to her questions, but that was not something I could do. I felt as if I was failing her all over again. It is easy now to look back and say that I should have just lied to her in order to make her feel better and keep her calm, but after just being evicted from the Garden, I was determined to be on my best behavior. Besides, I'm not sure that I could have lied to her at that point, at least not convincingly. Deceiving others is a skill that I came to master over time; at that point I had no experience with it.

I told her all that I did know while assuring her that the rest we would simply have to figure out together. I did pray for answers and understanding of this new world in hopes that I would have some sort of sense of things as I did in the Garden, but no such answers were given. I remembered God telling me that He would always be with me, but that it would be up to me to figure things out. Understanding this, I took a firm hold of Eve's hand, and we began walking toward the new people, new life, and new path set before us. I was terrified, but with God in my heart and Eve by my side, I knew that everything would be just fine. We would be back in the Garden of Eden soon. At least that was my belief at that moment.

Walking toward this group of people, I was filled with questions. Naturally I was worried about whether these were good people or the bad people God had warned me about. If they were dangerous, what was I going to do? I had never faced any danger in my life. Somehow I had a sense of what danger was as an abstract notion, but there was no real knowledge of what that would actually mean in real life. I found myself hoping that this first group would be good people and that God would allow us some time to adjust before facing any danger in our new world. Still, even if they were good but did not know God, I worried about how hard it would be to explain to them about God and the Garden. I caught myself thinking of them as new people because Eve and I had been living in the Garden already before they were created, but to them we were also strangers and new. Beyond those thoughts and concerns, I found my mind becoming occupied with practical issues. Would they speak the same language? The only other person I had ever met was Eve, and seeing as how she was made for me, she obviously spoke in the same tongue. God had said that this world was not meant to be easy. A language barrier would surely count as making things difficult. What kind of food was out here to eat? With the food provided in the Garden, would we be able to find food and provide for ourselves here? As we got closer, the biggest question filling my mind was about their appearance. They looked to be very similar in shape and size to Eve and myself, but from what I could see, parts of their bodies were covered by fur. This wasn't hair like I had, but fur like that of the animals I had known. Seeing this, I was filled with dread and fear. Maybe these were not actually humans after all, but some combination of people and animals. I held Eve's hand tighter and thought about backing away slowly, hoping we could avoid being noticed by these creatures. It was too late. We had been spotted, and several of them were coming toward us. I considered running, but given the ordeal we had just been through, as well as the new environment, I knew it would be useless. To run and be caught would be worse than to stand our ground. I'm not sure how I knew that, I just did. With a deep breath, I gave Eve's hand a squeeze and then a soft tug as I led us straight toward these human-animal creatures, hoping that the human attributes were stronger than those of the animal.

When we were close enough to speak, they stopped moving and seemed to be taking stock of us to decide if we were a threat. Looking back now, I have to laugh at the thought of Eve and I being a threat to anyone or anything at that point. Yes, in the Garden, we had been rulers of everything, but here in the outside world, we were nothing more than two naked people with no weapons of any kind. Once they got close, I was able to see that the people did not truly have fur themselves. The fur was actually from the animals. These people were simply wearing it for some reason I could not even begin to guess at yet. Apparently, just as I was confused by them wearing furs over their bodies, they were confused as to why Eve and I wore none. I responded to their question by simply telling them the truth: that we had never seen or had any thoughts about wearing "clothes" before seeing theirs. This seemed to leave them a bit shocked; but after a moment of quiet staring, they began to laugh and insult us for being so stupid as to live naked with our bodies exposed like that. Eve started to defend our past, but I cut her off, apologizing to them and asking for their help. I figured that it was best not to take a superior position, but rather to admit that they seemed to understand this world much better than we did and hope that they would teach us. This plan worked very well. They welcomed us into their group, offered us food and water, and taught us how to wear clothes. We learned that clothes provide a practical aspect of protection from the world; but in addition, they explained their belief that to be naked was wrong except for bathing and "intimate" moments. While this seemed strange to us, we quickly understood this to be the way of our new world, where we now had to find a way not only to survive, but to accomplish all that God could expect in order to get back to the Garden.

Through the next few years, we settled into life outside of the Garden of Eden. It was strange to deal with all of these new people, who had been placed on the earth by God yet had not been in the Garden with us. Truth be told, I had been quite happy in the Garden. I know that is a pretty obvious statement, considering it was perfection. It was more than the food and the comforts. I really was quite content with the world of just Adam and Eve without all of these other people. I had never even imagined that there would be any humans beyond the two of us. What more did we need? Now I know that you are thinking about us having children and how important that is for people. I am not sure what would have happened had we been able to remain living in our personal paradise. It is possible that it was always part of God's plan for us to have kids at some point. Then again, perhaps the notion of continuing a family only entered into the human equation when the perfection was lost and death became real. No, I'm not saying that kids are bad or placing judgment on the desire to have them. I'm just saying that in the Garden we never thought about it, and no children were ever born. I personally believe that in time God would have blessed us with a child, but it would have been nothing like the human process you know in regard to bearing children. No, I clearly remember God stating that women giving birth would be quite the ordeal as a reminder of Eve eating the fruit. I often see the process as a mirror of my life: the joys of conceiving, the wonder of anticipating and growing with what might be, the pain, and then again the hope of a new life. To me I see the perfection of the Garden, the discoveries of Eve and all of God's blessings, being expelled from paradise, and then the hope of new life through returning to the Garden. I know that it isn't a perfect analogy, but it make sense to me.

Beyond my thoughts on what God's plan might have been, I do know that once we were out of the Garden, God wanted us to bear children. It was like opening my eyes to discover what was in front of me. Everything about having kids made perfect sense. I simply knew what was supposed to happen. I guess, in a way, it was our strange version of going through puberty all at once to understand the process of having children. As I said, I don't know what would have happened had we stayed in the Garden, but I know that it is just a part of being human to know and feel sexual drive and desire. The same actions and behaviors we had always enjoyed would now produce children when the time was right. If we had any doubts about this new knowledge, they were quickly erased by seeing the process played out from start to finish by many of the new people with whom we lived. Luckily for us, we did not conceive and have children until after we had been living outside the Garden for a few years. This allowed us time to become fully adjusted to our new world and what it took to survive. Thankfully, the new people knew what was required to live, and were very willing to teach us.

One of the first skills we learned was how to hunt as food was always in high demand. This was quite different from our old life, where food was simply provided in abundance. Still, I have to say that it was very rewarding to actually catch the food rather than just pick it up. It took a while to get used to killing the animals myself, but I found that a prayer of thanks helped me remain at peace and appreciate the gift in a similar manner to what I had known in the Garden. There were many other lessons involving all aspects of living, from cooking to protection to bodily functions. I won't describe it now, but that story is one that still makes me laugh to this day, especially after the genius invention of indoor plumbing. I can only imagine what our new friends truly thought concerning those experiences. It always makes me wonder why they allowed us to stay that first night; but they did, and we quickly became one large family.

CHAPTER 7

CAIN AND ABEL

The time finally came when Eve and I were ready to have a family of our own and bring children into this new world of ours. I'm sure you are well aware of Cain and Abel; their story is probably every bit as famous, or infamous, as my own. Just as with my story, I am sure that you know the basics, but remember that there is much more that you do not know. It is every father's dream to have his children become well-known for their deeds, but my sons obviously are not known for the things I would have liked. It is a horrible memory, and to this day I fight to keep it from my mind. At the same time, it is an integral part of who I am and my story along this path. My life and my impact on humanity were greatly changed by the actions of my two sons. I know that many versions of their story have survived to this day within all of the religious texts as well as collected folktales from around the world. Just as I said about the true story of creation, there are facets of truth within nearly all of these versions, as well as some good fictional storytelling. I know my sons, and I know how I still love them to this day, but that does not mean that a sin was not committed.

Cain was my firstborn son, and like any father, I was thrilled to have a healthy boy. Eve and I felt truly blessed to have a child of our own. After living among these people of the new world for several years, and watching the joys they experienced through their families, it all made sense from the very first moment we heard Cain cry. It is strange how Cain coming into our lives made us feel like we had finally become part of the society in which we were living. For me it also caused additional happiness, as I remembered God's promise that if I was able to raise my children to know and love Him, we would be allowed to return home to the Garden of Eden. I began telling Cain about God from that very first day, and I never missed a chance to praise and thank God for everything in our world. I knew that it was mostly just for me and that Cain was not really getting anything out of these talks, but I was determined to not fail this time. Shortly after Cain was born, we were blessed with another son, Abel. The joy that I felt watching these two boys play, learn, and grow together is beyond words. Still, every parent knows exactly what I mean when I discuss it. Eve and I did our best to love these boys equally, but as you can imagine with two young children, they both sometimes felt as if their brother was favored in some manner. This was especially hard on Cain, as he had been used to being the only child and was not old enough to fully understand why Abel needed more attention as the younger child. I hoped that as they got older this would lessen, and the two would begin to appreciate how lucky they were to have each other.

As Cain and Abel got older, things did begin to change, but not in the way I had hoped. Abel began to realize that he could not always be the center of attention and that he had to do his part as part of the family instead of just what he wanted. Cain, on the other hand, became more convinced that Abel was the favored son. This initially led Cain to work extremely hard in order to prove his value. He had no need to do so, as his mother and I loved him dearly, but he truly believed that he had to earn our love through his success. As he got older, his skills led him to a life working in the fields. He had a natural gift for getting the highest quality and largest quantity of crops from the earth. This talent earned him a lot of early recognition from the people of the region, and of course, from his family—especially Abel. My younger son saw everything Cain accomplished and simply gushed with pride over what his big brother was able to do. Cain, on the other hand, saw Abel as a nuisance who was always getting in the way. Outside of the family, Cain's success brought him great notoriety from the rest of the village. This fame also brought him many friends who simply did not have the best of intentions. It became quite clear to me what God had meant about some of the new people not having the right heart and mind. As Cain's attitude began to change due to this influence, his efforts in the fields also began to change. He slacked off to the point that his crops no longer showed their normal high quality. I tried many times to talk with him and guide him back to the efforts I had been so proud of earlier. Sadly, these attempts all fell on deaf ears, as Cain was becoming too set in his new ways to listen to his father.

As if this problem wasn't bad enough by itself, it grew at the same time in which Abel was coming into his own as a herdsman. While the two were separate skills, Cain naturally saw his brother's success as competition. The fact that I was praising Abel and being critical of Cain's efforts only served to further convince Cain that I loved Abel the most. To be accused of this by my son broke my heart, and I tried to do my best to praise Cain every chance I could. I even began to let some things go without comment, even though these same things had previously earned criticism for my oldest son. I truly wanted him to see that I loved him more than he could fathom. With his lack of response to my previous attempts, I hoped that my love and support through this method would help pull him back to being the hardworking boy who had been so proud every harvest.

Things seemed to be getting better for a while, but then everything came to a drastic change. It was time for my boys, now young men, to take wives of their own. Part of me was sad we had not earned our way back into the Garden of Eden yet, but another part of me was looking forward to seeing my sons married and starting families. Eve was particularly excited to experience the custom of a wedding, which we had learned from our new friends in the outside world. In the rush of the desire to coordinate this double wedding with the harvest, there was little time to search for brides outside of the immediate region, as was the custom. In our case, this actually seemed like a blessing, as one of the leading families in our village had two daughters who were set to be married as well. It was decided that his daughters and my sons would indeed be married, with Cain marrying the oldest daughter, and Abel the younger. The age difference was very minimal, but it was custom for the eldest to be married and partnered first. The problem was that while the older of the two sisters held more prestige as a wife, the younger of the two was more beautiful. I tried to explain to Cain the benefits of marrying the traditional partner, but he insisted that he only wanted the younger daughter. Eve and I continued our attempts to persuade Cain to follow custom. We even played on those newfound desires for position and profit by pointing out that if he would do things in this way, he would be in line to become one of the leaders of the village one day. No matter what argument we used, Cain was determined that he would only marry the younger daughter. To prove his point, he used the one argument that he knew would bother me the most. He stated that if we forced him to marry the older daughter rather than the beautiful one that he desired, it would prove without question that Abel truly was the favored son. Hearing this, I sought out the father of the girls in hopes of finding a solution. It was decided that both Cain and Abel would prepare an offering to God before the upcoming feast. The one who prepared the best offering would be awarded the right to select the wife of his choosing.

When the offerings were presented, there was little question regarding which of my sons had done the better job. Abel was first to arrive, and he brought with him his very finest and biggest sheep to offer to God. Cain, on the other hand, had let the quality of his crops suffer to the point where he would be fighting to maintain his new lifestyle throughout the coming year. Knowing this, he chose to hold back his best for future trades and personal consumption. Instead he brought some of the lesser quality crops, which he had already harvested, for his offering. Cain was furious and ashamed at seeing his younger brother once again succeed ahead of him. I truly did feel bad for Cain, but there was nothing I could do at this point. I had tried to help him in the past, yet he had always ignored me. This was simply the result of his previous choices. Later that night, when it was officially announced that Abel had won the right to select his wife first, he made the choice he thought was proper. He selected the younger of the two sisters, which in Abel's mind allowed Cain to retain his rightful place as the oldest son and maintain his future claim to a position of leadership. This infuriated Cain, since he was thinking only of the physical beauty of the younger sister. Cain wasted little time in facing me and claiming that he never had a fair chance against my favorite son. Following this outburst, Cain stormed out into the wilderness, vowing that he would find a way to put things right.

It was several days before Cain returned. This was a strange period for all of us. We wanted to be happy for Abel. We were proud of Abel for his offering, which showed a true love and understanding of God's love. We also wanted to be proud of him for trying to do the right thing to protect his brother's rightful place in the community. On the other hand, we were worried about Cain in the wilderness. We were also concerned about his parting threat to put things right. I kept telling myself that he was just angry, and after some time on his own he would calm down and things could be salvaged for the good. So, naturally, when he came back home, I was relieved for his safety and hopeful that we could fix things between my sons once and for all. These feelings were intensified when Cain greeted me with remorse and asked forgiveness for his disrespectful actions. There was no question that I forgave him—he was my son. Still, it was not me that he truly needed to apologize to, so I sent him to find his brother. The eagerness he showed to seek out Abel should have concerned me, seeing as how it had been years since they had gotten along as brothers should, but I was blinded by my hopes that my family would soon be happy once again. I remember putting my arm around Eve as we watched our two sons walk off to talk and settle their differences once and for all.

I'm not sure how much time passed, as I began to focus on other daily chores around the home, but I suddenly got this feeling that something was wrong. This was not nearly as intense as what I had felt in the Garden when Eve had picked the fruit; but then again, I now lived in the outside world of sin, and had become much more accustomed to pain. I looked up from my chores to see Cain coming out of the water of the nearby river. Despite his small attempts to hide it by walking through the river, I could still clearly see that his clothes and hands were red. I'm not sure how, but I knew immediately that it was blood—Abel's blood. I ran to Cain with fear in my heart. I asked him what had happened. Part of me was holding onto hope that Cain would tell me they had slaughtered an animal for a feast to celebrate the reconciliation, but I also knew that was a fool's hope. When Cain did not say anything, I knew that my fear of this blood belonging to my youngest son was indeed correct. My hopes at this point shifted to something no father should ever have to think about. I now hoped that the blood on Cain was from him trying to save Abel, and not the truth that I somehow knew deep inside—that Cain had in fact been the cause of the blood. Cain just kept staring through me, as if I wasn't even there. Finally he began to mumble about what had happened. To this day, I am not sure if he really knew I was there at all, or if he was praying or simply coming to terms with what he had done. He wasn't really speaking coherently, but somehow I was able to understand some of what he was saying. Through that I was able to piece together what had happened.

Cain had returned home originally in hopes of bargaining with Abel in order to get the wife that he desired. If Abel was not willing to trade easily, Cain had planned on threatening to damage Abel's livestock. Before Cain had even started to talk, Abel had shocked him by suggesting that Cain should have his choice of the two sisters; after all, he was the older brother. Apparently this caught Cain off guard. In his twisted state of mind, which had developed through the years of associating with the wrong people in this world, he saw this as a sign that Abel had in fact found a flaw in the younger sister. He was not capable of seeing that his younger brother was simply trying to do something good for all of us. Instead, he was only able to assume that it was a plot against him, just as he had come to see everything that didn't go his way. I'm unsure of the exact details regarding the actual fight, but I know that at this point, Cain snapped and attacked Abel. I also know that it ended with Cain striking his brother repeatedly with a rock until he was positive that Abel was dead.

As Cain had been trying to tell me this story, Eve and some of the neighbors had come close to listen as well. By the time Cain was finishing, Eve and I were holding each other so tightly that I am surprised neither of us suffered any broken bones. This firm hold was also the only reason either of us was able to remain standing and avoid falling to the ground from shock, sadness, and fear. The onslaught of feelings and emotions swirling through me are impossible to explain and simply can't be understood unless you have felt them yourself. The knowledge that one of your sons has just killed the other is something the human mind and spirit is not meant to be exposed to and is incapable of fully comprehending. Even now, after all of these years on earth and seeing so much violence firsthand, nothing compares to that moment of my life. As much as that time is impossible to forget, it is also impossible to fully remember all that happened. Everything was a blur. I know that at some point the neighbors took Cain home while Eve and I set out to find Abel's body. I'm not going to describe what was done or said at that point. It is something between Eve, myself, and God, and is very personal. As I said, if you have experienced anything similar, then you understand. And if hopefully you haven't lived through anything such as this, then no words would make you understand the emotions of that search.

I am not entirely sure how long Eve and I were gone, but when we returned home, Cain was sitting on the ground, surrounded by the neighbors. I noticed that those who had been his "friends" were nowhere to be seen, and those surrounding him were staying a good distance away. I remember thinking that they were confused and had no idea what to think of Cain at this moment either. This was the first time that anybody had ever killed another human, and it just happened to be his own brother who was the victim. Then it hit me. They did not need to know what to think of or do with Cain. That was my responsibility. This was my failure. Just as I had failed to look out for Eve in the Garden, I had now failed to protect Abel. Even more accurately, I had failed to protect Cain from himself and from the evils of temptation. Had I been able to provide the proper guidance for my eldest son, my younger son would not have been killed. I failed both of my sons as well as Eve, all of humanity, and especially God. Suddenly there was a familiar flash and feeling of knowing that God was physically present among us. Knowing of no other fitting action, I fell to my knees and begged forgiveness for once again failing God and not protecting His plan.

CHAPTER 8

THE DEAL REVISED

I heard God speaking, but He was not talking to me. Instead He was talking to Cain and asking where Abel was right now. At first I couldn't believe that God was asking this question. Surely He knew exactly where Eve and I had just found my youngest son. The surprise I felt at God asking the question was quickly replaced by the shock I felt at the arrogance and defiance of Cain, my oldest and now only son. Cain had been taught about God from the very day of his birth in this world, and he knew full well that God was all-knowing. Still, standing there in front of God, Cain decided to deny this fact and continue to rebel against all who loved him. Rather than simply admitting to what had happened and begging for forgiveness, Cain flatly asked why it was his job to look after his brother. I knew then that I had not only failed Abel, but I had truly lost Cain as well. I rose from the ground and approached God. Once again I accepted my failure to properly guide and protect His world from sin. I begged that I be allowed to bear any punishment in place of my son. I had already lost one son through my failure, and I begged to be allowed to protect my only remaining son at any cost. God told me that Cain's life would not be taken, but he had to leave the region entirely. He was not to return to this land and would forever be known by all he encountered as a murderer. We were not allowed any good-byes. Cain simply was sent on his way without another word.

The next thing I realized, I was once again looking into the Garden. This is a site I truly did not expect to see, given that I had failed to fulfill God's wishes for me to raise my children in His love. As I looked at my former home, I saw Abel. He was standing in the Garden, turning slowly in a circle, with a look of wonder on his face as he took in all that surrounded him in my former paradise. I shouted his name and tried to run toward him. Before I had even taken a full stride, God placed His hand on my shoulder and stopped me, telling me that Abel could not hear me and I would not be allowed to step foot in the Garden. God explained to me that after Eve and I had been expelled from the Garden, He had made that paradise the reward for all humans who died knowing His love. This was the eternal home that all who found His path would obtain upon their death. I felt a true peace hearing this as I looked upon my murdered son. Abel had believed and now lived in the perfection I had once known with his mother. I smiled at the thought that when Eve and I died, we would join Abel in our Garden to live once again as a family. Somewhere in my mind I was thinking that it would not be the whole family, as Cain would never be allowed to join us in that amazing reunion. Still, I could see Abel, Eve, and myself living eternally together, and that thought gave me hope.

Knowing my thoughts and feelings, God told me that it was not that simple, at least not for me. Yes, when Eve died, she would return to the Garden if she remained a true believer in God's love. My path, however, was going to be much more difficult and much more important. When God had told me that it was my job to guide, teach, and protect the people in order to return to the Garden, I had believed that it would be a simple job to accomplish. I thought all I would have to do was just talk to the new people and tell them about God's love to convince them while raising my own family in God's honor. When Eve and I had left the Garden, God had created new people to fill the world and set in motion a new path for humanity outside of perfection. It was not anywhere near as easy as I had imagined for me to teach my own family, let alone all of the people born outside of the Garden. I was supposed to look out for all of humanity; in addition to the new people we had been living with, I was responsible for all future generations that would spread over the entire planet. I honestly had never considered just how impossible this task might be to accomplish. I had never imagined that my oldest son would kill his brother out of misguided anger and petty jealousy. I guess if Eve eating the fruit was the first sin, one could say that the second sin was my arrogance to believe that I could easily restore everything God had intended. I wanted to see an easy solution to this problem, but I knew in my heart that this truly was beyond the ability of one man. God promised me that the love I had shown in my decision to leave the Garden to be with Eve would help carry me through to completion of this mission. He also assured me that no matter how bad things seemed, I could count on Him being there with me. While He would not often be in the physical form as He was now, He would be present always.

After giving me a second to let this information sink in, God continued. He told me that not only would I feel his comfort and presence, but I would also be physically protected. He would not give me any special powers beyond my own human abilities to perform miracles or to control, alter, or impact the free will and beliefs of any other human. Still, I would be safe from sicknesses and injuries, including aging, which would limit me physically and mentally from being able to carry out my mission. It all sounded great until that last part started to sink in: no aging. I had envisioned growing old with Eve and then dying at some point alongside her. Now I was learning that I would not age or die. I was beginning to realize that this job was for eternity, and I would never join my family in the Garden. I felt betrayed. Had

God deceived me? Maybe I was just misled. No, God had told me the truth from the beginning; I just hadn't thought through all of what He was telling me. I had seen Eve lying on the ground, and I was desperate to be with her again. I had simply heard the parts that I had wanted to hear, and I had ignored the details. After the initial shock wore off, I realized that it didn't matter. I would have made the same choice even if I had thought it through—all for Eve.

As these thoughts passed, I asked God how I could possibly convince people of His love, especially if the population of the world kept growing and spreading over the whole earth. He told me that I could not bring everybody to the Garden. By giving humans free will, He understood that many would choose to reject Him. It was my job to bring as many as possible to find God's love and grace. I must never forget my promises, as I let my love for my family give me strength. He explained that in addition to what I already knew, it would also be my job to help out at key moments throughout the span of humankind. This truly had me confused and overwhelmed. Thankfully God put it simply for me. On a day-to-day basis, I was supposed to simply spread the story of His love to all who I could reach. Then at key moments, there would be a specific assignment or task in which I was supposed to intervene and help guide or direct a situation or person for the greater good of humanity. I would know these times and places when it was needed, but until then I only needed to enjoy the years I had left with Eve and prepare. At that moment, I was filled with God's love. Even with all that was set before me, God had decided to allow me to live out the rest of Eve's years with her in peace before I would become God's servant and custodian of humanity. I took one last look at Abel, who was now drinking from one of the springs in the Garden, and I was ready to return to Eve.

Eve and I stayed in that region for many years, living quite happily sustained by our constant and ever-strengthening love for each other. I did eventually have to tell Eve about my mission from God, as well as the truth that she would not be joining me in that part of my life.

Being the clever woman that she was, she had already noticed that I did not seem to be aging at the same rate as everybody else. She also had picked up on the fact that I was keeping something from her. I told you that I had not yet grown accustomed to the human ease of lying. Still, once I explained everything to Eve, we both felt better and decided to enjoy the rest of our time together to the fullest. We did eventually have more children. It was hard for us to imagine at first. We had loved Cain and Abel so much, and we were still traumatized by seeing one murdered by the other, who was then exiled forever from this land. Still, in time, we felt ready to once again have children. We had several daughters, who went on to marry and provide many grandkids for us to enjoy. We did have another son, as well, named Seth. Seth led a very noble and righteous life, and he never doubted in God's love. Of course we would at times wonder about Abel. After I had told Eve about seeing Abel living in our Garden, she would from time to time wonder aloud if he had found our favorite spring or places to rest. It made it easier to think of him by imagining him in a perfect paradise, and we found comfort in knowing that he no longer had any problems or pain. Cain did not come into the conversation as often as Abel, but we did still wonder about him. Eve would always express hope that he had found his way back to God so that he too could rest in the Garden when he died. Many years later, I did learn more about Cain and what had become of him, but I'll cover that later.

Finally, it became strange to stay in the same place any longer, as Eve and everybody else were aging while I remained the same age. Many people had begun to notice earlier, but they kept quiet out of respect for all that we had endured as well as all that we had given to the community through the years. While many were respectful and did not comment on my lack of aging it was difficult when it came to my family. Eve faced the challenge of knowing the truth about me with pride in knowing that I would be serving God and working on behalf of all humanity. Our kids and grandkids posed a different challenge. With Cain and Abel we had tried to be honest with them regarding our past. Part of me had always worried that the burden of such a secret had added to their issues growing up. When our first child after Cain and Abel was born Eve and I decided that we would keep our past a secret. I never questioned that decision, but it added to the stress of deciding when to move. Luckily, Seth and his family moved away early to get away from the lingering stigma created by Cain's murder of Abel. As our daughters began to marry into stable families of the region Eve and I knew that the time had come for us to leave the area.

When we moved, we were able to converse with many more people and spread the love of God as best we could. Still, I was getting a sense of just how difficult this life was going to be for me, especially when I would no longer have the love and support of my beloved Eve. I did not like to think of that, but it was becoming obvious that it would not be too much longer before Eve would be leaving me to return home to our Garden, where she would be reunited with Abel. I was also starting to understand what God had meant about how I would know where I was needed. It was not as clear and precise as when we would converse in person, which had not happened in many years, but I was beginning to definitely feel a pull toward a general direction. I also sensed that my ability to work with animals would be very beneficial.

CHAPTER 9
THE DEATH OF EVE

I awoke suddenly, unsure of where I was. I was not sleeping in my bed, and I was not in my home. In fact, I was not inside at all. Then it hit me. I knew exactly where I was. I was back in the Garden of Eden. Had God changed His mind and let Eve and I come home already? I didn't know what to think, but I was just happy that we were back in the Garden again. Then I realized that Eve was not here with me. I had no doubt in my heart that Eve fully loved God and that she would be here in the Garden when she died. That was another strange feeling, as God had told me that I couldn't die as a human, and that this Garden was reserved for those who had died in their human lives. I surely had not done enough to save humanity and earn my way back. Besides, I was pretty sure that God would have something more impressive in store for that end rather than me simply waking up in the Garden again. After a few minutes of trying to think through all of this confusion, I decided that it was impossible to understand God's plan entirely and I was wasting time. I knew where I was. Even if I didn't know about Eve, I knew that Abel was somewhere in this Garden. If I could find him, I could once again embrace my son.

When I found Abel, he looked just as he had all of those years ago before being murdered at his brother's hands. He looked peaceful and happy. The big difference was not with him, but that he was no longer alone. Looking around, I saw many familiar faces. These were people that I had known and talked with about God over the many years since leaving the Garden with Eve. I realized once again that this Garden I had known was now reserved for those who had passed on from their human existence. I was glad to see so many people living in this paradise. I was happy for them, and of course I felt some personal pride that I had helped so many people find the peace and perfection of the Garden. I just sat there and looked on as a proud parental figure to most and a literal parent for one. After a while the group began to disperse. As I watched the others walk away leaving Abel to walk off on his own, I decided to leave the secrecy of the tree line and follow him. Soon I figured out exactly where Abel was headed. I recognized the trees and the rocks as the ones lining the path to the camp where Eve and I had once lived so happily together.

Seeing this place brought on an onslaught of memories and emotions. Before I was able to fall too deeply into my own thoughts, Abel began to tell me how he had been living in this same camp since he came to the Garden. He simply knew exactly where to find our old camp and that it was now meant for him. He even showed me how he had kept all of Eve's old things exactly how he had found them, so that when it was time for her to join him in the Garden, she would be returning to what she had known and loved all of those years ago. My heart filled with fear as I heard my son telling me these things. I wondered where Eve was now. Then I realized what it meant when Abel said that everything was just the same as when Eve and I were expelled: the forbidden tree would still be there. I felt a wave of panic wash over me as I wondered if that was where Eve had gone. Was it possible that even after everything we had gone through, she would go straight to that tree to look for answers? Noticing the panicked look on my face, Abel told me not to worry about the tree. Then he began walking directly toward that dreaded place. I tried to stop him, but he simply told me that I needed to go there now. I'm not really sure why, but I trusted my son at this point and followed him. I had many fears and reservations; but Abel had been living here for many years, and surely he must know what he was doing.

I knew that we were almost to that horrible tree, but I still didn't know what was going on. Was Eve there? Or worse—was Abel going to eat the fruit now to return to the outside world? I simply could not allow that to happen. Yes, it would be great to have him back in my life, but this was his world now. The outside world he had known was gone, as there had been a very obvious shift in attitude over the years toward a more selfish and evil existence. As much as I missed Abel, I could not allow him to return. I could hold him back today, but what if he tried when I wasn't there? This thought brought me right back to my confusion over why I was here. When Abel had died, I had only been allowed to look in from the outside and was not permitted to enter. With the world how it was now, I knew that I had not done enough to be allowed back on my own. There had to be some reason for me being here now; only I could not figure out what that might be. The only thing I could figure was that this was just a dream. And if that was the case, I was going to enjoy it the best that I could. Just as I had started to relax and accept this as a dream, Abel stopped walking so abruptly that I almost ran into him from behind. As I stepped to the side, I could see it right in front of me: the forbidden tree.

I hadn't realized it before, but I had been looking off to the sides as we walked toward that place, wanting to avoid seeing the tree that had been the site of such evil and pain. I resisted looking at it, but Abel kept asking me to look. Slowly I lifted my head to look. To my shock there was actually no tree there. I had simply seen it in my mind. The tree that had haunted my dreams for so long was not in the Garden any longer. Standing there instead was God. Seeing God instead of the tree filled me with happiness, but I also felt confusion. God immediately reminded me that the purpose of the tree was to allow Eve the free will to live alongside me in the Garden. When she ate the fruit, everything changed. The Garden of Eden was no longer perfection on earth; now it truly was paradise alongside God. The world of humanity now occupied the physical earth. In that world, the choices of humankind would determine and decide who was allowed to enter the Garden for the peaceful reward in eternal paradise. Eternity in the Garden was no longer something to be given up from within, but rather gained from outside. Still reeling a bit from the shock of being back in the Garden and the missing forbidden tree, it took a second for me to understand what God was saying. But then I remembered how every face I had recognized here in the Garden belonged to somebody I knew had died. They were also people who had made the choice to accept God and His love. Clearing my thoughts so I could follow the conversation, I finally understood that paradise was now the reward people received after they died if they chose God's love during their earthly life. Almost as if on cue, a new person appeared exactly where the forbidden tree had once stood. I recognized him as one of Abel's friends from his time on earth. Abel greeted his old friend and then told me he would leave me there to finish the conversation. He gave me a big hug and told me to always be strong and embrace God's love through all things, no matter how long and difficult the journey. He broke the embrace and told me that he still loved his brother, and that forgiveness of others was the greatest gift any person could give to God. With these words, my son left me alone in the presence of God.

When I turned back to face God, I knew there was something more to my visit in the Garden than what I had just learned. I told myself that I should remember Abel's advice, but I was so overwhelmed with confusion and questions that my mind began to race as I attempted to figure out why I was home again. God told me that He was proud of me for my devotion to Eve and that I had shared His story with so many people over the years. Sadly, despite all of my efforts, things on earth were not going well. The rise of evil had begun, and it was growing at an extremely fast pace. It was becoming clear that something would have to be done to remedy the situation. God assured me that I had not failed Him. The people created outside of His presence in the Garden simply had not known His power or love well enough to appreciate all that they had been given. I confessed that I still could have and should have done better in my role as His servant. God again assured me that He was quite pleased with the job I had done. He had wanted me to enjoy my time with Eve while we were together. As soon as I heard that, I was filled with a knowing sadness. I now knew why I was there. It was not to see Abel or to learn more about God's plan. I was there because the day I had dreaded for so long had finally come. I was going to have to say good-bye to my beloved wife, Eve. Just as soon as the thought went through my mind, Eve appeared before me, just as Abel's friend had done earlier.

My breath was gone, and I shook to my core. My precious Eve was no longer alive. She had left the earthly home we had been sharing to return to our Garden home to live out eternity in perfection. My Eve was truly home. Even if she was not to be with me for now, at least I could take comfort in knowing that she was living in peace with our son. I ran to her and held her tighter than I can even describe. No longer was she the aging woman I had grown accustomed to seeing as the years had passed on earth. There, back in our true home, she was the exact vision of perfect beauty I had known all of those years. Don't get me wrong; she had always maintained beauty in her appearance. Still, it was so difficult for me to see her suffer through the aging process with aching joints, loss of strength, and simple pains I could not know in my state of existence. Now, none of that would bother her. She was perfect in all ways once again. As sad as I was that she would no longer be with me, I was filled with joy knowing she would never again suffer. All of these thoughts and more filled my mind, but no words were spoken, as none were needed. We held each other, knowing that we shared the same thoughts, and that was perfect. Finally, God simply said that it was time. I kissed Eve one last time and watched as she walked back toward our old camp and her new home.

After a moment of quiet, I turned toward God and told Him that I was ready to get to work. I can't be positive, but I swear He smiled when I said that. He then surprised me by showing me the state of humanity now throughout all of the lands. He wasn't kidding when He said that the people created outside of the Garden had fallen prey to evil quickly and quite completely. I didn't really need any reminder of how bad things could be, remembering how Cain had murdered his own brother because of that evil in the world. Still, it was hard to understand just how widespread that evil had become throughout the entire world. I simply did not see how I could even begin to make an impact against what humanity had and would become. In response to my fears, God promised me again that He would always help me and that He was planning on setting the world back on course. This would give humanity a fresh start and provide a clean slate from which to work toward returning humankind to a place in the Garden. I had no idea what He meant exactly by this promise, or how it could possibly make a difference against the widespread evil in the world now, but I did have full trust in God when He told me that my feelings and instincts would guide me as long as I had faith in Him. I was curious about those few people living on earth who did believe in God, but He reassured me that He would always take care of those who loved Him. Yes, many of them would die through this plan to start over, but they would be given their place in paradise. Still others would survive and would live to carry on the world.

Suddenly, I found myself back home, not in my home in the Garden, but in the earthly home where Eve and I had been living for the past few years. There in our bed I found Eve's body. She looked totally at peace, reminding me once again that she was no longer going to be with me on my path. I took the time to give her body a proper burial, knowing that she was living again in her true home of the Garden. When I had finished, I said good-bye to our friends.

I then gathered my family and explained to them that I had to leave. Despite their concerns for me leaving on my own they saw my resolve to leave. When pressed for a reason why I was leaving I simply allowed them to believe that I needed to find a purpose in life again. With Eve dead and them happily married there was no cause for me there. I reminded them again to have faith and believe in God's love, hoping that they might somehow avoid whatever God was sending to rid the world of evil and allow humanity a fresh start. With my farewells taken care of, I packed my things and began walking. I wasn't exactly sure where I was going, but I knew that I was on the right path.

CHAPTER 10

MY FIRST MISSION

I walked alone with my thoughts and prayers for longer than I can put into words. Truth be told, after a while, I simply quit counting the days. Still, I was never away from God's love, as I always managed to find food or water whenever it was truly needed. This initiation into my new life reminded me in some ways of how I was taught to survive in the Garden all those years ago. The food wasn't anywhere near as good or as easy to find as back then, but I was learning how to survive on my own in any situation. This period of time also allowed me to come to terms with everything that had happened to me in my life. After being born in the perfection of the Garden of Eden, partnered with the most beautiful and loving woman ever, and enjoying that life before we were exiled, it had taken time to get used to living in the outside world. Then Cain had murdered his brother, Abel, and was banished from that land forever. Finally my Eve had died and returned to our home in the Garden. Looking back now, I am very thankful for this time after Eve's death to clear my head and truly ready my heart, mind, and soul for the missions God would put before me as the guardian and custodian of humanity. I tried to think about what might be in store for me during my time in this role, but I honestly had no idea what to expect. There were days when I felt as if my sanity was barely holding on by a thread and that all would soon be lost.

Then one day I figured it out. I had burried my precious Eve and Abel. Cain had been banished. All of the friends that I had made after leaving the Garden had died. With the time spent wandering I could only assume that the rest of my children had died as well. There could be grandkids and most likely great grandkids alive, but I had no knowledge or connection to them after so much time. With all of these thoughts running through my mind I knew that Adam must die as well. Not in the literal sense as God had told me that was no possible. I simply needed to put that life behind me and bury it deep inside so that I could move on and recreate mysel. If I was going to truly live and do what God wished of me, then I could not hold onto the person I had been. Yes, I would still have my memories, and I would also love Eve and miss her being by my side. I had to live as a new person in order to survive through what the world would bring my way. At my core I would still be Adam, but outwardly I must shed that identity entirely and adapt to the situations as I encountered them. Once I accepted my new reality, the first animals appeared—camels.

When the camels began to follow me, I felt a renewed sense of peace. I know that might seem strange, but the presence of these other earthly creatures confirmed that I was indeed on the right path to accomplish God's first mission for me. I mean, why else would camels simply seek me out and start to follow me through the wilderness? Over the next few days, I began to notice a flock of birds soaring overhead. When I looked closer at them, I was shocked to see that this was not simply a large flock of one type of bird, but instead many species of birds were all flying together in harmony. As I continued to travel, more and more animals came to join the camels and the birds. It was a strange feeling to travel with all of the animals in this way. In the Garden they had all been peaceful toward me as well as toward each other, but outside of paradise I knew that many of these animals existed within predator-prey relationships. Still, they walked alongside each other tranquilly as we continued in the direction I simply knew to be correct. Food and water were always nearby when needed, not only for me, but also for all of my nonhuman companions. The sight of lions and zebras, tigers and gazelles, and so many more all drinking from the same water supply gave me even more confidence that everything was going according to God's plan. Soon animals I had not seen since leaving the Garden began to join our procession. I had no idea where they had been living, but I knew they must have traveled many months to reach us. Finally one night, as I settled in to sleep between the bears and the lions, I could see fires in the distance. Rather than being concerned about my parade of animals, I knew that this was my destination, and it was why the animals were following me.

The next morning, I began walking toward the location of the fires from the previous night. I had only made it about halfway when a man named Shem came to meet me. He didn't seem surprised at all by the animals following me. In fact, he seemed to be happy to see them and relieved—as if he had been expecting them to arrive sooner. Turning to me with a nervous look on his face, he asked if I knew about God who had created the world, animals, and even humans. I almost started laughing to have someone ask me if I knew God. Part of me wanted to tell him that I knew God much better than he did, and I had spent many days in the Garden of Eden talking with God. I imagine that Shem would have seen the humor as well if he had known that he was asking the original man such a question. Or he would have thought I was a crazy person for making such a claim. After all, it had been several generations since I had been expelled from the Garden. With all of the evil I had seen in the world, I was actually quite surprised that knowledge and acceptance of God had spread this far, especially since I knew from God that a clean slate was coming soon. After what can best be described as a sort of feeling out or testing of each other's faith, it became clear that we were of the same belief and thinking. Shem then invited me to speak with his father, Noah.

I have to say that I liked Noah from the very start. He was pretty funny and relaxed. Then again, with what God had asked of him, a sense of humor would be quite helpful. Don't get me wrong; along with his humor, I could sense his deep faith and high level of intelligence. He shared with me how God had asked him to build an ark to save his family and the animals from a coming flood. At first he had pictured a small boat, as his family was not that large, and they didn't own many animals. He was quite shocked when God told him how big to build the ark; but he trusted God, so he built it exactly to the dimensions God had given. Noah looked me straight in the eyes and said that he had finished his ark but had no animals to put on his boat. I simply smiled at Noah and responded that I had all of these animals and no boat to save them. Yes, I truly did like Noah from the start. I was glad that I would have my new friend Noah and his family alongside me during my first mission for God.

Now, I am not going to go into great detail about our time on the ark. There were some obvious negatives about riding in a boat for that long: some related to the animals, and some related to being a human stuck on a boat. I truly can't complain too much, though. The animals all remained very well-behaved and were honestly fairly quiet, at least more than I thought they would be. Besides, what was the alternative? Was I going to swim for months? I will admit that I did have thoughts of what it might be like to dive into the water at times. I knew God had said I couldn't die, but I also knew not to test it by being careless. At least it only rained for the first month and a few days. The rest of the time, as the water receded, we could go outside onto the deck in the fresh air and sunshine. Eventually we found land, and the boat settled. When it was safe, we let the animals out, and they began to peacefully disperse in order to begin again. I knew it would not be long before the prey would once again be running from the predators. As for Noah and his family, it too was time for them to spread out to new lands and bring forth life and God's love to the planet.

I said my good-byes to all of them and set out on my own once again. With the clean slate God had promised, I knew it would be a short while before my services would be needed again. This was fine by me. I had accomplished the first task God had given me in this role quite easily. I did not figure that they would all be so easy or that I would always be given time off between assignments, so I was going to relax for a while and enjoy exploring the new clean world to discover what wonders I might find. I could see a great deal of beauty in the world around me. It wasn't anything like the Garden of Eden, but it was still a sight to behold. When I was a day away from where the ark had settled, I built myself an altar and gave God thanks for His provision and protection. I promised to set myself to any and all missions He needed done so humanity could return to its proper place in His paradise forever. Following my prayer, I settled down for the night, knowing that no matter what the future held, I would meet it with God in my heart and a determination to once again enjoy paradise with Eve and all of humanity.

SECTION 2, CHAPTER 11

ALL THE GREATS

A s I am telling you this story today, you can only imagine how many missions God has sent my way. Actually, I am not sure that you can imagine it. I sometimes have trouble fully comprehending and coming to terms with the immensity of assignments that I have completed. I actually lived through them all, and I can remember each event in great detail. When I actually do allow myself a moment to think back on my life, as I am doing now for you, it is not the details that I struggle with, but the sheer number of endeavors. I know that I have made mistakes. I also know that despite those mistakes, I always strove to do the will of God and work toward returning humankind to paradise. I possess complete understanding of several different numeric systems, and I am quite proficient in numerous advanced methods of mathematic computation, so I could quantify my life's work in many ways. But when I think about quantifying my accomplishments, I am not sure what to count as missions. I have done many major things in my life for humanity. As you now know, I helped Noah on the Ark, and I will continue to describe more significant events in which I played a part. I try to do at least one thing every day to help me on my path. If I were to simply count one act a day, which is a conservative number, then I still would have given up counting centuries ago. Besides, you likely aren't interested in stories of me simply helping somebody cross the street or comforting an individual who was sick. I don't blame you, as those are not exciting stories for me to describe, either. In the grand scheme of things, though, I am every bit as proud of those moments as I am of the world-changing events.

As God had promised me, I did have time between larger missions to rest, refocus, and travel to the location of my next major endeavor. I greatly enjoyed those breaks, as they allowed me time to focus on talking to the people I met between specific assignments. It seemed that these times of respite always came just when I needed them most. While I was working on a mission goal or task, I would become consumed by my activities, and I had little interaction with people outside of those involved in the assignment. So, despite spending time in Florence during the early years of the Renaissance, I was not truly able to enjoy the masterpieces being created at the time. The same can be said for all seven wonders of the world. Yes, I have seen all of these achievements at some point since, but it does seem sad that I was not able to enjoy them at the moment of design and creation.

I have seen the rise and fall of mighty empires all over the world. It sometimes was hard for me to accept that these strong and great empires would fail and vanish from the earth. Sometimes they were conquered in battle, but mostly the collapses came from their own doing. Even the ones that did lose in battle had set themselves up to fail through their own arrogance, lack of structure, refusal to advance in education, or simple laziness of thought and passion. It always amazed me how so many problems came from the misunderstanding that military makes an empire strong rather than focusing on education and science and art to advance civilizations. Sadly, I have learned that empires will fail and vanish from the history books.

OK, yes, I will admit it. I did often have something to do with these empires failing, but that still doesn't mean that I liked seeing them fail. Maybe someday I will tell you more about all of those experiences. They really aren't as exciting as you might imagine. As I have said, they generally died out over generations of decline rather than from one big event. In fact, I often would set something in motion to aide the collapse, only to find that history has not fully understood. It is a delicate balance to maintain an empire or great civilization. Many factors that can contribute to a fall are often overlooked—those were my specialty. I will share one example that truly demonstrates what I am talking about.

I am sure that you have enjoyed, or at least seen, any number of movies, plays, books, or TV shows about Roman gladiators. Well, that was my idea. I know that there are always many reasons given for the fall of Rome, and for the most part they are all true. A combination of problems always makes it more likely that an empire will fail. Still, most of the reasons are easily prevented or minimized if only citizens would pay attention. That was the beauty of my plan for Rome. The images you have seen of the Romans enjoying their death matches relay the start of the correct reality, but they fall well short of the actuality. As the leaders were destroying everything that had made the Roman Empire strong and proud, the people were busy clambering for a better view of the next brutal battle to the death. There was even a saying regarding this: panem et circenses. It literally meant "bread and circuses," which was a nice way of saying that the people wouldn't notice how bad things got along the path to demise as long as they had the promise of just enough food and entertainment. This certainly did prove to be true. The Roman Empire fell while the people cheered, oblivious to the reality around them. As I said, bringing down an empire is best done with multiple actions while the public's attention is distracted.

Just as I have seen civilizations fall, I have seen them all replaced by the next great people or ideas. Looking back from this perspective of human history, I can tell you that for the most part, these empires began with big ideas of making things better. Sadly the leaders did not always see their better ideas as being fit for all people outside of their top circle. Yes, some structures and systems were much easier to corrupt than others, but it still always came down to the people involved and not the design of the government.

Within any empire there will be a group of people who will do good on their own while others do bad without any pushing. The key to the success or failure lies in the majority of the people who exist in between those two extremes. The way in which this large group moves toward good or bad will determine the true nature of the empire. This has been true no matter what region or time of human history I have been working in.

I remember talking with Plato and Aristotle about governing and why they saw democracy as such a bad choice. After many conversations, they came to a basic answer regarding people and doing the right thing. Put simply, they felt that it was more likely for one person or a small number of rulers to do the right thing then for the majority of people living within the system to agree on doing the right thing. This simple, straightforward logic has always stuck with me through the years. Still, I also knew an author and statesman in sixteenth-century Florence who, while not his true belief, showed a very basic outline for gaining and holding power easily by mostly ignoring the right behaviors. Anyway, what I have learned through all of my years on this earth and observing governments and people is that citizens truly determine the good or bad of a system and not the other way around.

One of my assignments illustrates my understanding of humans quite clearly. I am sure you have heard of and probably assumed that I might mention this one. When I talked about stopping bad people, your thoughts most likely went to everybody's number-one bad guy: Adolf Hitler. Then you also probably wondered why I didn't kill him early on and save all of those lives. Well, the answer is both simple and complex. Obviously, I would have liked to stop the horrors of World War II and the Holocaust. The soldiers, the civilians, and, of course, the victims of the Nazi concentration camps under Hitler all suffered and live in my memory of those I was not able to help. I hope that many of them found eternal peace in the Garden and that some-day I will be able to talk with them in person there.

It truly hurt to know what was going on and that I did not stop it in the beginning. It is easy to look back at Hitler from the present and feel that I should have stepped in before he came to power. The fact that he hadn't done those things yet hits on two issues as to why I didn't stop him at a young age. First, I don't know the future. Yes, I am immortal, but I am not omniscient. God guides me, and I have many years of experience understanding humankind, but that is where it ends. In addition to that, I am not allowed to simply kill anybody… well, at least not directly. I am not allowed to actually intervene in that way. I can only work to set things in motion to achieve the final goal. My job is not to stop people from acting in a certain way. First I attempt to guide them back to a good path, which would be pleasing to God. I know how crazy that might sound to you in regard to Hitler, but everybody deserves the chance to be good. Obviously I failed in that objective in his case. But can you imagine if I had succeeded?

In all of my years, there have only been a few people able to rise to power so quickly and with such support as Hitler accomplished. His process of using the democratic system in Germany to build his power shows just how easily a system can be corrupted or hijacked. I truly had hoped to be able to guide Hitler to using that overwhelm-ing power and support for good. For a short while, I thought that it might be working, as strong efforts were made to turn around the collapsed economy and to bring the people together to celebrate and be proud of their heritage. Sadly, at that point, I became firmly en-trenched on the wrong path.

Sorry, I'm not here to tell you what I wish I could have done, but rather to share with you what I actually did do. So, let me back up and tell you the story from my experience. I had been in Europe for many years, dating back to the time just before World War I. Yes, I played key roles in that war as well. I made a few trips to Russia during the early 1900s, but I always found myself quickly returning to Europe. Finally, in the early 1920s, I was settled in as a member of the German people. Here I will begin the story of life and actions in Hitler's Third Reich.

CHAPTER 12

WHO AM I?

Each time I had a major mission in a new land, I had to first live and exist in that place for some time. In the early years, this was much more important. In the past, when the populations were smaller and everybody knew everybody else in the region, I could not simply move to the region and immediately be in a position to have any influence over events. In those years, I would have to move in and slowly work my way into the society over years before I would be accepted. As the population grew and became more mobile, it was much easier to simply move in unnoticed and quickly achieve whatever position was needed to complete my mission. The larger populations allowed me a great degree of anonymity. When I entered the region, people simply would not notice. I remained unknown at first so I could observe and study the situation—and gain a firm grasp on the mission. I was able to gauge my goals and decide on a plan before having to become actively involved in any of the issues involved.

When I came to find myself directed to Germany in the years following World War I, the country was in shambles and seemingly beyond repair. Given my history and knowledge, I could easily recognize this region as clearly teetering on the brink of complete loss and on the verge of vanishing from the world entirely. I am not simply talking about the physical destruction done to the buildings and the infrastructure from the war or the crippling terms imposed by the Treaty of Versailles ending the war. The thing that struck me most and led me to believe that it could easily have been the last days of the Germanic heritage was actually the people themselves. They no longer seemed to possess any spark of life. Everywhere I looked, I saw people who were clearly demoralized and without any hope in their future. These people truly needed a reason to believe in themselves and their country once again before all was lost for them.

Many people offered ideas and suggestions about what might work to rebuild Germany, but nobody had enough power or control to guide the people toward achieving any them. The damage and division among the people left the government totally crippled and broken with no real direction or leadership. This situation was quite desperate and had the potential to implode on itself, destroying the lives of everybody living there with untold repercussions for the rest of the world. Seeing this made me think back to my discussions with Plato and Socrates about their fears regarding democracy. With the government having to answer to a divided and hateful population, no party could truly sustain any control, and compromise was limited out of fear and distrust. Given all the chaos and disorder, I spent a long time living in the region, unsure who the object of my mission was or what goals I was supposed to help achieve. While it was obvious that saving Germany from its destructive path needed to be done quickly, a nagging feeling deep inside of me told me that my real mission went beyond the immediate need for economic reform. I assumed that through the process of helping and observing the re-building of the economy, my true mission would become easier to discern. I knew that I could not simply fix the problems, as I was not allowed to so directly intervene. Besides, even if I did have all of the answers, I did not want to become a prominent figure until I had a better understanding of what had truly brought me to Germany. Even with the larger populations making it easier to move in and out of regions, I tried to avoid the spotlight as much as possible and remain in the background as an advisor to help guide people to the right path. The problem was that I had been in Germany for a while and still had no idea how to accomplish anything.

As I said, there was no shortage of ideas or people claiming to have all of the solutions to the problems facing Germany. These tended to follow a basic truth of human nature: those speaking the loudest had the least to actually offer. I can tell you there was a lot of empty shouting going on. Everything was truly a mess, and I needed to help find a solution quickly. The problem was finding the right faction or leader to back and help guide to power. I know what you are thinking. I know that looking back, with the benefit of historical hindsight, it is easy to say that I made a huge mistake. Just remember what I told you before: I cannot see the future any more than you can. My goal is always to help guide and influence people to the right path, giving them every chance to find God's love. So hold off on blaming me for everything bad that happened in Germany, and let me tell you my story and the truth of what occurred.

It all started with a chance meeting one night at a bar. I know that sounds a bit ridiculous, but I often found that hanging out in such establishments allowed me to gauge the feelings, thoughts, and beliefs of the regular people.

Much of history focuses on the grand speeches and well-written essays of the elites. These are without question very important to study, but it is essential to remember that more important than the merit of the idea itself is how it is received and acted upon by the people. I have seen the most amazing ideas entirely ignored by the masses; and the simplest concepts can rally the people to revolutions and social upheaval. So in troubled times I spend as much time as possible in public places, such as markets, bath houses, and town squares, where I can observe the average people of the region. Still, at least through most of the modern ages, the best place to hear what the general population is thinking is sitting at a bar. While other public places offer a great deal of conversation and insight into the thoughts of the masses, bars and taverns offer the additional benefit of alcohol-loosened tongues, which speak without inhibition.

So, with that in mind, I was sitting at a table in a small Munich tavern the first time I was exposed to the mind of Adolf Hitler. I was quite impressed and blown away by the concepts he was trying to explain to his friends. He made no mention of any of the more sinister ideas he would later come to be known for, but instead he was focusing on the people and the economy. It was clear that he desired to stabilize the economy, create jobs, and bring back the sense of pride the Germanic people were missing. Knowing what I know now, it would not be that difficult to interpret some of the evil in Hitler's mind. There is a very thin line between patriotism and fanatical fascism. At that point, I had no reason to even begin to imagine what evils might be carried out under the orders of this man. Besides, that night his focus was predominately on creating jobs. It was easy to see that he cared about the future of Germany and he had spent a great deal of time trying to find solutions to the economic crisis. Still, there was something even more important than his financial planning. He had fire and charisma that people would respond to and follow. That was why he stood out, even in that crowded bar with so many voices proclaiming to have the solutions Germany needed. That passion and charisma truly separated Hitler from all of the others. I knew that night that Adolf Hitler could lead the people of Germany to new places.

When I had heard enough of the conversation to know for sure that this man was one whom I could easily help guide to a position of power and control so that he could help the people, I quickly finished my own drink and decided to join his table. I planned to break the ice by buying a round of drinks; hence the need to finish mine first. But in the time I took to finish my drink, they too had finished theirs. As I turned to approach their table, I found that Hitler and his friends had already gathered their coats, paid their tab, and headed out the door. I missed my chance to talk with Hitler that night, but I had found the voice that I knew would be able to rise above the noise in order to lead the people. I decided to go back and have the drink I had intended to share with Hitler. I could relax for the night, as my mind was filled with excited plans of how I could help guide this man to power, unite the people, build the economy, and so much more. I truly saw no limit to the amount of good that he would be able to accomplish. I knew that he was a little rough around the edges, but I had helped kings, chieftains, and emperors through the years, so I fully believed that I would be able to mold this fiery man into a strong leader who would save his people and make God proud. I simply needed to decide what persona I would take on to make myself an asset and gain a position of trust so I could guide Adolf Hitler to greatness.

With my initial chance at engaging Hitler in conversation lost, I had to find a new approach. As I'm sure you can imagine, he was not an easy man to find. Even on the rare occasions when I did know that I was close to him, it was impossible to find an opening and simply walk up to him to start the conversation I needed to have with him. Even though it was no easy task to keep track of Hitler, his name was starting to be mentioned more and more in the conversations I overheard out among the people. After a few more days of being frustrated by my lack of success, I began to make more serious inquiries of those who I did hear using his name. This only led to more disappointment, as it seemed that everybody had heard of Hitler, but nobody had actually met him. They had always heard of him from a friend or been handed a pamphlet by a stranger. Despite the frustration of not being able to locate Hitler to begin my work, I was encouraged that his name and message of economic recovery was spreading among the people. Members of the populace seemed more than willing to work with the government to solve the problems facing the nation together. They only needed somebody to lead them and push for programs allowing all of the people to succeed. Then suddenly one morning, I woke up to the news that Adolf Hitler had been arrested and was in prison after trying to organize a takeover of the government.

Now, at that point you might think that I would have changed my mind about Adolf Hitler having any promise or potential to do good things for the people. It would be easy to think that a man being held in prison would not be part of God's plan for helping people find their way. Then again, in all of my centuries, I have seen God work amazing things through people who society would so easily lock away and forget about. Besides, through my time on earth, I have seen and helped many governments change hands. I know from firsthand knowledge that in most cases it is not an easy change. The ruling party often has to be forced out, and sadly, far too often, the incoming party has to abandon noble beliefs in order to achieve the goal of occupying the seat of power. I guess sometimes even I have had to accept that the ends do justify the means. So, even after hearing that Hitler was in prison, I still fully believed he wanted to do great things, not only for Germany, but also for the world. Honestly, as I learned of his arrest, I was upset with myself more than him. If I had met him in person sooner, I could have guided him away from his flawed plan and kept him from being imprisoned. I would have crafted a strategy to help him to power on a much smoother path. And who knows? I might have been able to influence him and direct him away from the negative plans I did not learn of until it was too late. Still, this is an account of what did happen and not what I wish I had done differently.

I could not simply approach him and tell him about all of my experience in helping leaders, as my "clients" were spread all over the world and all throughout history. My exploits in the Ancient Greek and Roman Empires, helping to push for countless revolutions, and directing massive shifts in ideological paths made me quite qualified and able to help Hitler. Yet as far as anybody knew, I was just an average unknown person. Telling any of my true stories would ensure that I was never allowed anywhere close enough to him to help. But then I realized that Hitler being imprisoned was actually a blessing and I could use it to my advantage. If I could get to him in prison, I would be able to talk to him and have his undivided attention. I could use the time to gain his trust over the course of many conversations, so that he could see the value I had gained through my experiences. I would be able to carry messages to his friends on the outside and keep him informed of the news while he was behind bars. I would establish myself as a trusted friend, so that when he was able to move forward—and I had no doubt that he would—I could be in a position of influence to help protect him and make sure that Adolf Hitler would find his way to power.

It turned out that gaining access to Adolf Hitler in prison was not nearly as difficult as I had feared. With the economy in Germany suffering so severely, the police and prison forces had been stretched beyond the breaking point. I was able to simply walk in and make my way to the wing of the prison holding political prisoners, which is where I assumed I would find Hitler. Just as I was about to lose hope, I looked in one last cell. There I found myself face-to-face with Adolf Hitler. I admit that I had been so focused on the practical task of finding him that I had not truly thought through what I would say to him when I did get the chance. He didn't say anything. He simply stared at me. His expression was slightly puzzled, as though he was wondering who I was; he also seemed to be daring me to say something. Even though I had been looking for him and wanting to talk to him for so long, he had no idea who I was or why I was standing in front of his cell.

I started to regain my composure and was about to introduce myself to Hitler when a guard working at the prison rounded the corner and walked straight toward us. Before he was able to question my presence, I jumped on the offensive and introduced myself as a new guard for the prison. I asked him where I was supposed to report to be issued my uniform and sidearm. I explained to him that I had been sent specifically to guard this wing of political prisoners. Since I hadn't seen anybody at the central guard station, I was taking the initiative to familiarize myself with my wing of the prison. Obviously he was suspicious at first, as he should have been, considering that I was lying to him about everything. I had come a long way in regard to lying or twisting the truth since those early attempts to keep things from Eve. Using my now well-crafted skill of fast-talking, I was able to convince the guard that I was in fact legitimate. A short while later, after repeating my story a few more times, I found myself actually in uniform and filling out all of the appropriate paperwork, making me an official guard of the political prisoners. With this obstacle cleared, I headed back for my third attempt to introduce myself to Adolf Hitler.

In front of his cell once again, I was amazed at his calm demeanor. While other prisoners paced or sat fidgeting with their eyes rapidly shifting over all that could be seen, Hitler simply sat on the cot and reclined against the wall, reading a book. The behaviors of the other political prisoners reflected their previous positions and statures above this criminal class. There was simply no way that those men could be comfortable in a prison cell. The fact that Hitler was so at ease probably should have been a warning sign, but I attributed his demeanor to the intelligent mind I had heard previously at the bar so many nights ago.

I was suddenly roused from my thoughts when Hitler plainly declared that he knew I was a liar. When I blinked myself back into the moment, I realized that he had put down his book and was standing directly in front of me, staring right into my eyes. He then told me that he knew who I was. This naturally caught me off guard, and at the same time, filled me with a desire to burst into laughter. I had used so many different names and personas through the years that it always struck me as funny when anybody claimed to know me. There was no way that he could have known my real identity. It had been centuries since I had answered to my true name in any way. As technology and record-keeping had improved through the years, I had become quite vigilant at covering my tracks. Plus, even though I cannot know for sure, I fully believe that God protected me and kept my face from showing up in a recognizable way in any images or videos through the many years and many regions of the world I have been in. Still, for some reason, when Hitler said he knew who I was, it brought a feeling of nervousness and apprehension. Trying to remain composed, I stared right back at him, hoping that he would believe the hardened and trained prison-guard act, at least better than I believed it at that moment. After a few minutes, which seemed like ages to me, Hitler continued speaking. He told me that he remembered me from that night at the bar and that he knew I had been looking for him. As I let out my breath, which I didn't even realize I had been holding, I gladly told him that, yes, I had been there and had indeed been searching for him. Seeing this as a golden opportunity, I told him about overhearing his plans for fixing the economy and saving the people. I expressed my belief that his plans were brilliant and that they would surely work. Hearing this praise brought a small grin to his lips, which turned into a full smile when I stated that the name Adolf Hitler would never be forgotten.

Following that brief exchange, Hitler began to talk in more detail about his economic plans and his desire to restore the German people to a place of prominence and power in the world. As I listened, I offered very little in opposition or correction on anything, as I honestly saw no points of contention with his plans for the banks, industry, or service. Still, what I did mention was received warmly and with open, honest consideration and genuine appreciation. When he finished outlining his plans, Hitler asked me if I could help him. I was afraid he was going to ask me to help him escape from prison. I explained to him that it was in his best interests to stay in prison and serve the time rather than escape. Shocking me again, Hitler quickly took my advice and agreed that he should remain in prison. He sat back down on his cot and glanced around his small cell, making it clear that he agreed with me about staying there, but it was not a pleasing proposition. Looking up at me, he asked me if I could carry a message to his friends. He wanted them to know that he was fine and they should not attempt to free him from prison. He understood that his plans were ambitious and knew that people would support him in his mission, but after hearing me out, he knew that would all be lost if he were to escape from prison and had to live in hiding. He thanked me for showing him the right path to take and politely asked for some dinner. I took that to be his not-so-subtle way of ending our conversation.

After bringing his dinner, I set off to deliver Hitler's letter to his supporters with a smile on my face and pride in my heart. I was confident that even while he was in prison, I would be able to help keep his movement going and growing stronger. I had found a place of trust with Hitler, and I was set to be a person of value to him while he was imprisoned. During this time I would impress upon him just how much I could help him when he was released. As I left the prison grounds, I thanked God for bringing me to find Adolf Hitler and promised to do all that I could to guide him along the path in order to return humanity to the Garden and me to my beloved Eve.

CHAPTER 13

WITH FREEDOM IT BEGINS

As it turned out, Hitler only spent a few months in prison, but that doesn't mean that it was a quick, easy, or boring period of time for either of us. During these months, Hitler never seemed to stop thinking or even slow down in the slightest bit out of self-pity over being imprisoned. In all honesty, it seemed to be much the opposite. Every time I passed by his cell, he would call out to me to stop and talk to him about a new thought he was considering at that moment. Given my real reason for being at that prison, I was ecstatic to have these conversations. But in order to retain such access to Hitler, I did have to perform all of my normal required duties as a guard, so I tried to keep the conversations as short as possible. Unfortunately a short conversation with Hitler, especially at that point in time, meant spending at least twenty minutes with him before I could even begin to look for a reason to draw the discussion to a close. Even in those rare instances when he didn't have a lot on his mind to talk about, he would ask multiple questions regarding any and all news from the world outside of the prison. He would always be polite and ask about his friends and partners in order to be sure that they were still safe, but it was clear that his main interest was keeping track of local, national, and international politics. With my help, Adolf Hitler, from his prison cell, was able to retain his grasp on all of the news; and he remained one of the most informed people in all of Germany.

Soon routines began to develop in order to streamline the information transfers between us. I think he understood that if I spent too much time outside his cell, talking with him, it could eventually cost me my job and leave him cut off from the outside world. Of course being fired would be fine by me, as I didn't need the money at all, and the only reason I had the job was to have access to Hitler for conversation. Still, the odds of me being fired over this were quite low because of the shortage of staff. More likely I would simply be reassigned to a different part of the prison. This would still give me some limited access to Hitler, but nothing near the time that I desired. To facilitate quicker conversations, I got into the habit of taking notes on all of the news of the day while I was home at night. That way I could simply pass along a few pieces of paper for him to read what was going on instead of taking the time to recount each of the stories verbally. This practice freed up my limited time with him for clarification of finer points and more idealistic conversation rather than the mechanical retelling of events. I would occasionally suggest that I could simply bring him the actual newspapers, but he said he preferred my summaries and enjoyed my analysis. This compliment filled me with pride and gave me confidence that when the time came to move forward, I would be trusted and included in his plans.

In addition to our routines of keeping up with the news and discussing his latest thoughts, Hitler began to ask more about my own views. I saw this as a great chance to help guide him toward the possible goals I saw for the future. Through my many years of trying to help people find their way to paradise, I had a great deal of experience influencing powerful leaders to guide them down a path that was pleasing to God. I didn't go into any detail with Hitler about returning to the Garden and my desire to once again hold Eve in my arms, as he would likely decide that I was crazy and put an end to our association and friendship. Instead, I talked to him in more general terms about how humans are capable of so much more than how they were living. I would express my belief that it was possible with some hard work and tough choices for humans to live in a near-perfect state, combining the grace and power of God. When I would talk about such things, Hitler would seem to hang on every word, especially when I would vaguely reference God's lesson that some people are evil and seek to lead humanity to ruin. If only I could have read his mind at that point to know just how severely he was twisting what I was saying.

It wasn't too long before Hitler asked me for a favor in addition to our normal conversations and my efforts to keep him informed. He knew that it would be dangerous for his partners to actually visit him in prison, so he asked me to carry some messages to them. I had relayed the one early message regarding Hitler's desire to remain imprisoned rather than risk any type of escape, but he had not asked me to talk to his partners since then. I agreed to bring them his messages, seeing no reason not to, and I was happy Hitler saw me as a trusted ally. Hitler told me that these were very private messages and should not be read by anybody other than the intended recipient. Naturally, I assumed that he meant for me to not read the messages, but he went on to tell me that he also was referring to any other associate of his as well. The messages were for the named recipient and nobody else. Now, here is one of the times when I have to admit to being human and not being able to live up to the standard I would hope to set. I don't know if I was simply too excited to be starting this service or if I was simply overcome with curiosity, but as soon as I had left the prison, I found myself unfolding the note to read what it said. To my surprise, Hitler was one step ahead of me. His note did not contain words for the original recipient, but was actually intended for me. He asked me to bring him more paper the next day, and he wrote that I would be rewarded if I could prove to be more trustworthy in the future.

That night brought me very little rest, as I tossed and turned until sunrise trying to decide on my course of action regarding the letter. If I took Hitler the paper that he asked for, then he would obviously know that I read the note. I considered lying to him and saying that I had delivered the note as promised and the recipient had told me about the request for paper. It seemed like a logical lie, but then again those simple logical lies tend to be the ones that get found out in passing conversations later. On the other hand, he had written the note for me and assumed that I would read it this time. If I acknowledged that I had done exactly as Hitler had predicted, I hoped he would feel confident that he could read and predict my actions as we moved forward in a trusting relationship. Besides, given that he had expected me to read the note, it wasn't like I would be risking any future collaboration or friendship by simply being honest. Still, it wasn't like me to settle for simply meeting expectations, not while on my quest to return to perfection. How could I hope to hold him to a higher standard if I was not able to hold myself to this same simple standard? I must have changed my mind at least a dozen times that night as I rolled around in bed.

Before I knew it, morning had arrived, and it was time to get ready for work at the prison. After a full night of obsessively analyzing all of the options, I still had no idea which one would bring the best result. So I did the most natural thing in the world for me to do: I prayed. I knew that I didn't need to be kneeling with my hands in any certain position to talk with God. In fact, I considered my night of all-consuming doubt to be a form of prayer, as I knew God was always with me. I guess, to be honest, the act of kneeling in prayer doesn't feel like I am talking with God any more than at other times, but it does bring a sense of calming peace akin to what some people feel from meditation or yoga. I clearly knew better than to expect a burning bush, a chorus of angels, or any other overtly obvious answer to my prayers. Still, this simple act brought me the calm I needed to be able to move forward with my day. With this peace and confidence that things would work out, I grabbed a pad of paper and attached it to the back of my bicycle. I was still unsure whether I was going to deliver the paper to Hitler or leave it for another time. But I did know that I would need the paper if I decided that giving it to him was the best option.

That morning, like every other morning on my way to work, I stopped at a local shop to buy some fresh bread for my lunch. Now, in the midst of this economic depression, fresh food of any kind was expensive. But over the years, I had managed to accumulate a reserve of money to fall back on in order to survive. I mean, it wasn't like all of my missions allowed me to have a paying job as I did this time working at the prison. Often I simply had to rely on my reserves to cover all of my expenses.

I am still so thankful that during my time with the Knights Templar during the Crusades we were able to create a system of banking so people don't have to physically carry their wealth. I do still feel horrible for what happened to many of my friends from those days, but I did warn them not to give King Philip of France such reason to be concerned. I warned them not to allow anybody to build up such a large debt, especially not a man with such armies and influence over the Pope. I guess on the positive side, I should be grateful that many of them did find a way to escape and thrive elsewhere.

Anyway, like so many other mornings, I stopped at this local store to buy some bread, and when I came back out of the store, I found my answer regarding the paper. While I had been inside the store, a presumably large vehicle of some kind—a truck or a bus, most likely—had passed by and driven through a rather deep mud puddle. My entire bicycle, including the parcel of paper, was covered in dirty water. Knowing that the paper would no longer be suitable for Hitler to write on, I took it to the shopkeeper and offered it to him, thinking that some parts of it might be clean enough to use for some scrap paper. I know that it wasn't much, but I preferred to let him find some use for what could be salvaged instead of simply throwing the entire package in the trash. With my decision made, I wiped off my bicycle seat and continued on my way to the prison, contemplating the new question of how to explain not delivering the message or having any paper.

When Hitler saw me walking toward his cell with my package of bread, he began to laugh. I can only assume that he was laughing because he was pleased with his ability to predict my behavior so easily. He believed that my lunch parcel was the paper that he had requested, showing my failure to resist the temptation to read his note. These thoughts actually brought a smile to my face, considering I had been tempted by some of the great evils of all humanity and even the devil himself. Granted, I had indeed caved to this temptation, as well as many others through the years, but even then I knew that it was not behaving perfectly that would regain paradise for humanity. I'm not saying that I didn't try to avoid temptations, but I have learned to accept the reality of this world and see each failure as a learning experience instead of a roadblock. As I got closer to Hitler's cell, his smile only got bigger. I could almost see his mind working to decide just how he was going to gloat over his small victory. Saving him the embarrassment of saying something, I went ahead and opened my parcel to show him that it was just a small loaf of bread, which I offered to share with him. His smile immediately left his face, and it took him a few seconds to regroup and regain his composure. After a moment of wondering what his next move would be, I was shocked when Hitler simply asked me where I had his paper. I managed to keep a straight face and play dumb for a bit, denying any knowledge of what his note said. I will admit that it was actually kind of fun to see this highly intelligent man squirm in his cell, but I finally let him off of the hook and told him the whole story.

I honestly think that moment, while it might seem insignificant, actually played a key part in Hitler forming his opinion of me and cementing his belief that I could be of great use to him in his future plans. Still, before any of those plans became reality, several more months would pass with conversations from his prison cell and a lot of actual message deliveries. Of course, the next day, I did bring several brand new tablets of paper for Hitler to use; and the whole incident became a running joke for years to come, even after I no longer saw any humor in the man.

During the rest of Hitler's time in prison, I had to bring him several new tablets of paper and many extra pencils. Some of these he used to write notes for me to deliver, while other tablets were dedicated to his copious notes on the news I brought him of the politics going on outside of the prison. Still, I noticed that more and more of the paper was being kept back in the corner of his cell, where it couldn't be read. I occasionally asked him about what was on that growing stack of paper, but he always changed the subject and made it clear that he was not going to talk about the pile of paper. Before long, his writing project began to take up the majority of his time, and our conversations became shorter. At first I worried that I had done something to damage his opinion of me, but then I realized that while the length of the talks were getting shorter, they were actually becoming more detailed. We spent less time talking about theories or hypothetical situations. The conversations began to focus on actual people and problems that would be facing Germany in the years to come. I then understood that Adolf Hitler was ready and wanting to put theory into practice and seek the reigns to drive Germany to the prominence that had been lost and so many people sought to find again.

One day, after I brought a response from one of the many contacts Hitler kept through me, I was filled with an unexplained nervousness. As he read the note, the expression on his face told me that it was filled with good news. Rather than breaking into conversation, as was our routine, Hitler asked me for some time alone. Fighting back my curiosity to understand his change in demeanor, I gave him his time and space. Considering that the prison was nearly empty, especially my sections, there was not a lot of actual work to be done.

This had been a great benefit when Hitler had been looking to fill his days with conversation, but as those had gotten shorter I had been forced to fill my time with other pastimes. Luckily the other guards at the prison were in similar situations with their work, so we had plenty of time to talk and get to know each other. It turns out that many of them had fought for Germany in World War I. Now they were working as guards because it was the best job available that came anywhere close to utilizing their skills as soldiers. The good news for me was that it meant they always had war stories to tell and were happy to share with a youngster like me. Given the fact that I had actually seen every war in human history and had participated in some manner in the major ones, I could have blown their minds with my war stories. But since I was supposed to be too young to have even fought in World War I, I figured it was best to just listen.

The other bit of good news for me was that the other guards liked to play card and dice games. Being in Germany, and having served in World War I, most of them preferred to play the card game *Skat,* which they had used to kill hours of time in the trenches of the Great War. Being the new guy to the prison, I gladly accepted their invitation to teach me the game. It was actually not all that different from other trick-based card games around the world. I could have shown them some games that were popular in the Roman Empire, with Spartan soldiers, or any number of variations from Chinese and African dynasties, as well as native tribal games from the Americas. Truth be told, many of these games were actually quite similar. I did sometimes have to laugh to myself when historians would discover that similar games were played by people separated by thousands of miles and years with no apparent link between them. If only they knew that the games did not develop out of some basic human characteristic, but simply by my movements. Still, as the world had become more developed, it was hard to keep up with all of the regional favorites and varieties.

After losing more hands of *Skat* than I care to admit, I decided that I had given Hitler enough time, and I headed back to see if he wanted to talk before I left for the night. I guess that I had actually taken longer than he expected or wanted, because as I came closer to his cell, I could see that he was pacing like a caged animal. I had never seen him act this way in any of the months he had been in prison. Other prisoners did it all of the time, but not Hitler. This told me that something was about to change, and he was not his calm, composed self. When I actually reached the cell, he quickly handed me a piece of folded paper. He told me that delivery of that note would complete a deal securing his release from prison.

Hearing that news left me quite conflicted. Obviously, I was happy that he would be free to begin the work of returning Germany to a proud and productive state. Still, I wondered how I would fit in the plans. I would no longer be needed as a messenger. More importantly, I would no longer be the only source for conversation available to Hitler. He would now be able to talk freely with all of his long-standing friends and partners from before his arrest. I wondered if I would still be needed when he was released. I felt that I had proven myself to him many times, and I had heard his promises in the past, but those were all easy things to say when locked behind bars. I did not want to lose this chance to do God's work and help put the world on a path to goodness.

Even before I was able to think of a way to broach my questions about the future with Hitler, he once again surprised me. He simply looked at me and announced that following his release from prison, he would be moving in with me at my home. He felt that it would be too dangerous for him to return to his own home or to live with any of his other known associates. He was a man with few options, and he felt confident that I would do my best to provide him with all that he needed. There was no discussion; he simply stated what was going to happen.

Maybe I should have noticed him becoming much more demanding, but my mind was honestly too busy trying to figure out how to make this man, who I had identified as possibly my last mission, comfortable in my small, one-bedroom apartment. I was honored that he would choose my home as a refuge, where he would feel safe to begin his work. I looked forward to the upcoming conversations and planning that we would soon share, as we would lay the groundwork for restoring Germany. Yes, I was quite confident that, with God's help, I would be able to guide Adolf Hitler to greatness, and together we could create an amazing world for all to enjoy and praise God. In my mind I had seen a clear picture of my mission in Germany and my future success for God. For this moment, I once again let myself imagine my return to the Garden and being reunited with my precious Eve. I felt that it was now only a matter of a few months or years before we would succeed, and I was anxious to begin this triumphant path.

CHAPTER 14

CHARISMA AND COMPROMISE

I am not really sure what I expected to happen. I guess I assumed that after spending several months in prison, Hitler would want to spend some time outside in the fresh air and enjoy his renewed freedom. I know that after the times I had spent confined, whether it was in prison or simply traveling on a boat full of animals, I always enjoyed a nice walk in the wide open and didn't want to be within walls for a while. Adolf Hitler, on the other hand, wanted nothing to do with going on a walk or relaxing outside. Instead, he wanted to go straight to my apartment. He told me he didn't want to waste time that should be spent on getting organized and preparing to move forward. While I admired his drive, it did seem a bit odd to me to not celebrate being out of prison.

Even though I didn't understand his thinking, I have to admit that I too at that point felt excited at the prospect of sitting down together at my table and beginning this mission. With that settled, we gathered all of his possessions, most of which consisted of the writing he had done in prison. His composition nearly tripled the amount of belongings he had since he was first incarcerated. After gathering all of the bundles, I paid for a taxi to carry us home. Even with all of the excitement building as I thought about the future, I still had a nagging feeling that everything was going to change now that Hitler was out of prison. Looking back, I can see now that my small fears of how things would change came nowhere close to the reality that would develop over the next few years.

When we arrived at my apartment, it took two trips to carry in all of the papers and other possessions Hitler had brought with him from prison. I started to carry his bags into the only bedroom of my small apartment, causing Hitler to put up a polite protest over taking my bed. I could tell this was only out of a sense of appearance, as he fully expected to be the one occupying the bedroom. I didn't mind this, as my couch was far better than many of my previous sleeping arrangements throughout the years. When he had protested enough to satisfy the social norm, Hitler immediately dropped down onto my former bed. He told me that after sleeping on a poor-quality mattress for months, he was anxious to have a good nap; but while he was sleeping, I should organize all the papers on the table so we could begin working as soon as he woke up without wasting time. I started to ask him how he wanted his things organized; but before I could get the question out, he had already rolled over with his back to me, and was sound asleep.

Feeling a bit more like a lowly aid than an equal at that point, I told myself that his craving for a good nap was only natural, and when he woke up, things would be better. After all of our conversations, I truly believed that Hitler saw me as a valued asset and ally, not just some assistant. Setting myself to the task at hand of trying to organize all of the bundles of notes, I noticed that Hitler's large notepad was not there. After a brief panic that somehow the precious notebook had been lost in the haste to leave the prison, I started to wonder if he was in fact keeping that one hidden. I knew that during our prison conversations Hitler had been sure to deflect any questions and keep the contents of that notebook private. I started to wake him to ask about it, just in case I needed to go back to the prison and look for it, as I was certain he would be quite irate if it had indeed been lost. Just as I was about to wake him from his nap, I saw that the notebook was not missing at all. It was in fact securely held in his hand between him and the wall, as if he was protecting it from danger. This couldn't really upset me, since I had actually been thinking that when I came across it that I would go ahead and take a quick look inside to see just what was so special to him.

As I am sure you might have guessed by now, Hitler was using that notebook to write his book, *Mein Kampf.* Looking back now, it is clear why he kept it so private and hidden from me early on. Had I been able to read it that day, I would have realized that my ambition of helping Hitler lead the world to greatness was a lost cause, and that instead I should immediately move to prevent him from gaining any more influence. I am not sure why he didn't trust me with it, given all that I had done to help him while he was in prison. Something kept him from letting me see that side of his plans. He continued to mislead and to manipulate me into believing that he was the one I thought I had been waiting for to guide humanity to God's path, allowing me to finish my mission on earth.

A few hours later, Hitler woke up and came out of the bedroom to find all of his notes organized by the countless topics. He seemed pleased that everything was out and ready to begin work. I suggested eating lunch before we began and set to making us both simple sandwiches. He seemed to accept this gesture as a polite courtesy; but to be honest, hunger was not my true motivation. I took this time while eating lunch to bring up the topic of the notebook once again. I mentioned that as I had been going through the papers, I had noticed it was missing. I was in the middle of asking him if I needed to run back to the prison to look for it when he abruptly cut me off and quite emphatically told me that the notebook was of no concern to me. It was filled with his personal writings, and if I continued to annoy him with such questions, he promised me that I would find myself without any place in his plans.

This hit me like a ton of bricks. I had always thought he was just trying to perfect some more of his plans and was holding back until he felt they were ready. Since our conversations had covered so much, I had thought that I knew this man very well. After this short exchange, I began to understand that I only knew his economic plans and theories, and I did not know the man himself. I put this in the back of my mind, planning on working to change that truth at a later date. Even without knowing him better, it was crystal clear that Hitler intended to work now and was not interested in any friendly chit-chat. Looking to move on quickly, I sat down to show him my work. Thankfully he accepted this gesture as an apology of sorts for mentioning his private notebook, and we began to formulate a plan of action.

Over the next few days, we hardly left my kitchen table. With only short breaks for meals, sleep, and other human functions, we managed to get through all of the notes with no more problems. As with other such planning sessions through my many years, I knew that creating the theories was by far the easy part. The real question was how to take these theories of rebuilding industry and putting people back to work from mere words to practical actions. We discussed the technical needs and requirements for rebuilding a devastated infrastructure as well as restoring the morale of a beaten and worn-down nation.

The biggest problem facing us, though, had nothing to do with any of those components. Before we could work on those massive issues, we had to find a way to gain a position of power for Hitler so that he would have the influence to guide and shape the future of Germany, and I hoped the entire world, into the peaceful paradise that I had envisioned at the end of his plans. Now, I know that this can be a daunting task for any individual, but we were talking about a man who had just spent several months in prison for his involvement in an attempt to take over the government. The task of raising him up as a legitimate source of authority would require a lot of grass-roots effort and a complete rebuilding of Hitler's image.

Having lived through all of human history, my knowledge of political structures and governmental design is quite extensive and came to serve a vital role at that point. Using the knowledge I had gained from my experiences with such men as Plato and Aristotle, I was able to show Hitler that the key to his coming to power was not held in the current elites of the government, but in manipulation of the masses. Hearing this, Hitler began to discuss what he remembered from reading the Greek philosophers. Several times I had to hold back my laughter, as I pretended to have simply read their works. Over the years I have read more books than I care to even attempt to count, but I did not make a habit of reading the works of people whom I had actually known and spent days exchanging ideas with. Still, I managed to combine my understanding from the discussions and debates I had enjoyed in the past with Hitler's understanding of their writings so that we were able to come up with a mutual decision and plan of action.

The next day, we met with Hitler's remaining allies and explained to them that we would use the existing system to gain our influence and then power by taking the plan to the people. The need for employment and money would make it an easy sell to bring people to Hitler's party. Then if we added in a few loaded concepts like God and patriotism, the masses would flock to support and believe in us. I had some mixed feelings about using God as a means of manipulation, given my true past and beliefs. I knew the emotional connection to God would lead people to willingly support us. I had seen this approach used countless times with great success, and I had discussed the concept with several of humankind's great minds over the years. Sadly, at this point, I still believed in the good that we were going to do, and I thought it was God's plan for me to help Hitler lead the world toward a time of peace and prosperity. It would be another few years before I would become fully aware of the other side of Hitler and his plans for the world.

With the plan laid out, we set out to the same tavern where I had first overheard Hitler discussing his economic plans. It might not have been the biggest tavern in the area, but somehow it seemed a fitting place to launch our campaign to lead Germany back to the traditional strength that Hitler desired. Surprisingly, when we were just about to reach the tavern, Hitler changed his mind. He decided that we would come back the following night to begin our newly formed plan. Instead of starting that night, he wanted to simply drink and enjoy the evening with his closest friends and supporters. I welcomed this unexpected sentiment. That night of relaxing and celebrating the success we knew was to come was one of the last good times filled with peace, happiness, and above all, hope for the future.

As with any developing movement, the beginning seemed slow and went fairly unnoticed by any of the larger opposition parties at first. Why would anybody notice a few people just having conversations at the local taverns? We kept it simple in the beginning and stuck close to our homes, talking to people who we already knew to be sympathetic to our message. Soon Hitler started getting impatient and wanted to see quicker and larger growth and progress. I knew then that it was time for the next step in my plan, and we started spreading out to some larger areas to feel out how the citizens would receive Hitler and his ideals. To our disappointment, the initial reaction was not a positive one. This was not as much due to the content of what was being said as simply the pack or mob mentality to reject an outsider. Despite being well-known in the smaller taverns closer to home, Hitler's name meant nothing to these new audiences. To help fight this, I began to arrive at the locations ahead of time and make use of my well-honed skill at blending in anywhere. I would simply strike up conversations and get to know the patrons. Then I would shift the conversation to the political spectrum and begin showing them the logic of Hitler's economic plans. During this time, Hitler would begin his speech. I would wait for the patrons to catch a key word of the speech; or if they didn't catch it soon enough, I would pretend to be shocked at hearing somebody expressing the views that we had just been discussing. As they began to pay more attention to what Hitler was saying, I would make subtle comments about his insights or the clarity of his vision. Since I had worked my way into their acceptance through the evening, they took these comments to heart and truly listened to Hitler's speech. This simple push was enough to open many minds and wallets to the cause, not to mention making Hitler a well-known name with a quickly growing base of support.

At each location, Hitler's associates would collect some money, but more importantly support. During that period of time, I must have been "persuaded" to join the cause a dozen or so times, with none of them ever realizing that my design from the very beginning had gotten them to believe in the message.

At first this filled everybody involved with a sense of great pride and accomplishment. To see that level of growth gave us confidence that soon we would be able to take the message to the national level. We had failed to anticipate that with all of these new people coming on board, it would become much harder to keep control over the message. It seemed that other people began to take credit for the ideas and then also alter them in small ways to fit their own objectives. Sensing that things could soon spiral completely out of control, we decided to move beyond simply talking at taverns and meeting halls. Looking through all of the notes that we had gathered, we picked out a few key phrases and formulated some slogans that would be easy to remember and repeat. Using some of the money donated during the speeches, we had some pamphlets printed. With the message seeming to spread on its own, the words were less important than the branding we achieved by putting Hitler's name and face together with the message. Having Hitler's name plastered all over the pamphlets led people to make the connection between the ideas and the man behind them.

The upstarts who had been trying to take credit for the ideas faded away. Even more importantly, we started to get requests for Hitler to speak at bigger venues. This also meant getting paid as opposed to simply taking up collections. Soon we truly began to be seen as a small but growing and relevant political party. This was solidified in the next election, when a few members of our group actually won seats in the Reichstag, having run campaigns based on Hitler's economic platform.

It would have been easy at that point to relax and be proud of the success we had found in transforming a few conversations into a legitimate political party speaking for the people. In fact, as our numbers grew, I considered the possibility that I had done enough and should be leaving for my next mission. With Hitler speaking for the people and seeking to fully rebuild the economy, I could see no path where he would fail to gain the power that he needed to change the direction of Germany and the world. Still, I did not have the feeling of success that God always gave me when I had done what I was supposed to do, neither was I feeling a pull in any direction to start heading out to my next mission. Without those feelings, I knew that I had not yet accomplished the full mission that I had been sent to do. I needed to stay longer and work harder to see what else I could do to help take care of Hitler.

Just as quickly as I had felt that the situation was getting better for the people, things changed. Maybe my arrogance caused me to be blinded by the surging numbers of Hitler's supporters and miss the clear signs of problems approaching. We thought that the economy was bad before, but it took a turn toward the catastrophic. I honestly don't know how Hitler would have reacted to this downturn had he been in power at the time, but I do know that he took full advantage of the current government's mistakes. I won't go into details about everything other than to say that the steps taken by those in power were seen as horrible attacks on the democratic system. At best it led people to doubt that those in control of the government even cared, but at worst it caused many to believe that the current regime was intentionally trying to protect itself at the expense of the majority.

Looking back from the present, I can now see great irony in how Hitler used that situation to cement his position as a key player in the national government. Again, I won't bore you with play-by-play details. Just remember that democracy at its best is fragile and easily manipulated if the people allow it to happen. Manipulating the masses and using the rules of the democratic system had always been the plan, but even I had doubted how easily the people would come to embrace Hitler and push for him to lead them.

Naturally, Hitler's fast rise to prominence in the government led to some ruffled feathers from the other political parties who had seen their numbers shrink over the past few elections. These ruffled feathers quickly transitioned from under-the-breath mutterings to defiant resistance to working with anybody thought to be a supporter of Hitler's party. This in turn only strengthened Hitler's resolve and ambition to gain enough power to avoid such political games. He was becoming convinced that the only way to succeed was to find a way to go it alone without any support from other parties at all. In time enough support might have shifted his way for that to be possible. It was also becoming more likely that his attitude would be taken as too controversial and confrontational, causing him to actually lose some of the support we had worked so hard to gain over the previous months. Sensing that things were quickly nearing a tipping point, which would either make or break all that we had been looking to accomplish, I decided to take things into my own hands and try to ensure that we would be in a position where we could do the most good to help the people. I felt that if I approached some of the other more centrist party leaders in Hitler's name, I might be able to work toward some sort of compromise and alliance for the common good.

Knowing that the prominent members of the centrist party met on a routine schedule I took the opportunity to approach them in order to describe the future for Germany and the world that would be created under Hitler's economic plans and leadership, at least how I envisioned it happening. They could not deny the benefits of the plans I put before them; neither could they deny that Hitler's growing popularity with the people would make it virtually impossible to accomplish anything without his blessing. The government essentially was sitting at a standstill. The other parties could still prevent Hitler from simply implementing his plans; yet at the same time, he was able to block anything that he did not wish to be passed. I convinced these other leaders that they could work with Hitler through me as I brokered a compromise. At the end of the meeting, they were quite eager for me to proceed. As I left the room, I was once again filled with hope and looking to use this success to achieve my ultimate goal of returning to my Garden with all of humanity.

That feeling was quickly lost as I began to tell Hitler about the progress I had made forming an alliance for him with the centrist parties. As the words started to leave my mouth, Hitler visibly showed his disapproval over what I had done. He told me that I had no right to speak on his behalf and proceeded to question my loyalty. This took me aback, as I had to this point felt that I had gone way beyond what should have been needed for him to know that I was dedicated. Once I regained my composure, I reminded him of all that I had done for him while all of his other friends had abandoned him leaving him alone in prison without even visiting that it was my plan we had been following to gain our current level of success, and that I would always speak on behalf of what I believe to be in the best interest of the people. As I finished my mini-explosion, I could see that I had gotten through to him, and he even apologized to me for being so short-sighted as to forget my contributions.

While we had been having our shouting match, I had realized it was not the benefit he would gain from alliance with other parties that he resented, but rather the thought that he needed them to achieve his goals and that he had needed somebody else like me to secure their help. Had I presented the compromise as the other parties looking to help Hitler in exchange for a little compensation rather than us asking them for help, the argument could have been avoided.

With both of us calm once again, I started over. This time I focused more on the benefits of this compromise for him personally and downplayed the actual compromise aspect as much as I could. From this new position, Hitler would be able to be a true force for the good of all people and help set humanity on a great path. In the span of about an hour, I had been filled with hope, then I lost hope, and then I was once again confident that I would soon be home with my family, and especially my beloved Eve.

CHAPTER 15
WHAT HAVE I DONE?

The whirlwind of activity and emotion only intensified over the next few months. Despite all of the success in getting Hitler's party members elected to offices, it was becoming obvious that Hitler was frustrated by his own lack of electoral victories. While I had become very accustomed to living life just a step or two out of the spotlight, Hitler had great personal desire to be the one and only voice of power. It was simple in his mind. The ideas had been his, so he should be the one leading the path toward all that we had envisioned for the country. I began to worry that this frustration would derail all of the progress we had been making with the elections, so I decided to once again act on Hitler's behalf with the centrist parties. Building on my previous success, I was able to secure a deal that allowed Hitler to be appointed to the position of Chancellor. This was not too difficult to achieve, given the government's current gridlock and the high level of support the people had for Hitler.

While I thought that this might appease Hitler and hold him over until we were able to carry our success to higher levels, it quickly became apparent that I had not bought nearly as much time as I had hoped. Despite sounding impressive, the position of Chancellor really was little more than an empty title with no real power. I think this only served to frustrate Hitler even more, as he began to openly complain about the function of the government and express longing for true authority. Witnessing the ineffectiveness of the government to accomplish any of the goals we had set out to achieve, Hitler began to express his desire for power to simply enact the policy changes that he desired. I had always known that he was a man of little patience, and it was clear that it was running out quickly. But I did not in any way anticipate what was to come.

We continued to experience growing frustration during these weeks and months. Finally, one of the key events that vaulted Adolf Hitler from a minimal player in the government to the most powerful man in the world, at least for a few years, was the Reichstag fire. Many modern history books explain this fire as just one of a long series of events that show Hitler to be the monster that he truly was. To those of us living at the time, it was not quite so obvious. We were not blessed with all of the research and information that has since become available. In the actual moment, it was a time of panic and uncertainty.

Maybe I was a bit blinded by my belief in the good that I saw possible, but I too overlooked much of the evidence. That does not mean I fully believed the official story of the communist parties being behind the attack. I was puzzled by this accusation. Having dealt with some of the leaders of that party in the past, I would not have expected them to be involved with anything like setting the Reichstag fire. So, while I did not see through the smoke to perceive Hitler as the cause of the incident, I did begin to feel a little unsure about what was going on around me.

I am not going to lie to you and try to make myself look better than I was. I could tell you that from that moment on I was able to keep my eyes open and clearly see what was going on, but that would not be the truth. If I am to be honest, in the aftermath of that fire and all that began to happen quite quickly for us, I didn't really have a lot of time to devote to the question of who was actually behind the fire. But I did realize how arrogant I had been lately. I had been brought to Germany on one of my missions from God. Early on I had decided that helping Hitler save the economy and pull the people up out of despair was clearly what God had planned for me. I was confident in that decision and honestly excited to use all of my knowledge of political systems and what I had learned about power throughout the many centuries. But I had been neglecting one aspect that had been central to my life: prayer.

Prayer had always been a constant for me, no matter where I was or what mission I was trying to accomplish. Well, there was one other time when I let myself slide away from this, which turned out to be a major turning point in my life. I will get to that later. When I realized my arrogance about my role with Hitler in Germany, I began to pray again and ask God to help me to understand what His wishes truly were for me on this mission. I still felt to my core that with the right advice and guidance, Hitler could accomplish great things for the world. Despite this belief I was starting to see the likelihood that things could go the other way and troubles could be unleashed if I messed up. So, yes, through my found-again prayer, I did begin to question some things. Without any real proof being offered at the time, I stayed the course and decided to work even harder to help guide things in the right direction, hoping that God would give me the right words and inspiration to achieve this goal.

With Hitler essentially assuming control of the government following the fire, I felt confident that we could now focus on the problems facing Germany and the world rather than the petty power struggles that plagued democratic governments. I told myself that the frustration of being so close to having the ability to change the world and yet being denied that by the other factions of the government had been the cause of the changes I had started to see in Hitler. I wanted to believe that now with that power, he would be reenergized and driven to accomplish the goals we used to spend hours talking about while he was in prison. Still, it wasn't as if all of the opposition had suddenly vanished. Some still desired to hold firmly to the same old ideas that had failed to bring any relief to the nation of the past years. Even though this group was clearly the minority within the government, and it did not have the support of the people, its members appeared to be set to block any attempts Hitler desired to make at reform.

Not wanting to see progress stall again, I offered to negotiate another compromise in order to move things forward. I wasn't surprised when Hitler rebuffed this idea. I had anticipated that he would not be overly receptive to me "saving" him again and moving his party more than he was doing. I had even figured out a few possible ways to secure the compromise without it being known that I was involved instead of him. Everything is about perception over reality, so I felt confident that I could obtain the compromise and at the same time make Hitler look like the powerful and gracious leader I still hoped he would become. Still, I was a bit taken aback when I did not have the chance to make any of my arguments to counter those views. I was simply told that my skills, as great as they were, would not be needed for any endeavors dealing with this situation.

In a few days I knew exactly why Hitler had not needed me to broker another compromise with the minority parties. It all became clear with the announcement of the Enabling Act of 1933. While I had looked to find a compromise and ways to convince others to support our directives, Hitler had decided to secure his position of power by effectively rendering all other views as obsolete. With his supporters in the government falling in line, the Enabling Act gave Hitler the authority to create and change policy unchecked, even in the case of working outside of the constitution. In all of my years on earth, I have seen plenty of dictators and kings. Some of them were very intelligent, and others were dumber than rocks. I have seen the most immoral queens, and I have seen chieftains rule with more morality than any democracy could dream of having. The nature of the ruler is always more important than the design of the government.

I couldn't help realizing the change that I had experienced recently with the Reichstag fire and now with the way in which the Enabling Act came to exist. During all of those long conversations with Hitler while he was in prison, I had been filled with excitement and a sense of peaceful knowledge regarding the future, knowing that Hitler had the ability to make broad, sweeping changes to a very broken world. A few months earlier, I would have been ecstatic about the passing of the Enabling Act. But I had begun to open my eyes a bit and see that there was a different side to Hitler. The more I returned to devotion and prayer, the less sure I was of what I had been doing. I still saw greatness in the plans and policies that we had discussed so many times, and I knew that it was possible for Hitler to lead the world toward everything that God had wanted me to bring to humanity. Yes, I still believed, despite my growing concerns about him, that if Hitler would simply listen to me and a few other members of the party, we could really set the world on the right path, and I could finish up my mission to return to the Garden.

Any remaining hopes that I held did not last much longer. In the months following the Enabling Act of 1933, some serious tensions arose between Hitler and some of the other factions of the Nazi Party. Two groups especially seemed to be upsetting to Hitler: those party members who tended to lean more liberal, led by Gregor Strasser, and the members of the SA, or brownshirts, led by Ernst Röhm. Strasser and his followers irritated Hitler because he did not approve of their views that the party should fully embrace socialism. On the other hand, Hitler was actually fearful of Röhm using his SA foot soldiers to enact a coup so that he could replace Hitler as the head of the government. I had not spent a lot of time with Röhm, so I can't say for sure what his intentions were regarding Hitler. I do know that even with my limited exposure to the two of them together, it was clear there was tension between them. While Hitler wanted to outthink and "convince" others to do what he wanted (a skill that I sadly admit to helping him craft and cultivate), Röhm was much more inclined to use the brute strength of the SA to force his desires on the world.

With these two threats to him starting to make more noise publicly, Hitler was beginning to show some signs of stress. At times he even retreated to his private office alone. When I would ask to join him, hoping to find a way to guide him to the path I wished him to follow, he would simply assign me some busy work to get rid of me. I kept telling myself that he just wanted to be alone, but then I started to see some other men leaving his office. I knew some of the men that were sharing those private meetings with Hitler, but others were new to me. Of those I did know, they were a mixture of cunning thinkers and crass reactionaries. That extreme difference between the known factions made me a bit more concerned about not knowing the others involved and which way they might tip the balance.

A few times I thought there was an additional participant in the room who remained secret. As the group would enter Hitler's office, I would catch a glimpse of an extra hat or coat hanging on the wall that did not belong there. And it would always be gone when the meeting had ended. I began to worry, not only about what was being discussed, but also about who was involved in the decisions being made without my presence.

The decision was made in that office, without my input or knowledge, that both of the threats to Hitler needed to be eliminated. I can't be positive, but I have always had a feeling that three "threats" were put on the elimination list. Maybe I am just paranoid and reading too much into everything. Maybe it has something to do with the fact that Hitler and everybody involved in the decision knew that I would be opposed to eliminating those men, and I would do everything that I could to work with them. Still, it is only a gut feeling that I have, but I am pretty sure that my name was very close to being included as a threat to the party. Every so often, as I would enter a room, everything would go quiet, as if they had been talking about me. Or I would hear whispers of "hummingbird" just before people would look away. I am not sure how things would have turned out, given my current state of immortality. In the end my name was not on the final draft for those included in "operation hummingbird," or the infamous Night of Long Knives.

I will never forget that date. On June 30, 1934, I knew for sure that I had befriended and had been helping a monster. I no longer had any hope in my mind of guiding Hitler to do great things for the world. Clearly I had been mistaken in the past when I thought that a king or president or even a writer or inventor might be the key to fixing the problems of humanity and leading me to the end of my missions. Still, this time had felt different and much more promising. The world had been on the brink of greatness or the depths of disaster many times before, but I was positive that Hitler had been already on his way to greatness before I ever came into his life. I still find myself looking back to those early days after meeting him and looking for signs that I might have missed or misinterpreted. I think back, wondering what I should have done differently to push Hitler to the greatness that could have been for all of us. In the end I am always left with a nagging feeling that my every move had been challenged and bested by evil. And on that fateful day, June 30th, I knew that I had lost the battle. Achieving greatness was no longer an option. On that day, I realized that I needed to change my goal from helping Hitler lead humanity to amazing heights to finding a way to stop him before he led us all down to the depths of hell. All thoughts of returning to the Garden vanished from my mind, as I now had to focus on finding a way to put an end to the monster I had helped to create.

CHAPTER 16

SURVIVING

My mind was reeling from the understanding of just how wrong I had been about Hitler and the future that I had envisioned him providing for the good of all people. Even without full knowledge of what was yet to come for so many millions of people, I knew that I had been deceived by a man capable of evil at an astounding level, a level rarely seen in humanity. I remember sitting there at my desk in what had up until a few days ago seemed an office full of hope. Now as I looked around, the hope was replaced by fear. Looking out the window as other people hurried about their days, they too seemed to be lacking any sign of hope and joy. I found it even more disturbing that many of those faces had replaced hope with a look of pure determination, as if they knew that this was only the beginning, and much larger things would come in the weeks, months, and years to follow.

The look on the faces of those passing by helped me fully grasp my personal situation. I had indeed been considered by some to be a threat to the mission and suggested as a name to be included in the list for the Night of Long Knives. I had caught the attention of some people as being dangerous to the cause, so I needed to watch my step and be sure to do everything I could to give the appearance that I was unquestionably loyal. I assumed that Hitler himself had made the decision to not include me on the list as an enemy. I am not sure if it was because of my service in the past or if he was looking toward my future help, but either way my name stayed off of the list. This did not mean that he had total faith in me any longer, especially since I had gone off on my own a few times to work with the other parties rather than holding the hard line. I assumed that he figured his ability to control and manipulate me would be enough to ensure my continued loyalty and service. As much as it sickened me at that point, I knew that if I was ever going to stop the monster I had helped put in power, I would have to be seen as a loyal member of the party willing to do whatever job Hitler decided for me.

I soon found out what Hitler had planned for me. He told me that I had skills and talents he did not want to lose for his upcoming war effort. At the same time, he did not want me too close to him; otherwise it might appear that I had direct influence over him. While Hitler thought that he was sending me a message and banishing me from the glory that was to come, I saw God's hand in this action. The demotion that Hitler thought he was giving me would actually serve me in many ways as I attempted to do the most good. After all, given the fact that I was forbidden from simply killing him myself, where else could I do the most good in my new mission than from within the intelligence department?

Obviously, if I was allowed to actively take the life of another human being, I could have killed Hitler, and so much senseless death and suffering might have been avoided. I say might have been avoided because nobody can see the future or know which of the countless paths the world might have followed from that point. We can only hope to understand the moment and guess at the future based on knowledge and experience. Sadly, I'm not sure that Hitler being killed at that point would have stopped what was to come. Many of his disciples could have stepped in and continued the plan without missing a beat. As strange as it seems to say, I knew that Hitler needed to become an even bigger name so that his fall from power could not be ignored. Once he became entrenched as the face representing all that was going on, his demise would surely open enough eyes to what his plans truly were. At least that was my plan. Still, I would be lying if I denied that I truly wished that I could simply kill Hitler right then and there. I had often wondered about God's restriction on this for me. Trust me, Hitler was only one of many people that would have been met with an early death if I had been allowed to do so, but God had instructed me that I could only guide humans, and their free will decided the path of things to come.

With that in mind, I began to think of all of the ways in which I could do good from my new position within the intelligence division. The possibilities seemed endless. All I had to do was to figure out which ones would provide the best results in the moment as well as move me closer to the ultimate goal of being able to help put an end to Hitler. I made sure to not repeat my sin of arrogance, which had helped put Hitler in power, and I prayed thanks to God for giving me this new chance in such an ideal position. I understood that the uncertainty of my place as a possible enemy in the days leading up to the Night of Long Knives was needed so that Hitler could put some distance between us. After all, if I were still right next to him in all of the meetings, it would soon become obvious that I was no longer working with him but trying to guide him toward defeat. No, the intelligence office was the perfect place for me. It would allow me access to all of the information that I would need to help and to hinder while trying to guide humanity back to the right path.

Now, I know what you might be thinking. God forbid me from directly taking action to eliminate a threat, so I was not able to kill Hitler myself; but that didn't prevent me from helping to set things up for an assassination attempt. Well, in that thinking you are absolutely correct. In fact, I had used that approach several times throughout my years.

I don't want to get off topic too much right now, but yes, you most likely do know of some of my work through the years. Then again the actual details of some of the assassination attempts you are aware of might just surprise you. For that matter, some of the deaths you know of across the years were in reality my orchestrated killings. Just remember that history is written by those who win as well as those with influence and a point to prove. Shockingly little attention is paid to real details or facts in favor of telling the "right" story.

My point is that planning and carrying out this sort of activity is not always as straightforward as one might wish. While some of the attempts on Hitler's life make for great and exciting stories or movies, many of them are actually quite boring and lacking in regard to storytelling quality. For that reason, I will simply tell you that of the twenty-seven documented assassination attempts on Hitler following my move to the intelligence office, not all of them were connected to me. There were in fact some others who had come to see Hitler as the threat that he was and decided to take their own actions in hopes of stopping the world from sliding down the wrong path.

Clearly, as I am sure you assumed, I did have my hand in a great deal of those twenty-seven documented attempts on Hitler's life. I can also tell you that I worked toward many others that you will never find on any list or in any book. Some of these never made it too far beyond the planning stages, so they really can't be counted. Several did go through, but they were not seen as being the actual attempt that they were. Yes, in all of my years on earth, I have learned more ways to end a life than I care to admit. My mission is to save humanity and return to my beloved Eve in paradise, and I take no joy in some of the things that I have had to do along that path. Still, sometimes the situations simply require less than upstanding actions. During these years, God ordered countless wars, which involved innocents dying. But in the end they were necessary for the greater good and to put humanity moving in the right direction. Now, don't misunderstand things. God is never in favor of anybody dying, but sometimes the severity of a war is the last effort in hopes of helping people find their way back to faith. On the other hand, don't be so naïve as to believe that all of the wars fought over the years in the name of God actually had anything to do with God. Even some of the ones that you are well versed in and have always been taught were just and holy wars were not pushed for by God, but rather by the selfish desires of man. In either case, you can bet that I was somewhere in the picture. At some points I was orchestrating, and at other points I was trying to salvage something good from the mess.

That is essentially where I found myself at that point with Hitler. I had tried to do the right thing and had failed; now I needed to stop him as best as I could and look for any possible way to push things toward something positive. I will admit that in the early days of working in the intelligence division, I had a hard time seeing how anything good would come from the situation. Over the years I have found my peace with the positives—even if I still struggle to forgive myself for the damages I allowed.

As I settled into my new life and role in this mission, I was thankful to have survived without having to abandon everything I had built to this point. But it was time to move on and adapt to my new reality. I needed to develop a new plan.

CHAPTER 17

A NEW PLAN

I tried to help engineer and orchestrate assassination attempts on my former friend Adolf Hitler in every way I could think of. I had leaked plans to individuals who I knew to be opposed to Hitler as well as being outstanding shots with a sniper rifle. I made sure that travel plans reached those who had experience with sabotage and precision explosives. All of these ideas managed to fail. They either missed the shot when they took it or found the timing to be ever so slightly off on their explosive. Most of those whom I had worked to enable on this mission always seemed to come up against some obstacle preventing them from being able to even make the attempt.

One thing I learned in all of my years of experience with these types of situations is that diversity can be a great help in ensuring success. To be honest, I felt that the likelihood of a lone gunman being able to pull of an assassination of this nature was in fact quite low, but I have seen much stranger things happen in my time on earth. Still, I was determined to succeed in my mission to stop Hitler, so I when the first few attempts failed, I quickly began looking for other possible options. Modes of travel were leaked in hopes that more drastic means of eliminating Hitler might be possible. I figured that the surgical strike of a sniper or controlled explosions of a saboteur had not been working, so more blunt force was needed. Yes, part of me felt guilty that more than only Hitler might be killed in this type of attack, but I was resigned to doing what it took to save the world from the man I had come to know as a true monster. It also helped to ease my mind knowing that generally the only people who traveled closely with Hitler were every bit as vile and evil as he was.

The more time that passed and the more that I found out about what really was going on in Hitler's Third Reich, the more determined I became to do all that I could for the good of humankind.

As I began to accept that my plans to aid in the assassination of Hitler were not going to find easy success, I looked to find other ways in which I could make strides for the greater good. I also understood that even if Hitler had been taken out in any of the attempts on his life, it would not necessarily change anything in the grand scheme of things. Yes, Hitler had been the inspiration, and with my help had orchestrated a fast climb to power. But several other member of his new inner circle would have been more than happy to fall in line behind new leadership and carry on all of the Nazi plans and ambitions.

My initial thought had been that having Hitler killed after securing his position of complete control would create a power struggle among his followers that would bring down the whole party. As time passed, I began to see that an organized hierarchy existed that would be able to carry on even if Hitler was killed. With that in mind, I began to think that the failures of the assassination attempts might have actually been a blessing. What was I going to do—keep having every new leader killed? With my new position in the intelligence office, I was no longer in a place where I could get a good read on all of the possible people who might come to power in Hitler's absence. I knew several, and I could say with confidence they were just as bad. If those few were eliminated, I would have no way of knowing for sure if and when a good soul came to power. No, the attempts on Hitler's life did not stop and would not stop until the very end, but my involvement in facilitating them did die down quite a bit. After that first initial wave, I rededicated myself to my other projects.

I won't bore you with the endless details of how I managed to navigate my way through the ins and outs of the intelligence division. I know that it might seem that I couldn't have really done too much, given all the horrible events that unfolded during the years of World War II. As I told you before, I live with those thoughts in my heart and on my mind daily. Still, I did manage to have a major impact on the course of events that were to follow. Clearly I would have loved to do more, but you also have to remember that while my goal was to do as much good as possible, I also had to avoid attracting too much attention and thus reveal what I was actually doing. Much as with my mission from God, I tried to do as many little things as possible while always looking and waiting for the bigger opportunities to present themselves.

Rather than going into all of the details involved with each of the examples that I plan on sharing, I will try to keep it more basic for the sake of storytelling. To be perfectly honest, most of the particulars were forging signatures and forcing paperwork mistakes.

I know that the big battles and the heroes who lead their troops to victory are the subjects of great epic stories and movies, but they do not truly win the wars. No, wars are won and lost by the details. It used to be war councils and calling in banners to support the cause, but in the more modern eras, this has turned into bureaucracy and paperwork. I respect and admire the nobility and bravery of the soldiers who fight and the generals who lead them, but the strength of those troops comes from the boring paperwork and requisition orders that bring them the supplies necessary to fight.

Taking yet another step back from the soldier, even if the paperwork is correct, the orders can't be filled if the supplies and resources are not available. This is the key to fighting and winning wars. The best strategy and most skilled soldiers on the battlefield are only as strong or as weak as their supplies. The old saying used to be that an army marched on its stomach, as an army fighting starvation is not able to fight the enemy. As the years have passed, and the tools of warfare have changed to more modern inventions of killing machines, the supply of equipment has also become more critical to war efforts. A sword was much easier to maintain and did not require bullets to be effective. Even before the sword required a blacksmith, weapons were as simple as a rock or a piece of wood. I am always amazed at humanity's discoveries and scientific advancements, and yet the driving force is so often the desire to improve warfare and the ability to kill.

Given the importance of behind-the-scenes details, it was actually easy to make major impacts on the war effort without ever really being noticed. Despite being delegated to the intelligence division and exiled from the inner circle of Hitler's government, I did not lose all of the power and position I had gained in the previous years. While I clearly was not the head of the intelligence division, I was left in a position with enough authority that very little went on in Hitler's war effort that I was not aware of ahead of him. In fact, I often thanked God that I had not been put in charge of the whole division, as it would have kept me from being as successful. If I had occupied the big lone office, then it would have been easier for my work to be discovered. By being in the middle, I was able to control what got sent up the chain of command as well as helping some information simply vanish before any of the lower analysts had a chance to truly examine it and make reports. This kept the "mistakes" of the division from looking too similar and arousing suspicion. A perfect example of this notion of the importance of the details was one of the most successful of my plans to hinder the war plans of Hitler and his new friends.

Germany is not an oil rich country, yet war machines require oil and gas to function. This fact was not lost on me as I planned what sort of ways I could get in the way of Hitler fulfilling his plans for world domination. Just a few years earlier, I had been looking at the problem of oil, looking for ways to import more and maximize every drop for the betterment of the nation. As I came to see the monster Hitler had become, I knew that my work in this area could also be used to hinder his plans. Hitler's need for oil had led him to look to North Africa and the regional oil wells there, which could keep his tanks and planes fighting. Knowing the importance of this to the future of Hitler's war effort, I made it an area of concentration for me as well. I will admit that with some other areas I had adopted a sort of hit-or-miss mentality. If I was going to try to interfere with something, I would pick my approach and take one good shot at it before moving on. Whether I found success or failure on that attempt, I did not often return to take another pass and risk exposure. When it came to North Africa and the oil, however, I felt that the risk was well worth it to prevent Hitler from securing the steady supply of oil that he would need to fully maintain his war. Of course I failed a few times at trying to keep Hitler from his oil; but as I said, this one was worth a few extra attempts.

I will admit that my first attempt was not all that inspired. While Hitler was focusing on the efforts in Europe, it was left to the Italians to secure and protect the oil reserves of North Africa. It was no secret that Hitler did not really trust the Italians to be a fully competent ally in the war effort, but he also realized the strategic advantage offered to him if he did not have to use his own troops to maintain North Africa. His plan was to allow the Italians to control North Africa for as long as they proved capable, but at the first sign of trouble he would send the German forces. I am sure you see how easily the idea came to me to sabotage this plan. With the intelligence reports coming through the office regarding the situation in North Africa, all I had to do was change some numbers, lose some information, and in general make it seem that the Italian army was actually able to maintain complete control of the situation. I knew that I could not continue with that cover-up for very long before some information would find its way around my office, but I did what I could. Even if the result was not a total success, at that point it felt like a victory. It was an important step, as it allowed the British troops to secure enough of a foothold in the region that they would be able to stage further actions toward cutting the oil supply, especially once the United States finally joined the war effort.

Just as I had assumed would happen, the reality of the Italian struggles became obvious, and Hitler sent in some German troops. Given the importance of the oil, the decision was made to send in Rommel to lead the forces. When I first realized this to be the case, I figured that I should move on and find a new way to impede Hitler's plans. Not wanting to simply hand over this vital resource without trying again, I stole a moment to devote to prayer. For the most part, I prayed for peace of mind and spirit so that I might be able to think clearly. It wasn't like I expected to open my eyes and see the answer written on the wall for me to read, but God did send me a very clear answer as to what my next step should be. No, the answer wasn't written out for me to read; but when I finished my silent prayer, I was overcome with a very strong thirst. Then the seemingly obvious thought came to me. The troops would be fighting in a desert and would need water in order to maintain their strength and abilities. I knew that I couldn't simply cancel all orders for water and containers scheduled to go to Rommel's forces; but with a little creativity, I was able to find an effective way to interfere. While the British forces relied on tanker trucks to supply water, the German army had no such vehicles available, and I made sure it stayed that way. So the water for the German troops was stored in large, cumbersome twenty-gallon barrels, which worked to slow the process. And many of the troops lagged in the field from lack of quality hydration.

I had figured that the difficulties related to the water supply and the headway British forces had accomplished before Rommel and his Afrikakorps arrived in North Africa would lead to a quick defeat and loss of the oil fields. Much to his credit and my surprise, Rommel found a way to win many of the battles, and it seemed like he might be able to salvage the situation after all. The turning point came when Rommel decided to push his advantage and try to force the British to the breaking point in the region. His plan was sound and looked like it would be successful, if not for one ill-timed conversation on my part. I knew that the British had worked very hard in getting their own spies to infiltrate various components of the German war machine. Using a strategy that I would come to employ a few times during the war years, I made sure to be walking near one of these spies while openly discussing Rommel's plan to attack the southern line of the British troops at El Alamein. A few days later, when the action took place, I had to fake the shock and surprise that others felt throughout the offices at the news that Rommel had been repelled by a surprisingly well-prepared and waiting British army. I don't know what would have happened in regard to the whole war effort from that point forward if Rommel had not been stopped in that moment, but it is hard to imagine Germany losing the oil of North Africa.

The last dagger in the heart of the German army's attempt to hold North Africa was actually something that I cannot take credit for in any way. Despite the shocking loss to the British at El Alamein, Rommel was not going to give up the fight. While the Americans were reinforcing the British, Rommel found his supply chain to be slow in recovering after the loss. Yes, that part I can take credit for, but it was not the last dagger that I was referring to that brought an end to the German control of North Africa. Rommel continued to plan and find ways to hold out, hoping that the supply problems could be solved (they weren't going to be if I had anything to say about it). I know that I was working against him and actively looking to sabotage his efforts, but still I could not help but have a great deal of respect for Rommel and his abilities. This respect, as it turns out, was not wasted, as later on he would see what I had seen and come to be involved in one of the many attempts on Hitler's life. Again, I am not sure what might have happened had things played out differently, but what did happen helped ensure that the oil fields were lost to Hitler for good. It turned out that the inspired fighting of the Afrikakorps had a lot more to do with Rommel than Hitler would have liked to admit. With the combined forces of the British and American units preparing to push the Germans out of Africa for good, their success was made much easier when Rommel fell ill and had to be evacuated back home to Germany. It seemed unlikely that even Rommel could have held out forever against such odds, but with him in a hospital ward miles away, his troops seemed to lose heart entirely. In the end, they put up little more than a token resistance.

With Rommel incapacitated, the Afrikakorps decimated, and the Allied forces pushing through North Africa, the war plans of Hitler took its first major setback. Obviously the war did not simply stop at this point. In fact, it would continue on for years. Still, I shudder to think about what might have happened had I not intervened and helped make sure that the precious oil fields of North Africa were lost to the German war machines for good. The loss of the oil would come to be a problem for the German tanks and planes at many occasions as the war dragged on through the years. Even without firing a shot, I had been able to find a way to put many of these killing machines out of commission. It simply took a bit of time before the results of my efforts came to have their true impact on slowing down Hitler and his plans. While some of my other plans had much more direct and immediate impacts on the war effort, I find that I often think of this sabotage of the North Africa campaign as one of my finer moments in my attempts to help stop the monster I had put in power.

At the start of the war, most expected a quick victory for Germany. Considering the preparations prior to the war, Germany clearly was ready and willing to fight. On the other hand, no other countries were quite so prepared or even willing to fight at all. The period of time leading up to the war showed a true desire from the rest of the world to avoid another war at any cost. It seemed that after the horrors of World War I, the nations of the world had entirely lost the will to fight. This was not lost on Hitler. In fact, he was counting on being able to exploit this and gain as much as he could before having to engage in any actual fighting.

For a while, the world seemed more than willing to comply with this wish. Whether blinded by their desire for peace or simply due to naïvety in reading Hitler's intentions (something I can easily relate to), the nations of the world sat by and watched Hitler take in land without firing a single shot. The whole time this was going on, Germany was the only nation actively using their industry to prepare for the coming war. I see now that Hitler had always planned to push as far as he could; and then when he met resistance, he was ready to take what he wanted through the use of force while the rest of the world was woefully unprepared to stop him.

With Italy quickly agreeing to stand with Hitler, and France easily eliminated from the picture, England was the only European power standing in opposition to a German conquest of the continent. Given that the Soviet Union had signed a nonaggression pact with Germany in the years leading up to the start of the war, Japan had joined Hitler, and the United States wanted nothing to do with fighting in another war over what they called European problems, I understood that there was not much chance for Britain to hold out for very long against Germany. I knew that I had to find some way to tip the scales back toward a balance before I could even hope to finally tip them all of the way against Hitler. To do this, I had to buy some time to keep the war going until I could find a way to bring the other world powers into the war. While these actions were not nearly as detailed or delicate as what I did in North Africa, I think you would agree that they were much more important to stopping Hitler. After all, if no other country had fought him, then clearly he would have won the war.

As I said, before getting the other powers involved, I had to find some way to keep Britain from surrendering. Well, you know that I was able to succeed in this task, because Britain did hold out all alone until the situation changed. To be honest, I did not think that this was going to be possible at the beginning. As the German forces were able to quickly subdue mainland Europe with little to no resistance, it allowed them to turn all of the attention on the English. The fact that England is an island bought the time that was needed. Even though the English Channel is not a huge distance to cross, it does create a rather sizable obstacle when planning to launch an invasion. It had been decided that before any channel crossing and land invasion would even be attempted, the German *Luftwaffe*, air force, would fly bombing runs in hopes of clearing the path for the land troops. This was a very sound strategy, which would have eventually worked. I knew that I could count on the stubborn nature of the British to resist surrender for a while, but even they would have their limits when they saw the German tanks rolling through the streets of London. At the rate things began, Hitler would have controlled all of Europe, making it nearly impossible for any other world powers to stop him.

At that point, I fell back on my understanding of people, a skill I have developed over my long life. Obviously it is not a perfect skill, given the mistakes I made with Hitler and some others, but in general it has served me quite well over the years. In this case, my understanding of the collective psyche of the British people and not simply the military assets and strategies really came to be important.

The British people are known for their resolve, and it would be difficult to deflate their spirit. The defeat of their military from the bombings, allowing the German troops to simply set foot on the English shores, would have gone a long way in destroying that famous resolve. On the other hand, if the *Luftwaffe* were to switch from bombing military targets and begin to attack civilian cities and towns, it would serve to increase the defiance of the British people. This defiance would come to inspire the military in their fight against the Germans. So, all I had to do was find a way to convince the *Luftwaffe* to switch strategies. It turned out that this was not as difficult as it should have been. All I had to do was forge a few reports claiming just the opposite of what I knew to be true. I flooded the planning offices with fake papers stating that if the civilian targets were bombed, the British people would lose heart quickly and push their government for a quick settlement of peace. Just for good measure, I also made sure to exaggerate some of the mission reports so that the successful bombing runs on British military bases seemed to have already succeeded in tipping the scales in Germany's favor.

When the *Luftwaffe* began to focus on the civilian targets over the military assets, I knew that I had found the time that was needed to continue searching for other outside help in fighting Germany. The British people stood firm in their defiance of Germany, and the path of the war was forever altered. It was no longer possible for Hitler to conquer Europe quickly. Yes, he held mainland Europe, but without England under his control, there would always be resistance and a staging ground for launching attacks on his empire. If he had succeeded in taking England, then it is highly probable that a unified Europe under the Nazi flag would have become a true reality and might even still exist to this day. Hitler would have been able to secure all of the borders and essentially make Europe an impenetrable fortress, greatly reducing the chances of any other nation ever seeing value in opposing him on the battlefield. Thankfully I was able to manipulate and take advantage of one major character flaw that seemed to exist in all of those in positions of importance in Hitler's Germany. I had fallen victim to this same flaw as I helped guide Hitler to the height of his power—arrogance. I had been arrogant to believe that I could guide Hitler to be what I wanted him to be, and I had been blind to what was truly going on around me. The arrogance of the German leadership allowed me to trick Hitler and his inner circle into making such clear mistakes. They were convinced that they could not lose, and they were more than willing to believe any lies that reinforced their belief in their invincibility. I had used their pretentiousness to save England and to buy time, and I continued to make use of that flaw for a few other key moments in the long process of bringing down my monster.

Now you see just how easily I was able to manipulate and push the German war machine to make critical mistakes. Even after I had helped buy time for the British to resist giving in to the evils of Hitler's Germany, I knew that it was only a matter of time before Hitler would be able to overcome the defiance of the British and essentially own all of Europe. I knew that without help from another strong world power, England was doomed. The two strongest nations not involved already were the Soviet Union and the United States of America. Looking to bring either into the war against Hitler posed challenges, but the Soviet Union would be much easier to get involved, simply because of geography. The United States was literally an ocean away and had made it a very consistent practice to avoid getting involved. The distance allowed US leadership to claim that the events in Europe didn't really involve them; they also fostered a mentality of self-absorption.

I have seen it all through the world and all through time: when a power is growing and finding itself detached by geography from the rest of the world, it tends to develop a detached mentality. It is not entirely an intentional desire to be that way; in some parts the geography honestly makes it difficult to be actively engaged with the rest of the world. But it was worse for America because it was such a young country growing up in such a different world from the other powers. As America was finding its young footing, it did have access to information about the rest of the world, but it was still not easily accessible like it is today. The fact that it was truly a nation of immigrants with no historical national identity also created concerns for their government regarding getting involved in foreign affairs. For much of their history, the people living in the United States still held tightly to their nations of origin and felt their loyalties belonged there—sometimes more so than their new homes in America. So I did not turn to America for help. Not only would it be much harder to get that country involved, but even if I could find a way, right then it would serve very little good since they were not prepared for war and would take a while to get mobilized. No, the Soviet Union was a much better choice for what I needed at that time. The Soviet Union was much closer and did not have to cross an ocean, so they only needed ground troops and not a strong navy for transportation. The people of the Soviet Union also seemed to be much more inclined to go to war against the Germans.

As it turned out, getting the Soviets involved was actually quite easy. I knew from all of my time talking with Hitler that he did not have a very fond view of the Soviets as a people or as a nation. He would often talk about how Napoleon had failed in his attempts to conquer the Russian people when he had the chance. Hitler had examined the mistakes and believed that he knew better. Hitler always believed that he was a gifted military strategist, when in reality he had no true mind for military thinking. Using this knowledge, all I had to do was manufacture the slightest bit of reason for Hitler to believe that his nonaggression pact with Stalin was not secure. From there Hitler's own distrust of the Soviets drove him into a frenzy of convincing himself that he needed to strike first, before Stalin launched a surprise attack of his own. Hitler's arrogance carried him the rest of the way into believing that his troops could simply march straight through to Moscow and his empire would be expanded to even greater heights. The Soviet Union clearly fought back and became a full participant in the war against Hitler. With the massive numbers of soldiers in the Soviet army, and a few supply issues for the German soldiers, such as the oil from North Africa, this proved to be one of the most productive ways in which I worked to stop Adolf Hitler.

With the Soviet Union entering the war, the pressure was off of Britain to win the entire war alone. Still, I knew that if Hitler was going to be stopped, eventually the United States would need to bring its wealth and production to the war effort. As it turned out, I did not even have to do anything to bring the United States into the war. When Japan bombed Pearl Harbor, there was no question that the United States would be going to war against Japan in the Pacific. All

I had to figure out from there was how to bring that anger over being attacked to bear on Hitler as well.

As I am sure that you have figured out by now, this was done with some simple lying on the right reports and analysis playing into the arrogance of Hitler. With the right misinformation sent up the chain, it was a very obvious decision for Hitler to again strike first and declare war on the United States himself. Based on what Hitler was told, Japan would easily beat the United States and would be seen as the sole power for that half of the world. Hitler simply could not allow Japan to achieve that kind of recognition without having his name attached to it as well. Plus, if Germany helped defeat America, it would serve to secure help with the Soviets from Japan if needed. It also helped to include some transcripts of President Roosevelt condemning Hitler for his actions up to that point. Of course I made sure not to include the parts of the report discussing how Roosevelt was just grandstanding and lacked the needed popular and political support to enter the war on his own. Even after the attack on Pearl Harbor, it was unlikely that Roosevelt would have been able to include Germany in any war plans, at least not for a while.

I might not have been able to succeed in finding a way to have Hitler assassinated in the early stages of the war, but from my desk in the intelligence division I was able to manipulate information and supply chains to find a way to prevent Hitler from finding the quick and easy success that he desired. Had he kept to the plans of his military advisors and just kept pounding the British military targets with the *Luftwaffe,* it is likely that Britain would have sued for peace early on, and the war would have been over. Following that mistake, all I did was jump on the chances to manipulate Hitler into his own demise. Even if Britain held out as long as possible, it was not likely that the Soviets or the Americans would have ever entered the war without Hitler bringing them in himself and thus bringing on his own defeat. As the war years continued to drag on, there were many more chances for me to help create problems in the supply chain or faulty reports regarding the strength of Allied forces in various regions and I took every chance that I could to help bring an end to Hitler's Germany. Still, the whole time I kept looking for one more big opportunity to truly turn the war in the favor of the Allies. I finally found that possibility in 1944, and I made the most of it.

I would imagine that when I mention June 6, 1944, you know what I am talking about. Very few moments in history have been studied, documented, and glorified to the extent of the Allied invasion of mainland Europe at Normandy. The number of books, movies, and history classes covering the D-Day invasion is simply mind-blowing. With that in mind, I am not going to go into detail about the operation and everything that happened to make that day possible. I will say that there were a lot of reports that went missing in the days and weeks leading up to D-Day. I had been praying for many months that something would present itself where I could make a major impact again. It had been such a long time since I had helped bring the Soviets and Americans into the war, and my successful plot in North Africa had ended years ago. I had this feeling that the time was right for something major to happen to push forward toward ending this war. D-Day served as not only a military victory, but also a psychological dagger through the heart of the German forces. When it came to that fateful June day, I found myself at my desk enjoying the confusion and chaos surrounding me. I had to fight very hard not to sit there with a huge smile on my face, knowing that the truth had been in this office several times and managed to simply vanish without a trace.

As the Allies had been building up for the necessary invasion of mainland Europe, they had worked very hard to create confusion about the location of that landing. They did not hold back in trying to deceive the Germans as to which landing zone would be the point of attack. Still, the Germans did have their own spies who had worked their way into the ranks of the Allies. Even with all of the extensive work that the Allies put into building a fake base and using props to simulate the presence of tanks, planes, and ships, it was still possible for the German spies to decipher that Normandy was actually the planned point of attack. In those weeks leading up to the invasion, I lost track of how many reports I doctored and destroyed to help keep the Allied plan secret. Even with all of my efforts, I fully believe that the key factor in the successful ruse was that General Patton was stationed at the decoy base. Nobody in the German high command believed that the Allies would dare launch an invasion of mainland Europe without Patton leading the troops. When it was all said and done, that is exactly what happened. And as you know, from D-Day it was all headed straight to the end of Hitler's Germany. There were still some bumps in the road and some smaller things that I did to help sabotage the war effort, but my work on that aspect was for the most part done when the Allies secured the beaches.

CHAPTER 18

SAVING HEART

You are probably wondering why I have been so focused on telling you about how I worked to hinder the war effort of Hitler's Nazi Germany, but I have not touched on any of the other horrors that took place during those years. After all, it is impossible to even think of World War II or Adolf Hitler without bringing up thoughts of the atrocities of the Holocaust. Trust me, not a day goes by that I don't spend at least a few moments remembering all of those souls lost in large part due to my massive mistake of helping bring Hitler to power. Yes, through the years, I have seen many horrible events and mass killings on grand scales, but none of them were directly connected to my actions. I know that all death can be placed at my feet for my failure to protect humanity in the Garden, but this was different. This was the first time that I had been involved in bringing about deaths of this nature because of my arrogant mistake. So, you ask why I haven't talked about that aspect of the war to this point, and the answer is quite simple: I know that I did not do enough.

I guess that it is pretty obvious that I didn't do enough to help out and stop what was going on in relation to the Holocaust and death squads running rampant during the war. I do not mean that I did nothing, but I did not do enough. And blame myself for every soul lost for such insane and hateful reasons. No matter how much I wish I could have done more, the fact remains that I did not have the access needed to make the same level of impact as I did with the war effort. When the chance would present itself to do some good and work to save some lives, I was faced with the horrible task of having to weigh the risk and the reward of getting involved. Yes, I had to do that with simple supply issues. Yes, I was aware that soldiers were dying because of my impact on the war. Still, it was one thing to know that soldiers were suffering as opposed to innocent people who had done nothing other than be born with the "wrong" blood. My other problem was knowing that if I stuck my neck out too far in hopes of saving lives, I could easily get discovered and would lose my chance of bringing the war to the best end I could manage. That fact cost me many hours of sleep. I stared at my ceiling, thinking about how many innocent lives equaled a military loss for the German army. Even to this day, it bothers me to know that I had to think in such a way. Still, I knew that if I got caught, there was a very good chance Hitler would win the war and even more lives would be lost.

Looking back and remembering the times when I was able to help out in some way, it is hard to feel any sense of pride in those successes when I know how many victims were not saved. If I am going to be truly honest with you, I can't even really take any claim for any of the lives that were saved from the Nazi concentration camps. The actions that I took to help hinder the war effort I take pride in, as I was the one thinking of the ideas and putting them into motion. Yes, I had to rely on others to unknowingly carry out my plans, but for the most part they were my plans. On the other hand, when it came to saving souls from the Nazi death camps, the ideas very rarely came from my office. That isn't to say that I didn't have some ideas. But as I mentioned before, my office did not have a lot to do with the planning or controlling of that arena. No, my only way to really contribute in this effort was to do damage control and work to hide the actions of others.

I was filled with a sense of accomplishment and pride as if I was almost single-handedly sabotaging the entire war effort, yet I felt so useless as all I could do was hide the good works of others who were saving the lives slated for death camps. Those individuals were the real heroes in my mind. I knew that God had promised me that I would not die until I had finished my work on earth. With that in mind, I don't know what would have happened to me if I had been discovered. On the other hand, those people trying to save lives knew that if they were found out, that they would face a certain death, yet they risked it anyway. They didn't know I was there to cover up for them. Still, their desire to do what they knew to be the right thing won out over their personal fears. Those people—they are heroes. I am not just talking about individuals such as Oskar Schindler, Frank Foley, Raoul Wallenberg, or any of the others who are well-known for saving thousands of lives each from the Holocaust. I am in awe of even the farm family members who risked their lives to save just a single life. If the SS had caught them, it would have made no difference whether they were saving thousands or a single person, the penalty would be death in both cases.

To this day I have untold respect for the many individuals who risked everything to save others. While I was safe and sound in my office at the intelligence division, they were on the front lines fighting for what was right. I was the first human, I had many conversations with God in the Garden, and I spent all of human history working to bring humankind back to paradise; and yet these individuals from all different nations and faiths were able to do such amazing work fighting the Holocaust. While my focus remained on the war effort, where I could do my work, I kept an eye out for reports coming across my desk involving any suspicion aimed toward these individuals. Sadly, my desk was not the only one that such reports were brought to during those years. I did my best to get my hands on as many as I could;

and I quickly disposed of them to keep suspicions away from the people who were doing the work I wished I could be doing myself.

At first the office just received intelligence reports with neighbors alerting authorities about people being hidden away in homes. These were relatively easy to shuffle aside in the beginning, seeing as how the war was in full swing. As the war continued, I started to notice some other strange activities. I began to see some reports inquiring about a large number of travel visas and passports being issued to "questionable" individuals. It was pretty clear to see what was going on with these requests. While I was focusing on trying to bring down Hitler and put an end to his power for good, these brave people were doing all that they could to sneak people out of the region before they got shipped off to concentration camps to be slaughtered. Clearly, I made sure that those inquiries found their way out of circulation. While I did my best to keep anybody else from seeing the papers and raising further questions within the intelligence division, I had to also send back responses to the officers who had filed the reports in the first place. I knew that if they never received a response, it would only serve to create more problems. So for every item I destroyed, I had to also forge a response with some believable explanation to alleviate their concerns. In some ways this was actually more difficult than my work in derailing the war effort, because I was reacting and not in full control over the plan. I only wish, no matter how difficult it would have been, that I could have done more.

CHAPTER 19

THE FALL

With all that I had done to help bring about the end of the war and cover up for other individuals doing God's work, I sometimes had to struggle to keep some attention focused on Hitler himself. After the D-Day invasion, the Allies were able to bring an end to the war as quickly as possible. The German troops had suffered defeat after defeat, thanks in part to "mismanaged" supplies and equipment. Still, my work only accomplished so much. Hitler and his top advisors simply had not been prepared for any situation involving them pushing back on the defensive. Once again the arrogance of Adolf Hitler came into play. The same hubris I had been able to use to help him gain power worked to help me put an end to Hitler and his plans.

I often wonder if Hitler ever realized any of the damage I did to his plans in those last weeks and days of the war. Maybe it is my own human pride, but part of me truly does hope that at some point he thought of me. Perhaps he didn't realize that it was me who had destroyed his supply chain or manipulated him into such disastrous plans as to force the Soviets and Americans to declare war on

Germany. Still, part of me likes to believe that, at the very least, he had some thought regarding how I had helped him come to power so easily and that everything collapsed for him without me there to guide him.

I had no direct contact with Adolf Hitler following the scare associated with the Night of Long Knives, but I still had direct influence over his life in my own way. As soon as it became clear that the war was lost and the Allies were not going to settle for any outcome short of rolling tanks through the streets of Berlin, I began to think a great deal about what the end of the war should look like. Given all of the atrocities of the Holocaust and death squads employed by the Nazis during the war, there was no question that anybody holding a position of authority within the party would be seen as a high-priority prisoner. I figured there would be trials and a spectacle made of punishing as many high-ranking members of the Nazi Party as possible; and clearly Adolf Hitler would be the biggest prize of them all. Naturally the world would celebrate the capture and public display of Hitler being tried for his sins, but it would also bring up some very difficult questions between the Allies. The Soviets felt betrayed by Hitler, and they surely viewed some of the military tactics used during the war as giving them a priority claim on Hitler's life. On the other hand, countries such as France, Poland, and all of the others devastated and toppled during the early stages of the war could make a similar claim. It quickly became clear to me that the best solution for the world moving forward after the war would be the same solution that I had tried to orchestrate in the early days: Hitler needed to die. A living Hitler would serve to create dispute between his captors and even to some extent serve to keep his message alive and thriving. On the other hand, a dead Hitler would make it much easier for the world to move forward and attempt to recover from the damage he had caused.

The problem, though, remained the same: how to succeed in having Hitler killed. As I mentioned before, I had tried to orchestrate countless assassination attempts early on, and they always failed. No matter what I tried, he had always managed to get the help he needed to avoid my traps. I did not see how, if I failed when he was in the open and travelling, I could possibly accomplish this goal when he was hiding in his bunker under Berlin. My first concern was that he would find a way to sneak out of the city to safety, and then possibly even find the means to flee to foreign shores. I had seen many plans for the transport of key Nazi figures to various nations, where they believed they would be able to vanish from the world's view entirely. There was no way I could allow Hitler to find such refuge, for as much damage as a captured Hitler could do to the balance of the postwar power, a Hitler escape could send the world into further turmoil. Hitler simply could not be allowed to survive the war.

My first concern was keeping Hitler in Berlin so that he would not have a chance to escape. This turned out to be quite simple. All I had to do was once again play on Hitler's pride and arrogance. With many of the other officers in the intelligence division already gone, attempting to find their way to safety, I was left with very few people to notice what I was doing. This gave me the ability and the freedom to send essentially any intelligence reports that I wanted to various commands. Thus I kept the German forces disorganized and out of position in those final weeks of the war, allowing the Allies to march through Germany. With Hitler hiding in his bunker, he had less access to information than normal, which in turn gave the intelligence I sent that much more weight. It really is amazing how easy it is to create entire divisions of troops, at least on paper. I had Hitler convinced that Berlin was well-guarded and that there were plans to push out from the city to stabilize the fronts and allow him to refocus and regroup. By the time the others in the bunker figured out that Hitler's strategy was relying on fictional troops, it was too late, and the Soviets were already inside the city.

Even at that point, though, there was still a chance that Hitler could escape at the last second and attempt to find freedom in some foreign land. With such limited access to the bunker, I realized that it would be nearly impossible for anybody to get to Hitler to assassinate him. That left me with only one option. Somehow I had to convince him to take his own life. Luckily for me, one of the people living in the bunker with Hitler was Joseph Goebbels, the Reich Minister of Propaganda. Since Goebbels had been with Hitler from the beginning as well, I knew him and understood that his mind would always be looking for how to spin every situation. He was very talented at his job and devoted to the mission of making Hitler and the Nazi Party always appear strong. Still, even with his mind looking for the right angle to present the situation, I was positive that he saw the end coming quickly. A few well-placed memos to his folders showing that those still loyal to Hitler would abandon their stand if Hitler was to abandon Berlin was all it took to set Goebbels's mind in motion. The last push that I provided was to draw on some of Hitler's early speeches, written by Goebbels, where Hitler declared himself to be the Third Reich—as he stood, so did Germany. From that Goebbels followed right along the path that I put before him. He went on to convince Hitler that history would come to judge him in a good and proper light, but only if he shared the same fate as his Germany. All of the way up until the very end, Goebbels and Hitler believed that everything they had done was right and justified, and people would understand the truth in the future. With that in mind, the only true ending possible for Hitler was to die there in the bunker as his Third Reich collapsed outside.

Finally, on April 30, 1945, Adolf Hitler was dead. The war in Europe ended in the days that followed as German troops surrendered to the Allies. Following Hitler's suicide and the fall of Germany, I found myself wandering through the streets of Berlin. As I looked around and saw all of the destruction and ruined lives, I couldn't help but see the symbolism reflecting the previous years. That once proud and beautiful city smoldered because of my failure. I had seen possible greatness in a man who had come to be viewed as pure evil personified. Much like Berlin, Hitler had grown to show success, power, and potential only to end in flames—figuratively and literally.

I had been so confident when I first met Hitler, so much so that I had shown a level of arrogance that actually rivaled Hitler himself. I had allowed myself to fall away from my reliance on God and prayer for direction and guidance. Maybe if I had been more faithful and dedicated to my own true path, I might have seen things more clearly and not allowed everything to get out of hand. Maybe I could have kept Hitler on the right path, or maybe I would have seen his true nature sooner and been able to correct my mistake in supporting him before he ever came to power. When I think of the millions who died at the hands of this man who could have been so great for humanity, it can be paralyzing even today. If I had only been able to get him to stay on the path I had believed we started together. As I said, I've failed at other times in my centuries on earth. I have lost others to evil and the lure of power. I have missed chances to put right what once went wrong and bring humanity back home to the Garden. I wish that I could say that this was not the case; but clearly since we have still not returned to paradise, there is no denying my failure. I have always tried to balance my guilt over the failures with the successes that I have had over the years, but that does little to help when I think of my years with Hitler and all of the lives lost due to my arrogance. My failure with Hitler and my failure with Eve in the Garden are obviously my two biggest regrets, and both grew out of my own arrogance.

I try to remind myself that I have actually had many more successes than failures. There have been countless lives saved and improved because of my work. Still, even when thinking about lives spared from slavery, diseases avoided from cures, wars averted, or simply how the human existence has been improved by the arts, it is hard to quantify and balance with an actual death toll that grows with every failure I endure. That is the burden of my soul. I know that humanity was placed in my care so long ago, when it was just the two of us and death did not exist. Everything that has gone wrong could have been avoided if only I had not failed Eve in the Garden, or if I had put things right in those early years outside of paradise. With Cain's actions, my responsibility and burden became truly set, and I have been fighting ever since.

As I tell you this story of mine, I find so many memories filling my mind. There have been so many missions. Some of them you may have studied in history classes and never realized my involvement. Just as I did with Hitler, I have always found a way to be involved in the course of humanity without being in the spotlight. You can search the videos, books, pictures, and stories for me, but you won't exactly find me. I live my life between the shadows and the light. In the rare cases when I am remembered at all, it is as nothing more than an "advisor" to somebody of importance. You might even have read about me by whatever name I was using in that instance, but still not have the slightest clue that it was actually me. It really is amazing how much influence I have had with very powerful people; but then again, that is just my arrogance showing is through.

Even if history does not remember me, I remember it. The failures, such as with Hitler, haunt me, and I think of them often. I guess if I am to be honest, I do have certain missions that I remember more than the others. Some are good, and some, like Hitler, are bad. Some are easy to remember because of the grand nature of the story, but others are essentially unknown names from the past. Sometimes it is the relatively unknown story that brings me the most joy. Then again, other times you find that the small boy who starts out as nobody from nowhere actually grows into a very well-known king. Yes, that was truly one of my favorite memories—not because it was easy, but because it was pure humanity. Similar to Hitler, there was great potential for goodness tempted by power and arrogance. Still, no two stories are actually alike in real detail, so allow me to continue and tell you another story from my life.

TO GUIDE A SHEPHERD

I greatly enjoyed the missions that were clear-cut and easy to understand who was right and wrong. Sadly, those missions actually did not come up too often for me. In fact, I can only remember a handful of them over the course of my many lifetimes on earth. As you could see with what I told you about Adolf Hitler, even a man who is considered by many to be pure evil had the chance to be a great hero for the side of goodness. That says a lot for what each of us humans has inside of us. We are capable of being good or evil, all at our own choice and use of free will. In all of my years, I have learned that even the best of humanity is capable of doing great wrongs, and that good deeds can be done by those considered to be the most vile. To be honest, based on what I have seen, most humans are neither truly good nor evil. They are mostly neutral but capable of both good and bad reactions to the events around them. I say that not as a judgment, simply as an observation. Still, it does help to explain a great deal about all of the people that I have met, both the famous ones and those who were forgotten. I guess you could say that I am a perfect example of this balance myself. Most would say that I have done countless acts of good in my years working to return humanity to the Garden as God intended. Then again, as I just told you, I did help to bring Hitler to power so that he could subject millions to his hatred. It also should be remembered that it was my selfish desire and arrogance that led to this life outside of the Garden in the first place. I was given the choice to continue in perfection renewed, but I chose instead to bring humanity through the gates and into a world of sin.

Even with all that I have done wrong, I don't consider myself to be a bad man. I have helped many great people find their way to the right path. I have also helped many remain true to their desires to follow that path in the face of temptation. I sometimes wonder what would have happened if I had been blessed with somebody to offer advice all of those years ago in the Garden. Perhaps this is why these missions are so draining on me. I know how easy it is to lose sight of reality in favor of personal desires. I have learned that it is just a small step from that point to becoming fully obsessed with the belief that those desires are truly the right path for all. That is when I find myself needed the most, and when I work the hardest to restore a true sense of right and wrong.

This type of mission did sadly sometimes require me to put a stop to the individuals because they had strayed too far. Then again, sometimes I simply had to give them some guidance so that they could return to the correct path. Naturally, I would always prefer to be able to help them get back on track. I believe that all people can be saved if they are shown the error of their ways, but they must be open to the truth. My life would be so much easier if it was always so simple. It has always been my first course of action to spend time with individuals in the hope of learning not only when and how they have strayed, but understanding why. Once I know them, I try to restore their path to the desired course. This is how I approached the case of one of my better-known missions: King David.

King David is considered by many to be a truly great servant of God who simply made a few big mistakes. While this is quite certainly true, it falls well short of telling the entire story. The path of David is one many believe they know quite well, but in reality so much of the story has been left out. Having spent many years living with him, I can tell you that you actually know very little about David. It might surprise you, given what you know of his failings, that David came very close to fulfilling all of God's hopes for him. It also might surprise you that this man of immense faith nearly walked away from God's plans and even came close to straying so far that I would have categorized him as a threat needing to be eliminated. While these statements might seem outrageous and appear to be in extreme contradiction to each other, to me they simply represent how fine a line humanity walks daily between hallowed hero of faith and forgotten enemy of the light. Every step of the way, David walked this line more than most—and in my opinion, better than most. Through it all, David's drive and passion helped him face all of the obstacles in his life. Well, of course he did receive some help from me along the way, as well. Still, without his own personal integrity, I feel it is safe to say that David would have met a very different and sudden end to his life. Yes, David truly was a complicated man who has remained very firmly on my mind through all of the centuries. So, let me tell you about the David I knew.

It all started for me when I was led back to the land of the Israelites, who were at the time under the rule of King Saul. That did not shock me too much, considering most of my assignments involved leaders and people in positions of power. God does not judge humanity by its rulers alone. No, all people are important, and they are judged as individuals based on their own personal choices. Rulers, however, shape the society and laws under which the people live, and therefore guide their subjects down either the right path to please God or the wrong path. So, when there was an issue in a kingdom or territory, I immediately sought out the ruler in order to put humanity back on the right path.

Over the years, leaders' roles have changed in many ways. In modern times, with all of our freedoms and liberties, which have been developed to protect the people from the overreaching rule of leaders, it is like a whole new world. In today's world, individuals have so much more ability, and also responsibility, to live by their own beliefs and convictions. No longer is it the job of the leader to tell the subjects what they have to believe and practice. It truly is one of the greatest developments of humanity. Now, all of the technology and inventions by humans are impressive. Trust me, they make life so much easier and more comfortable. In the end these advancements pale in comparison to the evolution of society that offers education and opportunities to the people. I know that many people are limited in some ways, but they still have more options than were available in the past.

Leaders consistently exerted control over the people through my missions in the past. So I was shocked to discover that my assignment was not King Saul, or any of his top advisors or sons. In fact, my task was to help a young shepherd boy named David. I knew immediately that this could be no ordinary boy. God had selected this young child to lead a life of immense importance and accomplish many great things—if I could help protect him from the world and guide him through temptations. From the very first time I met David, it was obvious that he was incredibly talented and gifted in regard to musical abilities. It only took a few moments with the boy to see that he also possessed intelligence well beyond his years. While it was possible to find gifted musicians or children possessing advanced intelligence when passing from city to city, it was highly unusual that the combination of such gifts could be found in one person. It was even more shocking that a lonely shepherd boy in the middle of nowhere would possess such a rare combination of talents. I knew immediately that this boy truly was special, and that it would be very easy to help young David secure a place within the court of King Saul.

After my first meeting with David, I spent the night in solitude as I pondered the many possible paths to greatness that lay before him. I found myself quite anxious to begin this journey and aid the youth along his way; I was curious myself to discover what the future might hold. I have to admit, after some of my previous missions, in which I dealt with many vile and cruel people, I was very excited to be tasked with guiding this fine example of humanity to the greatness ahead. I saw in David a shining example of why I made my choice so long ago back at the doorway of the Garden of Eden. I found myself dreaming that this would be the mission to end it all. I would finish the path that God had set before me so I could lead humanity back to the Garden, and I could return to my beloved Eve in that perfection we had lost. At least that was my hope.

I was so naïve then. Looking back, I see so much that should have been done or at least could have been done to better guide and protect young David. Still, as you know from being human yourself, life is full of regret and hindsight. This lesson is one I still struggle with after all these years. I do not claim to have the sole right to regret; as I mentioned, I am fully aware that all humans are burdened by regret. Still, I do imagine you will agree that, because of my unique situation over many generations, my guilt has accumulated, and I have a unique understanding of and relationship with human regret. Rather than keep going down this path of regret again, I will simply take this time to tell you the story of David, as I know it from a firsthand participant. I am sure that you will have your own thoughts concerning my mistakes, but remember that you were not there facing the situation day in and day out. Plus, you already have the advantage of hindsight and information on how the story ends. David and I had to face each situation and make our choices in the moment. All I ask of you is to listen and keep your mind open to the story I tell you: the real story of David the boy who would kill a giant and become king of a nation.

CHAPTER 21
A GIANT CHALLENGE

As I had thought, it was quite easy to gain an audience with King Saul regarding David. I simply had to offer information regarding a gifted musician and writer. I knew that the promise of a talented young scholar would be enough to pique his interest, but the mere mention of a musical prodigy was the key to ensuring a personal meeting with the king himself. A capable writer and scholar would always be welcomed into the court, but one possessing such musical gifts would be greatly desired. Quality musicians and performers were a sign of status on par even with gold and jewels in that era. King Saul was quite eager to hear of young David, even more so when he learned that David was about the same age as one of Saul's own sons, Jonathon. The possibility of Jonathon and David becoming friends greatly intrigued Saul, as he spoke hopefully about David serving as a trusted advisor and companion to his son. He believed that being exposed to a diversity of backgrounds and ideas would help shape Jonathon into the next great king of the Israelites. I honestly believe that this idea was one of the main determining factors for Saul inviting David to join his court, even before meeting him personally.

Still, looking to avoid any possible future regrets or hard feelings, I insisted upon David auditioning prior to any official invitation to join the court of King Saul.

That David played well at the audition would be a major understatement and an insult to just how talented he truly was as a musician. He played well-known pieces on the harp and lute, which the king recognized, and he improvised some new songs on the spot. After playing the instruments, David also sang and recited poetry, and he recounted historical events with great accuracy. It was truly an amazing experience to witness, not only for the pleasure of enjoying the performance, but to see the mighty King Saul so entranced and almost hypnotized from the very first note. Given King Saul's desire to have David as a member of the court simply from my descriptions, I knew that David would not be leaving the compound that night. What took me by surprise was the generosity of Saul. He wasted no time in offering David and me each a place within his own home. We would not be living in the servants' compound, but we would be living nearby. David would be readily available to share his talents, and it was easy for Jonathon and David to spend time together. I thought for sure that this was the beginning of all things good for David, and that my job was essentially finished. I had helped the young shepherd boy gain access to the royal court and families of one of the most powerful kingdoms of the time. I figured that the rest would simply fall into place for David, and I would be moving on in a very short period of time. Yes, I thought everything was set, and that this was one of the easiest and quickest assignments of my many years to date. I had no idea that instead this was only the start of a long, wild ride alongside a brilliant, passionate, gifted, and yet also troubled man.

The days passed, and things were going very well for David—not that I had any doubt that this would be the case for the young prodigy. I was filled with a sense of pride, quite similar to the pride a father has in his own son. This gave me pause to think back to my own sons, Cain and Abel. I did not focus on the tragic parts of their lives;

in fact, I rarely thought of those days at all. Instead, I remembered only the happy times: the joy and laughter we shared, as well as the fatherly pride of seeing my sons grow into men. That was my past, and it was ancient history to the rest of the world. My job and purpose was to help David; and that was where my attention would quickly return, as I began to realize that this mission was not quite as simple as I had initially believed and hoped.

As I said, David was doing well in his new life. Rarely an evening passed that David was not called upon to entertain the court with one of his many talents. The legend of his musical abilities grew and spread quickly through all of the lands near and far. Instead of sending simple messengers to address matters of the court, high-ranking officials from foreign lands began to travel great distances to personally handle business, just so they could witness the gifts and talents of David. I often had to bite my tongue to avoid laughing at the thought of these foreign emissaries gushing over the boy who had just a few months prior been playing those same melodies for sheep in the fields. I wondered if David ever had any similar thoughts, but I never actually asked him. Whether he did or not, he was always ready and willing to play for the court without complaint.

Saul knew very well why so many dignitaries were suddenly visiting him, and he never hesitated to place David front-and-center in order to impress those nobles. This practice, while common to any king with access to talent, worked exceptionally well for Saul, allowing him to negotiate from a position of power and prominence over even those who were more than his equal in riches. Don't get me wrong; Saul was a good king and did not use this as a means of obtaining horribly unfair gains in his dealings. If anything, the enjoyment provided by David allowed both parties to relax and negotiate rather than fall into the typical practice of simply making demands of each other. I remember being impressed with the restraint Saul showed in only using this advantage to ensure fair dealings for his people without pushing for unreasonable personal gains. David truly had become a key cog in the foreign policy of King Saul. Despite this role in such high-profile negotiations, David remained humble—a trait that only served to increase his calming influence over even the most stressful meetings.

The public arena was not the only one in which David was experiencing great success. Just as Saul had hoped, David was quickly becoming good friends with Jonathon. The king's son had plenty of advisors and teachers, but it did not take long before Jonathon was placing his trust in David. The two seemed to bond immediately and become close friends and confidants, and Jonathon often sought out David's advice and assistance. This friendship was also beneficial to David. In addition to the privilege of being a talented musician, David was also educated in strategy and the use of weapons right alongside of Jonathon. All who witnessed these sessions could see that David's talents reached far beyond the arts, as he excelled with grace in the world of weaponry and military strategy.

Given this growth in skills and the fast-developing friendship with Jonathon, it was only natural that David would begin to accompany the king and his court to the battlefield. For the most part, David stayed quiet and in the background, but he was always paying attention and absorbing everything that he could. After a briefing or negotiation, David could often be seen talking with Jonathon; and they would review what was said and discuss the issue from every angle they could conceive. Despite how much Jonathon welcomed this free exchange with his friend, David always remembered his place in the court, and he would not dare speak about such things in the presence of King Saul.

On one of these trips to the battlefront, things began to change for David, and my task of helping him became much more difficult. I assume that you know at least some version of the story, but allow me to share my memories and tell you what I remember about that fateful campaign. The famous story is now used all over the world to encourage the underdog and give confidence that sometimes the little guy can win. I always laugh when I hear that saying in regard to sports or business, because I was there to see the original. I know the true story, having witnessed the real David versus Goliath.

The Israelites and the Philistines had essentially been living in a constant state of war for many generations, so it came as no surprise to learn that Saul was preparing to lead his forces into battle once again. A culture of animosity was so ingrained that any brief moments of peace between the two nations would quickly vanish over the slightest offense, and the fighting would resume. To be honest, I do not even remember what the perceived offense was in this specific situation to warrant a return to arms. I do know that by this time David had secured his position as a trusted advisor to Jonathon and a source of comfort to Saul. With the troops marching for the battlefront, David and I promptly followed with the rest of the king's council to face off with the hated Philistines.

After marching for several days, we began to receive reports from the forward scouts that we were nearing the enemy forces. When we finally encountered the Philistines, both sides quickly realized that a horrible stroke of chance had befallen the war effort. Spanning the distance between the two armies was a valley, the Valley of Elah, to be precise. Neither side was going to make the first move into battle, knowing that it would mean surrendering the high ground and all strategic advantage. To charge into the valley in hopes of attacking the other side was essentially a suicide mission, so we stood staring across the valley at each other, daring the other side to either recklessly attack or walk away in shame. There seemed to be no solution in sight. Confident that his army was better supplied and prepared for a lengthy stalemate, Saul was content to set up camp right on the spot. He would not allow the Philistines the "victory" of the Israelites leaving first. We settled in for the night with faith in this plan and a feeling that enemy would soon simply back away. Many stated openly that the camp would surely awaken in the morning to find the other side of the valley empty of Philistines. The Israelites fully believed we would be on our way home with our default victory the very next day.

The next morning, before life had come to the encampment, we were all shaken from our sleep by the sentry's alarm that he had seen movement on the other side of the valley. As we fought off the remnants of sleep trying to maintain its hold, we felt a sense of victory, thinking that the Philistines had indeed decided to pack up and leave. Then we heard it: a loud bellowing voice demanding the presence of King Saul. Slowly we gathered our things and headed toward the ridge of the valley, where during the night a viewing stand had been built to allow Saul to look out over the entire valley. Upon our arrival there, I was shocked to find, standing at the center of the valley, the largest man I had ever seen. Once he saw that King Saul and his court had arrived, the giant once again spoke in that booming, bone-shaking voice, which should belong to no human. He introduced himself as Goliath, from the land of Gath, and a loyal soldier for the Philistine army. Acknowledging the standoff as an unwinnable situation, he offered a challenge: a one-on-one combat between himself and any Israelite brave enough to face him. When no challenger immediately stepped forward, Goliath marked a large X in the dirt with his sword. He stated that he would return to that very spot every day to reissue his challenge until it was met or until the Israelite army had run away like cowards who wouldn't face a lone man in a fair fight.

As the giant Goliath returned to his side of the valley, King Saul took a deep breath, gathering his thoughts. He turned to address the members of his forces, who by this time had gathered to witness the monster whose challenges echoed throughout the valley. I personally believe that Saul expected to turn around and find a long line of brave soldiers ready and wanting to volunteer to represent the Israelites in combat. Instead, all of his troops seemed to be holding back and cowering in fear. Saul remained silent, with a look combining shock and disgust registering on his face. Clearly angry and disappointed, Saul abandoned any speech that might have been forming in his head and stormed off of the observation deck. He then headed straight for his personal quarters in silence.

Saul's generals, Jonathon, David, and I stared at each other blankly, trying to quickly determine our own next steps. The wrong move at this point could demoralize the entire army and lead to mass desertion. Even if that was not the intent, it would be incredibly easy in this situation to insult to the king by showing doubt in his leadership and therefore punishable by extreme measures, most traditionally a brutal death by execution. After a brief moment filled with quick exchanges and questioning glances, one of Saul's most trusted and veteran generals, Urim, started to step forward. I thought that if anybody could give the speech needed at this time, it would be Urim, living up to the fire for which he was named. Still, knowing that in the next few moments the words he was about to speak might likely lead to his death, the veteran general took a deep breath. I didn't know whether I should be trying to stop him to save his life or if I should wait and allow him to once again prove his great skill at motivating soldiers.

I was shocked when Urim began by berating and condemning his troops for showing cowardice and fear, embarrassing him, their king, and most importantly, themselves. I glanced across to David and Jonathon and saw that both of them were shocked by Urim's words as well. Judging by his body language, it seemed that Jonathon was preparing to intervene in hopes of stopping Urim from doing any more damage. Just as he was about to step forward, I saw David grab Jonathon to hold him back and allow Urim to continue. I was unsure why David would do this, as clearly this speech was not working. Looking out I could see only blank stares and defeated looks on the solders' faces. I too was concerned enough that I was on the verge of moving to stop Urim. To this day I do not know why, but in that moment I trusted David, as did Jonathon, and we both held our ground to allow the speech to continue.

After several more minutes of questioning everything from their loyalty to their manhood, Urim transitioned into a long list of triumphant war stories, reminding the men of how many times they had overcome seemingly unbeatable odds in battle. These words were more along the lines of what I had expected. Urim then offered the soldiers forgiveness for their momentary hesitation, and he stated that, when the time came and Goliath once again issued his challenge, there would be a long line of proud Israelites eager to represent their king, nation, families, and God.

Now, in all of my years, I have heard all of the greatest speeches given in times of battle and in times of peace. I can tell you with all confidence that this speech given by Urim at the Valley of Elah was by far the best speech ever given in human history. As soon as the last word left his mouth, I looked out across the sea of soldiers, and I knew that Urim was right—come tomorrow's challenge, thousands of men would be ready to take up arms against Goliath. Every soldier had his sword drawn. In a unified rhythm the pounding of the swords on their shields began to grow in volume. There was a sense of destiny and confidence in the inevitable victory to come. Unfortunately, this feeling of confidence evaporated in a matter of seconds. The acoustics of the valley allowed Urim's entire speech to be heard not only by all of the Israelites stretching out away from the observation deck, but also on the other side of the valley, by the Philistines. The fire lit in the souls of the Israelites by Urim's words was just as quickly and effectively doused by the bellowing and guttural laughter of Goliath. This laugh echoed and grew to such a volume able to be heard over the fired up Israelite army. Every ounce of faith in having a willing and able challenger the next day vanished in that instant. It was a brave and noble attempt by Urim hoping to inspire the soldiers. For that brief moment I believed his move had worked. Sadly as the soldiers began to slink back to their tents it was clear that Urim had failed. This would be seen not only as a failure to lead his men, but as a failure to represent his king. I knew then that the next day, instead of seeing a one-on-one battle with Goliath, I would be witnessing the execution of Urim.

Sensing that the fate of this brave general had been sealed, the rest of us filed past him, offering only silent handshakes. That somber sentiment served as both a good-bye and a thank-you, not only for the years of service, but also for the sacrifice he had just made for the rest of us. Any one of us could have tried to inspire the troups. If Urim's speech had not worked then I doubt anybody else would have been successful and would now be facing the wrath of King Saul. By Urim stepping forward first he was now essentially saving us from that same fate. As we neared our own tents to retire to the thoughts and reflections on the coming morning, I stopped to take a look back toward the platform. There stood Urim, all alone, just as he must have felt in that moment. He stared out over the valley as if trying to figure out some way to mount an attack. Knowing Urim as I did, I honestly believe that only part of his mind was concerned with saving his own life. He surely was also hoping to save his king and his soldiers from the reality of what was coming. I remember seeing his shadow stretch out as the sun continued to set and thinking about the long shadow his execution would cast over every single soldier as well as those in the court. I had seen plenty of deaths, some in such horrible manners as to never be spoken of, so I did not worry for myself. David, on the other hand, was still a young man, who had not yet witnessed death in the form of an execution. I thought about trying to find a way to keep him from seeing Urim's execution the next day. I also knew that if he was to continue to find the success on this path God had set for him, it was something the young boy must witness. If David was going to grow to become an important figure for humanity he needed to understand the unpleasant side of this future. Still, seeing Urim standing there filled me with even more desire to search for any alternative.

I entered David's tent to find him pacing and wringing his hands, clearly thinking similar thoughts to my own. When he saw me, he asked what solution I had come up with to solve these problems. In all of our time together to this point, I had been the one David could come to when he was troubled, and I would always have an answer for him. He had come to rely upon my answers too much in times of need. Yes, he had started to ask me for my answers less frequently, but the topics he did still ask about were the difficult ones that serve to shape a man's character. I was supposed to be helping him find his way and not simply telling him what to do. And in this case, I honestly did not have an easy answer to Urim's pending execution or the challenge of Goliath.

I took this chance to shift myself into the role of friend and support for his own decisions. I had feared this day for a while. I was not sure how he would react to the change, especially now when so much seemed to be hanging in the balance. On the other hand, I knew that the crisis might just be what was needed to bring out the hero I believed David was supposed to become. I reinforced my loyalty to his path, but stressed that the time had come for his own heart and mind to guide his way. My job was to help him, not control him. I could see some initial fear and uncertainty in his eyes at this point, which was expected, but also buried in those eyes was a quiet calm. I knew that it would not take much to get him through this transition and be truly ready to take charge of his path. To help him with this, I quickly reminded him of the strength he had always found when we prayed together. He took my hand, and we knelt together to pray. Normally, I would lead the prayer, but taking his cue from my previous statements, David began the prayer seeking guidance and direction during this time of need.

Listening to David pray was almost as compelling and hypnotic as hearing his poetry or musical talents. The abilities of David were clearly on display for me in his tent as he prayed, but there was something bigger and much more important being demonstrated that day. The faith of David so openly professed through his prayer gave me great confidence in the young boy. I had seen such growth in him since finding him in a field with his flock of sheep, and I had never doubted his importance in the plan of humanity. But at that moment, hearing his words, I truly knew that he was indeed the future king of Israel, who would always serve God. My own faith was actually strengthened through that simple prayer offered, kneeling in a tent, searching for help and guidance to a seemingly impossible situation. I had known God since the beginning, so to have this impact on me was truly a remarkable thing. With this immense faith in God being displayed, I had little doubt that no matter what the outcome of the next day, my time of helping David was going to be over very soon. Clearly I had done my job if this young man already possessed such conviction and faith. If only I knew just how far from finished I truly was, and how many more years I would be spending with David.

When David finished praying, we both rose from the ground to reflect and compose our own thoughts before openly discussing them with each other. I don't know if he had heard David praying and waited for him to finish before entering, or if it was simply a case of lucky timing, but at this point Saul's son Jonathon came rushing into David's tent. Before any greetings or the customary royal pleasantries could be exchanged, Jonathon simply stated that something had to be done to save the life of General Urim. The only way he saw that happening was if somebody were to meet the challenge of the giant Goliath. Hearing the problem restated in such an obvious manner certainly put an end to any sense of growing confidence, which had existed just a mere minute beforehand. It was easy to say that somebody should fight Goliath, but it was beyond even the power of the king to simply order a soldier into such a confrontation. As was custom and law, the champion must truly be a volunteer. I thought back to Urim's speech and how the soldiers were truly motivated and ready to face the challenge, only to have their confidence dashed with a single noise from the mouth of Goliath.

Jonathon looked toward his feet for a brief moment, and then he flatly stated that since none of the soldiers intended to challenge

Goliath in the morning, he would do so himself. Hearing this caused David to immediately reject the notion. Even if it were not for the bond of friendship between the two young men, it was obvious that Saul would not allow his favored son to risk his own life in such a reckless manner. Now, to be honest, if the challenge could be easily won, Saul would firmly support his son being the hero for the Israelites. This, however, was not an easily won challenge, and I simply did not see any way Jonathon could survive even a short time against the mighty giant from Gath. After a few moments, David was able to convince Jonathon that Saul would rather retreat in humiliation and shame than to risk his son and heir to the throne.

We sat in silence for quite some time and none of us could offer a single acceptable idea of what to do. From time to time other people would peer in, hoping to find that we had solved the problems. It seemed that every member of the upper levels of the Israelite nation was hoping and even expecting the three of us to find the solution. This felt quite strange to me, considering the young age of Crown Prince Jonathon. In addition to the age factor, for David as well as Jonathon, since he and I had only so recently come to be in these positions within the court, I was surprised others viewed us as the ones to design a solution to the problems. As more and more people asked about our progress, we realized the solution was not going to be an easy one.

Jonathon was clearly getting frustrated with the interruptions and began to turn the tables somewhat. He started responding that we did indeed have a solution—the same solution that had been apparent from the very start of the day. Jonathon would then stare right at the individual and instruct him that he would have the honor to face Goliath the next morning in order to save Urim from execution and bring honor and victory to King Saul and the Israelite nation with the slaying of the giant.

I don't think I have ever seen such fast backpedaling in all of my many years. None of these well-seasoned soldiers had any desire to face the imposing Goliath, and they all responded to Jonathon's instructions with a long list of why they were not the proper choice for this battle. I admit that the reactions were at first amusing and a nice tension-breaker for the three of us in the tent, but Jonathon's tactic also served to end the interruptions. After only a few of these exchanges, word spread through the camp that soldiers should avoid disturbing the prince and his advisors for fear of being pressed to volunteer as Goliath's challenger in the morning.

We were beginning to feel like nothing could be done to salvage the situation or save General Urim. Come morning, King Saul would have no choice but to execute Urim for his failure, which would only leave the impossible problem of facing Goliath or surrendering in shame. I had thought about the possibility of Saul simply sending Urim to face the giant, at least giving him the chance to save the day for the king, and perhaps save his own life as well. This of course seemed like a logical answer to both problems. If Urim won, then all would be well. But given his advanced age and previous war injuries, which had led to his place as a nonfighting general in the king's army, it would be nearly impossible for him to survive even a few moments against the giant, let alone win. This could in essence be seen as having him executed, but it lacked the honor of his rank; and it would also show Saul to be shying away from his responsibility as king to hand done justice.

Of course the other concern with essentially using Goliath as the executioner was the issue of losing the war with the Philistines. I had to remind myself that as nice as it would be to save General Urim, the bigger picture of the war had to remain the more important problem to solve. I considered whether I should volunteer myself to fight Goliath; after all, I was immortal and would not die. The mere thought of this sent a sharp pain shooting from the top of my head through my entire body in a flash. That pain was my quick and obvious reminder that this was something I was not allowed to do.

While I am immortal and here to help humanity return to the paradise I once knew, I cannot simply take it upon myself to win their battles for them. No, it is my job to guide and help them find their own way to the Garden. And in doing so, I too will return to my beloved Eve.

Even if I had been allowed to intervene in such a way, it would not have been a practical answer to the problems. As I thought about it again, I saw in my head an image of Goliath actually hitting me with his sword. How would I explain why I did not die? I am not even sure if my body would get cut or bleed like normal from the giant's sword. I have always been able to find a way to avoid situations where serious injuries could take place. I have occasionally gotten small scratches, but never anything life-threatening. To this day I still don't know what would happen. I have become quite skilled at avoiding the risk, so I do not intend to find out. There was another way to fill out God's plans for this situation, and I had faith that David would discover our solution.

As the hours continued to pass and the sun began to set, we still had no solution. It was clear that in a battle of strength, Goliath held every advantage. He was simply bigger, stronger, and possessing a longer reach than any soldier in the Israelite army. Even if one were to get a lucky shot on him, it would not likely do much damage to his imposing form. Yet a single strike from Goliath's sword would clearly end the battle in an instant. Physically there was just no way to match up to the giant, but we held to our belief that there had to be some way to overcome his physical advantage using our skills and brains. The problem was that strategy worked well when using many troops over an entire battle campaign, but in single combat the brains tended to be less important than the brawn. Trying to simultaneously find a way to beat the giant and prevent General Urim from being executed was exhausting for us, yet we remained awake and worked through the entire night.

As the sun began to rise, a messenger from Saul's tent arrived to summon us to meet with the king. We were not surprised, as Saul would be looking to make his decisions before the rest of the camp was awake. I am not sure if another hour would have made any difference or not, as we had been working all day and night without finding a solution. Still, the walk to King Saul's tent seemed impossibly long. I looked toward the observation deck, where I had last seen General Urim the previous evening. Part of me expected to see him still standing there looking out into the valley, but he was not there.

I remember wondering what it must feel like to know that you were going to die. I can't imagine this, having gone from living in the Garden with Eve to living in my current state. I obviously have seen more deaths in my years than anybody can hope to count; but it was never mine, and I never felt any fear of dying. This was a strange notion, considering that death only existed for humanity because of me. I wonder how many months or years I have spent ruminating on that one topic during my "lifetime" on earth. I know that I would have thought about it much longer that day had we not arrived at King Saul's tent and been rushed inside without any delay.

Upon entering the tent, I found out just where General Urim was: he was talking with the king. From the looks of things, the two had been talking for quite a while. I am not sure if they too were looking for a solution or if they simply were two old friends remembering a lifetime of adventures. The only thing I heard as we entered was General Urim stating that he would not embarrass the king by begging for his life, and he hoped King Saul understood that his only ambition was to inspire the men and return them to the honor they had forgotten in the face of Goliath.

Much to my surprise, Saul looked to me and asked how many men had been swayed by General Urim's pleas. The only response I knew how to give was the honest one: none of them had stepped forward to face Goliath, and in fact all that had spoken to Jonathan had made excuses and hidden from the challenge. Now it was truly set. It was in fact my answer that sealed Urim's fate and condemned him to die. I had been sent to help David; and in doing so, I had likely ended the life of another brave and loyal servant of Saul, who was, even more importantly, a faithful believer.

My thoughts were interrupted when I heard David's voice—not the quiet voice of a boy, but that of the man I believed he was meant to be. The man who led the prayer inspired me, but this David also intimidated me through the confidence and power he showed as he stated that without question I was wrong in saying no one had stepped forward. I was not the only confused party in that tent. In fact, David was the only person who did not seem to be confused.

This would be a true test of the new David. How would he re-act and respond with all of us, including the king of Israel, looking to him to explain his statement? To speak out in the minority view took courage; I admired his bravery to do so. Still, it was the next step that really mattered. Now that he had spoken out, stating his disagreement, all eyes were on David, waiting for him to defend his position and convince everybody that he was not out of line. It was one thing for King Saul to have been insulted by his top general, but no matter what I thought or how Jonathon saw David, the truth was that he was still just a lower-level advisor and performer. To David's credit, he looked to be totally at ease in this spotlight he had so suddenly stepped into. His next few words would either raise him to new heights in the king's court or separate him from his life alongside Urim. Remaining poised and controlled, David simply took a breath and stated again that the general's speech had inspired action against Goliath. In fact, Urim had moved the king's own son to desire the opportunity to face the giant. Naturally, Saul was very quick to state that no such action would be allowed. I was impressed with David's ability to fight for the life of the general without putting any others in actual danger. David had showed us a loophole that the rest of us had over-looked. The fact that we had all known Saul would reject Jonathon as a challenger had blinded us to the truth that Urim still had actually succeeded in convincing Jonathon to challenge Goliath. This meant that Urim was not guilty of any violations of law or custom and was free from punishment. Saul now was faced with the free path to choose any outcome he desired. No longer burdened by the custom requiring him to execute General Urim, Saul could simply move on to focus on the problem of Goliath.

CHAPTER 22

DAVID'S DECISION

The moment of success and feeling of triumph did not last long at all. In a matter of mere moments, worried expressions returned to all of the faces in the tent. While the concern for Urim had passed, Goliath still had to be considered. Yes, saving General Urim's life had been a great relief, but that would not matter if the forces of the Israelite army could not be counted on to produce a champion capable of defeating Goliath in single combat. The question was clearly on everybody's mind—what if no such champion could be found? A full assault on the Philistines was still not possible, given the geographic restraints of the valley. At the same time, retreat could never be considered. To simply leave would do even more damage to the prestige of the Israelite nation than to endure a crushing defeat on the battlefield. There was nothing but shame in retreat at that point in time. A champion had to be found—quickly. Saul looked around one last time before he simply ended our gathering and ordered us all out of his tent.

As we exited the tent, I could hear many whispered concerns just out of earshot. Even without being able to clearly hear the words, I knew the topic was Goliath. Since nobody was brave enough to even approach us as we left the tent, it seemed clear that no champion was ready to step forward. Maybe it was a random whisper that I heard, or maybe it was because I had already had the thought and was trying to suppress it, but my mind quickly went back to the notion that King Saul would enter the valley to offer his own personal surrender. In his prime, Saul was a very skilled warrior known for being able to handle any number of weapons at once. Sadly, those days had long since passed. Goliath was no average opponent, which only served to make the situation even more daunting. I had not witnessed Saul's earlier successes, but I found it hard to believe that he had ever faced any foe remotely close to the giant who would soon be waiting at the floor of the valley. No matter how I pictured it, Saul facing Goliath seemed to mean certain death for the proud king.

The loss of King Saul would be devastating for the Israelites. Not only would they lose a very powerful leader, but the loss to Goliath would also serve as a form of surrender for the entire army and nation of Israel. The loss of power and prestige would undo years of gains under Saul and force the Israelites to become more concerned with simply surviving rather than thriving. It would take generations for them to rebuild to this level of civilization, economy, and prestige again. A much more likely scenario was the Israelites being fully conquered and absorbed by the other civilizations coveting the region and resources currently occupied by Saul's kingdom.

A quick glance at Jonathon's expression showed me that he too was considering similar thoughts. The awareness that within a few hours, the fate of the Israelite people would soon be his responsibility was already causing this young man obvious distress. Under the best of circumstances, it would be a formidable task for any man. To be rushed into a position of power over a nation sacrificing the current king, countless offered as slaves, and an immense loss of land seemed to be an impossible situation. David tried to offer Jonathon some reassuring words and support, but Jonathon was not ready to hear such things at this time. Instead he simply walked away, muttering something about needing to be alone with his thoughts. It was not truly his desire to be alone with his thoughts, as he walked directly back toward Saul's tent. Having never had a father myself, I cannot speak from personal experience on the nature of that bond. But from what I have learned in my many years on earth, I can say that I fully agreed with Jonathan's decision to return to his father's tent so they could spend their last few moments together.

I could see the strain on David's face as he desperately searched for the words to shout at Jonathon, wanting to help ease his friend's pain. David then gave me a quick look and asked me to join him for a prayer in our tent. As we began walking, David glanced over his shoulder at Jonathon, and suddenly his pace quickened. I knew immediately that David had decided on a new course of action.

Before I could catch up to David, I had it clearly in my mind that his decision was to fight Goliath on his own. Despite the logical and rational part of me screaming in my mind to stop David from this suicide mission, I was aware of a growing sense of calm filling me. I knew from past experiences in my time here on earth as God's chosen custodian that this was His way of helping me to know that He was in control and that this was in line with His plan. I was not sure how this was a good idea, but I had learned to have faith and know that everything would work out when this calm feeling came over me. By the time I caught up to David, he was just entering his tent. He turned around quickly, obviously expecting me to attempt to alter his mind and talk him out of his decision. Instead I simply took him by the shoulders and then embraced him as a brother in faith and in the human world. I can't say for sure, but I like to hope that in that moment David was able to take some of my strength and faith, knowing that God would protect him. We knelt in prayer, and again David showed the depth of his faith. I wished that I could actually tell him that I knew for sure that God would protect him and that He had great plans for the future. I knew that David would somehow face down the giant and come out the bigger man.

As we finished praying, Jonathon walked through the entrance of the tent. Before taking even a few steps into the tent, his face showed a wide range of emotions and conflict. Apparently it was obvious to anybody who truly knew David that he intended to face Goliath himself. With a simple glance at David's face, Jonathon must have known that his friend had made that decision. A very brief discussion between the two friends showed that David's resolve to face Goliath could not be shaken. Despite the obvious nervousness and fear for his friend, Jonathon also had great confidence in David's abilities to face the giant. After a brief moment of silent yet meaningful glances around the tent, we all rose together, as if responding to some unheard signal.

We knew that it was time to begin preparing David for this immense challenge. But there the agreement seemed to end for a while. David and Jonathon had very different ideas about what it meant to prepare for facing Goliath. Jonathon wished to offer David the use of anything from within the royal armory, but David refused. Instead, he wished only to enter the battlefield with his sling and his faith. Jonathon also had great faith in God, but he was at heart a military man who knew that winning a battle required a sharp sword, a strong shield, and sturdy armor. To face anybody, let alone the giant Goliath, without such equipment simply made no sense to Jonathon, and he was prepared to do anything within his power to make sure that David was ready for the fight.

Jonathan took a good look into David's eyes. The focus and determination present there was enough to convince both of us of anything. I remember seeing those eyes and questioning if David would even need the sling. I could imagine Goliath catching David's gaze and immediately surrendering. Of course, I knew that was highly unlikely. Still, seeing David's confidence and grace greatly improved my faith in his decision, and Jonathon came to respect David's desire to only carry the sling. Even though he was not much more than a boy in age, David was a man of faith on a mission.

We decided to keep David hidden in his tent until the last possible second before facing his foe. David needed privacy to maintain his faithful focus, but we also wanted to prevent others from having a change of heart. Some of the great warriors of the Israelite army would likely feel challenged by the sight of this mere boy braving the immense giant, and they might decide in that moment to rush in to face Goliath. But Jonathon and I felt that any such rash move would lead to a quick and easy defeat for Israel. We chose to rely on David's focused and comfortable faith and resolve. I also had my own faith in this being God's will for David at this time.

As the morning moved forward, and we had been waiting for Goliath to issue his challenge, we became aware of a crowd gathering outside of the tent. Everyone seemed to know that Jonathon was in the tent with David and not with his father. This was more than enough to earn curiosity, given the circumstances. I had to laugh, though, as I would get as close to the tent entrance as I could in hopes of overhearing what was being said. Most assumed that Jonathon would never face Goliath, as Saul would never allow it, and David was considered merely a young boy performer. The whispers from outside the tent conveyed to me that they were convinced I would be facing Goliath. I was the stranger who said little but clearly knew more than the rest. I looked as if I could handle myself in a fight. I was easily sacrificed. The list went on and on as to why I was clearly going to be the choice. I had to work very hard to keep from breaking out into a laughing fit as I imagined what they would think when they saw the boy, David, who they had so easily dismissed, not only enter the valley to face Goliath, but triumph.

At last the booming voice of Goliath echoed through the valley, calling for a victim to present himself. The whispers from outside of the tent fell silent, and I could feel every eye in the entire army staring at the tent, waiting for me to emerge and save them. I had a sudden fear that their reaction might have a very negative impact on David's confidence and faith. I now questioned my previous "knowledge" that David could not lose. Maybe I was so desperate for this assignment to be a success that I was reading too much into things. Was I overconfident and arrogant at this point and actually sending David to his death? It is amazing how quickly confidence can turn to fear and then back again. No sooner than I had begun to doubt this plan than my faith was restored. The calm of David in this moment put me at ease. If he was not wavering, then how could I possibly have any doubts? He was about to walk straight through the crowd of soldiers, determined to face Goliath.

Then, right before David exited the tent, Jonathon stopped him. It was not fear or doubt in David that caused him to do this, but the sudden realization that Saul had to be stopped from going to the valley himself. Jonathon told us to give him a short head start and then move quickly to the valley. Jonathon bolted out of our tent and headed straight to Saul's tent, and I had a quick final moment with David. I started to offer more encouragement, but there was simply no need. After a few quick breaths, we decided that Jonathon had been given enough of a head start to reach Saul. It wasn't that I thought Saul would object; he simply needed to be told to avoid confusion, allowing him to save face as the controlling and powerful king before the members of his army.

As I pulled back the flap on the tent, I noticed another benefit of Jonathon's quick thinking. The soldiers who had been surrounding our tent only moments ago were now gone, apparently having followed Jonathon to the other side of the camp and Saul's tent. This would make it much easier to get David to Goliath without any problems. I could only wonder what David was thinking and if he was truly aware that in a few moments his actions would forever alter the course of the Israelite nation.

CHAPTER 23

DAVID VERSUS GOLIATH

I led David out of the tent and toward the valley, where in mere minutes somebody would be a champion and somebody would be dead. On our way we were essentially invisible. It was not that we weren't seen by other people, but simply that we were completely ignored. Everybody had seen Jonathon leave and head toward Saul's tent, leading their attention in that direction to see what plan the king and his son had settled upon. As for David and myself, nothing was remotely interesting about us in that moment. Since David had put his faith in God and decided to go into this battle without armor or weapons, we appeared to be dressed as normal and headed in the direction of Saul's tent as well. I would say that most people simply assumed that we had conferred with Jonathon and now headed to the king's platform for a final decision or announcement just the same as everybody else.

That all changed when we actually arrived at the edge of the valley. Rather than climbing to the platform to take our normal places among all of the other royal advisors, David simply kept walking straight down the path to the floor of the valley. The whispers asking who the champion might be quickly grew to murmurs and grumblings of doubt and confusion. As these expressions grew louder, I thought about how they would never doubt David had they simply been able to see the look in his eyes moments ago in his tent. In just a few more steps, David would be in full sight of Goliath. Some of the Israelite soldiers started to turn from the valley and head back to their own tents in order to begin packing for a quick retreat. They must have felt certain they would be ordered to withdraw just as soon as Goliath finished using David as a toothpick. Some seemed to give in to morbid curiosity, wanting to see just how quickly Goliath would kill David. Even betting pools formed, with David obviously getting very bad odds. Had I not been so keen on seeing Goliath's face the very second that he saw David emerge as the Israelite champion, I would have taken advantage of those odds and placed bets with as many people as I could.

Still, most of the soldiers must have figured that if they quickly packed and organized the retreat, they could be long gone by the time it became necessary for Saul to select the offerings of soldiers as tribute to the Philistines. They clearly felt that it would be better to defend their loyalty in the future rather than risk their present by waiting to become slaves or sacrificial kills as part of the unconditional surrender they were convinced was the only possible outcome. In a stroke of good timing, whether lucky or orchestrated I am still not sure, Saul emerged from his tent and appeared on the royal platform. Seeing some of his troops beginning to retreat already, he simply challenged them, asking why they were leaving instead of staying to watch his champion earn the victory for the entire Israelite nation. I have no idea if it was a newfound confidence and faith in David spurred on by Saul's words or if it was simply due to being shamed by the comments of their king, but quickly they all returned to their places along the valley ridge to see what was going to happen.

I met Jonathon's gaze, and I was amazed to see the confidence filling his face. I initially assumed that he had gained this faith through his attempts to convince Saul of David's mission. I was even more amazed when he told me that in reality it was the opposite. It was in fact Saul who had faith in David and had convinced Jonathon of the upcoming victory over Goliath. Jonathon told me he had not truly doubted David, but at the same time he did not truly believe in David's chances to win. He understood that David was going to fight Goliath and that Saul had to be told. Jonathon had taken that task as much to protect his father's image of the king being in control as he did for David's sake. When Jonathon had gotten to Saul's tent to tell him of David's intentions and to stall for time, Saul had been very pleased with the news. Saul had told Jonathon that there was no question about David being able to win with the help of God. This faith from Saul had quickly rubbed off on Jonathon, and now both father and son were as confident as David and I were in the upcoming victory.

After he had finished telling me about his meeting with Saul, Jonathon asked me what sort of strategy David was going to use to defeat the giant. To be honest, I didn't know what David was planning, but I had unwavering faith. Luckily I didn't have to attempt an answer because at that moment Goliath got his first glimpse of the Israelite champion who was coming to face him. Upon seeing David, a loud, guttural laugh rose from Goliath to fill the valley. It was only a matter of seconds before the whole of the Philistine army joined in laughing and taunting the small warrior who was about to be easily dispatched by the great Goliath. I am still amazed at how David stood his ground in prideful defiance and calm confidence despite taunting shouts from the Philistines, claiming that Goliath would use David's bones to clean his teeth or that a woman would last longer in the fight.

The moment had finally come. David stared through Goliath with confidence. I swear that simple act seemed to totally unnerve the giant. Goliath tried to regain the upper hand by banging his large sword against his shield. Within a matter of moments, the entire Philistine army had joined the cadence. The tensions rose, and the confidence from across the valley reached a peak, while the Israelites teetered on the brink of running again. David began to slowly walk in a circle around the immense warrior, forcing Goliath to turn in order to keep David in his field of vision. It only took a couple of times around before it became obvious that Goliath's massive helmet was hindering his view of the smaller, more mobile opponent. A quick glance at Jonathon confirmed that we both understood this to not be a stalling technique, but it was in fact a well-thought-out strategic maneuver. By constantly moving, David was forcing Goliath to use up energy by turning and fighting his helmet, trying to always maintain an unobstructed view.

A few turns later, a very frustrated Goliath ripped his helmet from his head and threw it at David. This was easy for David to avoid, as it sailed well over his head. A defiant Goliath once again pounded his chest and looked to the sky as he let out a bellowing scream, trying to intimidate David. Seeing his chance, David quickly grabbed the small stone from his pouch and readied his sling. Returning his attention to David, Goliath mocked the small boy with the puny weapon and demanded a real champion to fight. Saul quickly responded that David was the champion of God and that Goliath could still surrender. Hearing this enraged Goliath, and he raised his sword to charge. David took this opportunity and launched the rock from his sling, landing a perfect shot right to the giant's temple. As the stunned behemoth stumbled around the valley floor, David prepared another stone. Steadying himself, Goliath lifted his sword again. The weight of the sword being lifted over his head was too much for the injured giant, and he fell backward to the ground. The sword slipped from his hands, and Goliath let out a moan that shook me to the core. It was obvious that David had won the battle and that Goliath would soon be dead from the head wound.

David grabbed the sword, which was nearly as big as he was. Holding it poised to strike a killing blow to the fallen giant, David paused to say a short prayer for Goliath. Then in a flash of the sun reflecting off of the blade, David brought the sword down and through the large neck of Goliath, removing the head from his body in one single blow. David picked up Goliath's head by the hair and held it up for all to see. Turning toward Saul, David proclaimed his victory to be in honor of God and his chosen king. He then faced the Philistine army and demanded their immediate surrender. I will never forget that sight: this young man holding up the severed head of the unbeatable giant, demanding the surrender of an entire army.

After another moment, David dropped the head and the sword to quietly begin the walk back up out of the valley. When he reached the camp, David was met as a hero, but he refused to celebrate. His only interest at this point was to return to his tent with me for prayer and reflection. David was greatly conflicted between his belief that it was wrong to kill and his faith that he had served God's will. We spent hours talking through many ways to view these issues, often returning to the understanding that God does not wish for humans to fight, but that it is human nature to do so. It would be wrong to simply allow an enemy to destroy and kill in order to avoid violence. I worked hard to show him that he had saved many lives through his taking of Goliath's life and that he should see this act as protecting the Israelites as God desired. Finally, David was able to relax, and he drifted off to sleep, leaving me to my own reflections. Naturally my mind returned to the Garden and my firsthand knowledge of just how human death truly is.

CHAPTER 24

THE CHANGING MOOD

I know that to you death is simply a part of the human experience and the only way you know for life to exist. I once again feel the need to apologize to you for the world being this way. I remember a different world, the world the way God had created it where the only death was for a source of food so Eve and I could survive. I was aware that those animals were once running and jumping around, living a happy life within the paradise of the Garden, but it still never truly registered to me what death was. We simply knew that it was God's will for that animal to become a source of nourishment for us to sustain our health and strength. Knowing it to be God's will, we always were sure to be thankful and honor the food we consumed. Nothing of the animal was wasted. Every piece of meat was consumed, the skins were used to provide shelter and storage, and even the bones were used to make tools for our life in the Garden. Great pride was taken in offering thanks and respect for all that each and every animal provided us. No, that was not death and suffering in our minds. Those concepts were simply not present while we were living in our paradise. Eve and I never felt sick; neither did we experience any suffering until that tragic day when everything changed. I know that my words must give you some idea of how amazing our life was; but trust me when I tell you it was so much better than you are capable of imagining. This only makes the life you understand to be human seem that much more cruel to me as I have experienced it.

Yes, again, it is all my fault; you don't need to worry about me forgetting that. Death haunts me at every turn of my life. Following the end of paradise, my exposure to real death became constant. Animals had to be killed for food and no longer went peacefully. Sickness and pain also entered our lives. Still, as you know, Eve and I were blessed with a pretty happy life, and we were exceptionally blessed to have children. Through the death of Abel and the loss of Cain, I was able to truly learn and understand the meaning of human loss and suffering. However, it was also through this blessing of my family that I came to understand the depth of a father's love. This lesson served me well through each of my different assignments for God, but especially in my time with Saul and Jonathon and David and his family.

Following David's defeat of Goliath, the mood around the camp quickly began to change. Beyond the natural relief of not being killed or sent into a life of slavery as part of a surrender deal, there was a new hero to celebrate. My initial concern with the hero worship was how it might change life for David. I was worried that this young man of such immense faith in God might even be tempted beyond what was possible to resist, as he was suddenly surrounded by all of the temptations and trappings of the world. Even though he had clearly grown in age, belief, and wisdom since the days of being the young shepherd boy I had first met, I worried about the still young man being offered immense wealth, women, and gifts of countless description. I knew that David was not used to being the center of attention, having lived as a shepherd in the fields before I brought him to Saul's court as a musician. Despite growing in status in that life and becoming one of Jonathon's top advisers and friends, wealth and fame were still new to David. To be perfectly honest, I found myself quite tempted by all that was being offered to young David, and I am still not sure how he was able to handle everything so well at that young age. While I clearly knew the dangers of giving in to all of earth's temptations, I also understood that there was nothing wrong with enjoying some of those pleasures in moderation. Maybe it was my mistake that helped lead to future problems for him, but I did find myself encouraging David to allow himself to enjoy some of the possible rewards being offered. Given his initial rejection of all of his sudden fame and glory, I felt that my initial concerns over his reactions to his success were no longer needed. He had clearly shown me that I should trust his restraint, but that did not mean I felt entirely safe.

No, my concern did not remain with David long, but I quickly switched my focus to the rest of the Israelites. I wondered how their treatment of the young man would change. It had not been long since David first came to Saul's court and became the favorite musician of the king. While this was a position of immense importance among the rich and powerful of the kingdom, as well as with foreign dignitaries, it was not something often enjoyed by the common soldier. In fact, the time spent in that camp was actually the first time that many of the people had actually ever seen David. They knew that Jonathon had taken on a new friend and advisor who was rumored to be extremely gifted and intelligent, but I am sure that his young age caught many of them by surprise. This only served to add to the mystique and wonder of how this young boy had so easily defeated the giant and brought an immediate end to the war, thus saving all of their lives and possibly the entire society. At that moment, David was the hero and everybody wanted to be close to him. But even in those days, I knew that fame could be fickle; and I wondered how things might change as time passed.

The entire trip back to Saul's castle saw David swamped with people of all ages and positions in society seeking to talk about the battle with Goliath. I was amazed at how well David handled this new pressure. It seemed as if he always found time to retell the story, making sure to emphasize that his strength and courage had come from his faith in God. I began to believe that my time with David might nearly be over. I had helped this young, obscure shepherd become a strong man of faith, who was quickly rising to a place of importance within God's people. I simply did not see any reason why David would still need my help or guidance now that he had found such early success. This felt like a truly welcome change from some of my previous missions, where I had spent years and years working toward a single goal. As we neared home, I was making my plans on where to travel next and how I was going to say good-bye to David. I had no doubt in my mind that he would continue to flourish and thrive in his new life.

I was so preoccupied with these thoughts that I failed to notice one striking fact that should have warned me of the trouble coming. I had just been amazed at how David always made time to retell the story of defeating Goliath. I don't know how many times he actually told that story, but it seemed like it was a constant part of life during that journey. What I missed was that David was able to do this because he had plenty of free time. He had not been called to Saul's tent to perform or for any other reason. No, Saul in fact seemed to distance himself from David. Had I been paying attention, I would have known that something was not right. Saul was the kind of person that recognized greatness in many forms and was always quick to connect himself to it in any way that he could. Given that, Saul should have been keeping David closer than normal and bragging about how the young boy he had brought in was the amazing hero. Instead, Saul kept his distance, and I had been so wrapped up in my success with David that I had failed to notice.

I can't say for sure what I might have done had I noticed it then, but I like to imagine that I would have done something to try to bridge the gap and help put things right between the king and the hero. Maybe I could have accomplished that, or maybe things would have still gone wrong for David; but due to my arrogance and pride, I never even tried.

Over the next few years, David saw his place change quickly. He was no longer simply the talented musician and friend of the king's son. David and Jonathon became much closer than simply friends or brothers. The open distance between Saul and David had seemed to vanish. I believed that Jonathon's close relationship with David had helped to bridge the gap. While I still believe that it did have some role in Saul's actions, I truly feel that the change of heart was caused by Saul's love of power. Initially after David had killed Goliath, Saul clearly felt threatened. As time passed and David remained popular with the people, Saul knew that he had to be connected to the young hero. In order to do this, Saul looked to be welcoming of David as a friend of the family in addition to the hero and skilled leader whose skills as a military mind could not be wasted.

David was sent on several important campaigns and always came home with stories of his easy victories over the enemy. During one brief return home between campaigns, Saul came to David and embraced him, calling him son. While this caught everybody off guard initially, it was quickly forgotten, as Saul continued on by stating that he was offering his daughter Merab as David's wife as a reward for all he had accomplished. David, however, rejected this offer, claiming that he was not worthy to become the son-in-law of the king. This angered Saul a great deal and led to him quickly give Merab to another man as a wife. I knew that this rejection of Saul's daughter, and the insult to Saul's ego, would serve to create problems for David in the future. Soon Saul announced that David would be taking a small force of men out to attack a much larger army. Everybody who heard of this plan realized that the intent was for David to fall in battle for his rejection of Merab.

Despite the overwhelming opposition intended to destroy David, the Israelite forces were victorious yet again. As David had been collecting victories, many people began to wonder if it was not a sign that David was in fact blessed and loved by God. I even started to hear people question if David should be king and not Saul. I did my best to shield David from hearing the talk, as I did not want him to be tempted by such things, neither did I want him to overreact and silence the talk in any permanent ways. I knew how strongly David felt about situation, as evidenced by his rejecting a chance to marry into the king's family because he did not feel worthy. I worked hard to silence the talk when I came across it and to remind people that it had in fact been Saul who had seen the gifts of David and was using him in such important strategic manners. Unlike the trip home following the defeat of Goliath, when I encouraged David to mix with the people to share of himself and his faith that led to his victory, travelling home from this success, I tried to keep him as busy as possible to limit the interaction.

We spent a great deal of time on our journey home talking about his life so far and how his trust in God had served him so well to that point. One night I brought up the offer Saul had made for David to marry into the family and how I honestly felt that the offer should have been accepted. I tried to get him to imagine his life without having to go out to battles all of the time—where he would have more say in which battles he fought and when he stayed at home to delve deeper into his personal studies. I really thought that I was getting through to him when suddenly he became angry. He told me that it no longer mattered how much sense it made, or that he loved Merab, because he had made his choice and she had since been given to another man. Following that heated outburst, I felt it best to leave David alone for the rest of the journey home. During that time I focused on my own thoughts and prayers, as I remembered my own true love that I had lost.

The day we got home was much the same as every other return home with nothing standing out in my mind. At this point, I was just so glad to be home that nothing else really mattered to me. Now, I know that talking about the comforts of a rolled up blanket on the floor in a small, square room barely big enough to stretch out in might seem crazy to you. Yes, I have spent time in more spacious prison cells, but for that period of time, home was that small room and therefore my comfort. No matter where or when I have been in my life, I have always found a way to appreciate the value and comfort of any kind of home. I have lived in a cave with a rock for a pillow as well as some of the most luxurious palaces, but no matter which home it is, I always am thankful. Maybe it comes from the feeling I had when I was evicted from my first home, the Garden of Eden. Since that last moment of seeing the Garden gone I swore that I would never again take any home for granted. So, yes, that ridiculously small room was truly a welcome sight to me. I found myself wondering that night what my next home would be like on my next mission as I prepared to move on in a couple of days.

The next day I woke up and found David studying the texts in the royal library. He was not looking for anything specific, simply reading. Whenever he had any spare time, David could always be found reading anything and everything that was available. His desire to learn seemed to be impossible to quench. He was always talking about the ideas in his head and how he wanted to write books praising God. I had no doubt that someday he would do just that, but on that specific day he was wanted in Saul's court. After David had rejected the offer from Saul to marry Merab, I was worried about his standing in Saul's mind. Then, following the successful victory over what was meant to be impossible odds, I once again felt that David was on King Saul's good side. I therefore simply assumed that this was going to be another formal recognition or presentation to David for being a hero of the Israelite nation. For this reason I hurried David from his reading back to his room to get cleaned up and dressed for such an honor. I had a feeling that David was about to be elevated to an official position of honor within Saul's court and that he would achieve all that I had imagined. I joked some with David about how he was about to begin a new life of importance while I was going to begin a search for a new life wherever I was needed. I compared my future days of sleeping under trees and the stars just as he had done as a shepherd with the royal life he would soon enjoy. I knew that none of these things mattered to David, but still there was a glint in his eye, showing that he understood his life was about to get a lot better and he couldn't help but be excited.

CHAPTER 25

EVERYTHING CHANGES

When we arrived at the entrance to Saul's throne room, I sensed the tension in the air. The doors were seldom closed; and even when they were closed, David and I had been given free rein to enter of our own accord. Yet, upon our arrival that day, we were met by the royal guards blocking the doorway. They told us that the king was finishing up an important meeting and we would be allowed in shortly. Having our normal entrance blocked, it seemed best to honor the respectful traditions involved with being brought before the king. David and I remained silent just outside of the doors, waiting to be called on to enter the throne room. Standing there in that moment, filled with sudden fear and uncertainty, I did the only thing that I truly knew to do: I prayed to God for strength and the ability to make the best of whatever course of action was about to unfold. It truly was one of those moments that people often speak of when all of time seems to stand still. I am sure that it was actually only a matter of a few minutes, but it seemed like an eternity (something I know all about) before any actions were taken.

I am not sure what had been going on prior to our arrival, but it clearly had been of importance to Saul. At the same time, it was something he seemed to wish to keep hidden from David and me. When we were finally called upon to enter the room, I could not help but remember the similar scene from just a few years earlier when I first brought David before Saul. Part of me still maintained hope that this meeting before the king would result in a great success, just as the first one had brought, but my mind pounded with anticipation that everything had already changed—even without my knowledge. As we entered the large throne room, my eyes caught a glimpse of motion from the far side of the room. Naturally, I was curious to know what had been going on. It struck me as odd that we had been kept waiting while Saul finished up another meeting, yet nobody had come out before we were brought in ourselves. Seeing only those usually present in the throne room, I came to the only obvious conclusion that the motion at the other end of the room was in fact the previous party leaving. This struck me as being unusual because that exit was essentially the private royal exit. I was not able to see clearly enough through all of the motion and the distance to be able to identify exactly who it was that was being rushed out the other side as we were coming in before Saul. I tried to convince myself that it was just a coincidence, but something inside of me kept telling me that this strange event was actually quite important.

Trying to shake my mind of those thoughts and wanting to focus on the moment, I turned my attention to the royal platform in hopes of being able to get a read on the king. What I saw there only served to make me more nervous. Clearly there was something unsettling about the previous meeting. The simple fact that Saul and Jonathon were very obviously trying to keep as much distance between each other as possible while holding to the expected royal appearance set off many warning bells in my mind. I immediately began thinking of everything that I could imagine might be the root of the problem in hopes of being able to defuse the situation. If there was trouble between the king and his son, I worried that David might be the cause. Was it possible that the man I saw being ushered out the back exit had come before the king and his son with some sort of slanderous attack on David? I knew that David and Jonathon had gotten very close over the years. This had been especially clear watching how well the two of them had worked together so recently with the logistics of the just-finished battle with the Philistines. Saul had originally been in favor of putting his son and David together in hopes that they would become friends, but I was scared that the king's perspective had changed, starting back when Goliath's body hit the ground. The killing of Goliath had elevated David to a hero among the Israelites, a status that only become more cemented with each additional victory under David's command. Even in those days, a hero could have more power than a prince. I honestly don't think that Jonathon cared one way or the other and was in fact quite happy to see his friend become so beloved by the people. Saul, on the other hand, was a king, and kings spent a great amount of time thinking about and planning their lineage and legacy. I can only imagine that from his perspective it must have been a painful thing to see his son and chosen successor being surpassed by a former shepherd, and for his son to be happy and supportive of this outsider. As those thoughts ran through my mind, I began to believe that David had been called before Saul not for an award, but to be sent back home to his sheep. Still, none of my thoughts proved entirely correct. At the time I was completely caught off guard, but looking back later it all seemed so clear.

As I said, as king, Saul was greatly concerned with his legacy. Rather than risk David's fame and hero status growing to be a challenge, Saul had simply decided to bring David into the family. Despite David rejecting the first offer to marry into Saul's family, Saul was determined that he would be able to ensure his connection to the future no matter if it was Jonathon or David who found their way to the throne. From my point of view, I saw the arrangement as a clear path to removing all barriers that might have kept David from working to return us all to the Garden. I felt certain that David would either be the next king of Israel, or at least he would be in a position of great influence over Jonathon and able to keep things on the right path.

With Saul making the announcement that David would be joining the family, I caught sight of Jonathon. I had noticed before that he had been keeping his distance from his father, but as this proclamation was being made, Jonathon had a look of almost anger on his face. I was at a complete loss as to what he was thinking to make him so angry, and I worried that it might be a sign of a fracturing in the relationship between Jonathon and David. Still, from what I knew of Jonathon, I could not believe he was upset about David becoming his brother. While he could have been upset about the possible threat to his own path to being king, that simply would not have fit the character of Jonathon. No, he had a very noble heart and would have gladly allowed David to become king if that was best for the people. Sadly, I didn't have to wait too long before I understood exactly why Jonathon did not look happy as I found out what Saul had already explained to his son in the private meeting while David and I were kept waiting.

Saul stood in front of the entire room with a look of confidence and pride. After he had called us forward, he flatly announced that David would be marrying into the family. With a wave of his hand, Saul's two daughters entered the throne room, looking more beautiful than I had ever seen them before. Once I got over the initial shock, I remembered one disturbing fact: Merab had been offered to David before, and upon his initial rejection she had been given to another in marriage. I froze, unsure of what David was going to say in response to Saul's statement. The first time, Saul had come to David in private to offer Merab as David's bride. But this time, in front of many other dignitaries and members of the Israelite upper class, Saul had simply announced that David was to marry into the king's family. Adding to my concern was the presence of Merab. David had recently confessed to me that he truly did love her. Had he not felt unworthy to enter the king's family, he would have been happy to marry her. As silence fell over the room, I could feel my heart banging in my chest. I knew that the wrong move by David at that point could bring cata- strophic consequences, yet I also knew that for me to talk with him at this point would be seen to be equally insulting to Saul and his fam- ily. I was in the same position as everybody else in the room: forced to wait for any reaction from David.

During that moment of silent fear, my mind drifted back through my experiences with arranged marriages. For the most part, the tradition served humanity well and could be considered a success. I knew from my own experience what it was like to be truly in love with somebody. Eve and I had found true and complete love in the Garden, and it had translated, survived, and grown after we had left the Garden for the world of sin. Well, I say that we found love, but it is also true that ours was the ultimate in arranged marriages, see- ing as how God had created Eve specifically for me to love. Still, I had also seen the problems that could arise from arranged marriages throughout the years. The perfect example, of course, would be my own two sons, Cain and Abel. We had thought that everything was lined up just as it was supposed to be. My two sons were to marry two sisters of importance, and our small society would grow stronger from the unions. Now that you know that whole story, I won't retell it, but Cain and Abel's actions will remind you of the dangers jealousy can play in such arrangements. That knowledge of my sons had me truly on edge as I waited to see how David would react. With both Merab, the woman he loved, and her sister Michal, who had made no secret of her love for David, standing before him I only hoped that his first step would be toward the right woman. Then again I also worried if Saul had set this up so that there was no "correct" response for David to give.

That fear was quickly realized as David took a deep breath and moved toward Michal. While everybody sighed in relief that David had not decided to press for love over tradition or respect to the king, Saul took exception at this action and chastised David for disrespecting the throne, both Merab and Michal, as well as God for abandoning his true wishes for the sake of trying to give the proper image. Clearly it had been Saul's intention of showing David to be wrong no matter what action he had taken. As David moved toward Michal, Saul was able to point out that David was not acting in accordance with his true feelings; but had David moved toward Merab, it would have been used to show David's selfish nature and lack of respect. I wished that I could simply pull David back and talk to him before he made any further moves, but I still could not risk doing such a thing. I only hoped that David was smart enough to realize that his best course of action was to attempt to minimize any insult and seek to show himself to be respectful and eternally grateful to the king. It turned out that I didn't need to be so worried, and I should have trusted in David. Looking back later, I felt stupid for doubting that he would do the right thing. After all, I was here working with him because he had the potential to help usher humanity back to the perfection that I had messed up and lost for all, so I really had little room to judge.

David did not hold back in showing his understanding and immense skills at oration. It did not take him more than a few moments to convince the entire royal court that his desires to move forward with Michal were genuine and sincere. He made it clear that he regretted his mistake in not marrying Merab, but he presented a detailed explanation of what had led him to that action. David made sure that everybody understood that it was not a lack of love or desire for her, but his own feelings and doubts concerning his place in society had led him to so brashly deny the proposed marriage. He then proceeded to explain how his previous actions should not have any bearing on a future marriage to Michal. I have to admit that he spoke so cleverly and creatively that even I forgot for the time being that he truly loved Merab, and I was fully convinced that David's love for Michal would blossom as soon as they were joined. It seemed that everybody in the room was convinced. Well, everybody except for Saul.

I can only assume this was exactly how Saul envisioned things playing out that day in his throne room. If by some chance it was not precisely what he had intended, the smile on his face made it very clear that he was pleased with the result of his arranged trap for David. As David returned to stand beside me, I could see in his eyes that he too understood this had in fact been designed as another chance for Saul to destroy David and his reputation. A quick exchange also confirmed that we both were expecting Saul to announce some ruling or judgment that would further test the young hero of the people. At this point Jonathon came to speak with us and offered his apology for the games of his father. He had tried to talk Saul out of this attempt to humiliate David, even pointing out that it was demeaning to the two women as well. The disagreement between Jonathon and Saul was the reason why the two had so clearly been keeping their distance from each other as we had entered earlier. Thinking back to that moment, I was reminded of the stranger who was rushed out of the other exit as David and I were entering. I started to ask Jonathon about the identity of the man and what concerns he had before the king. As the words were leaving my mouth, I could see the look on Jonathon's face clearly showing that he wished that I were not asking him about the man. Before I was able to press further and actually find out why this topic would bring out such apprehension from Jonathon, Saul's booming voice announced that he was ready to continue court. With this, Jonathon warned David to be alert and always on guard so that he might stay safe. Then quickly Jonathon returned to stand in his position as the king's son.

With everybody back in their proper place, Saul wasted no time in announcing that he had decided he still wished for David to join the royal family through a marriage to Michal. I was amazed that some people actually believed that put an end to the proceedings, but clearly Saul was not finished. There was no way he would simply let things be that easily resolved. Saul did not disappoint us, as he quickly added there was one condition that David must meet in order to make amends for his insult against Saul and his daughters. Fighting to hold back from laughing, Saul continued by saying that David would marry Michal just as soon as he returned from battle with the foreskins of one hundred Philistine soldiers. It was clear that Saul did not fully expect David to return from this mission, but he could honestly say that he was only seeking to defend the honor of his daughter.

We could hear a few murmurs of disapproval growing behind us, but David acted quickly to avoid any escalation of the issue. Walking forward and kneeling before Merab, David offered an apology for any insult that she felt at his actions. He then knelt before Saul and acknowledged that he had been wrong in denying the honor of joining the king's family when it was first offered and expressed his gratitude at receiving another opportunity. Finally, David knelt before Michal. Taking her hand to his lips and then kissing her forehead, David promised her that he would return with the required bounty as soon as he could so that they might begin their life together. David then rose and began a determined march from his bride straight toward the door. The looks on the faces of the royal family were quite varied. Jonathon was beaming with pride at how David had risen above the trap set for him by Saul. Naturally, Saul's face was no longer showed how pleased he was with himself, as it had just a few minutes earlier. Saul was simply glaring hate and disgust at the back of David as he walked away from the king. Looking at Merab, it was clear that she now understood just who David was as a person and wished he had taken her as his wife when Saul had first offered. Michal, on the other hand, was in tears. She had always loved David, and despite the promise of marriage, she understood that her father was in fact sending David out on a task designed to end in death and not her wedding. I turned to follow David out of the throne room, thinking that if this was the last time David appeared before the royal family, he certainly did leave them in a state of raw emotions ready to boil over.

When I had caught up to David, I started discussing plans concerning the mission at hand. He almost knocked me over when he suddenly turned around and told me that I would not be joining him on this quest. This truly caught me off guard. I had accompanied David on every battle, campaign, and journey since I had brought him to Saul's court. When I questioned this decision, I was quickly hurried into David's room away from any passing soldiers. There he explained to me that he did not trust Saul.

I fully agreed with David's assessment, but I did not see why I needed to remain home and not help to protect David in the field. I knew I should trust his judgment, as he had proven through the years to truly be blessed and find the proper path to serve God in all that he did. Still, I felt a great need to keep David safe for this very same reason. He had been so blessed and devoted to God, it gave me hope that he could be the one to help me find my way back to my beloved Eve in paradise. Seeing my confusion, David told me that he would go out, and with God's help, complete the mission Saul set for him, but he wanted me to remain behind and look out for Michal. In fact, he wanted me to begin setting up a new home for the two of them and to move Michal there as soon as possible to keep her safe and away from Saul. This desire to protect and care for his future wife moved me, and I quickly agreed to abide by his wishes.

The next day David and a small group of soldiers left on his mission, and I began preparations with Michal for David's return. I knew that she did not believe she would ever see David again, but I did my best to keep her spirits up and distracted with the new home. I tried to reassure her by telling her of all of the great victories I had witnessed David win, especially focusing on his defeat over Goliath to show her that God truly did favor David and would protect him. We had begun to settle into a comfortable routine. There was a great deal of silence between us, but the fact that she was willing to work so hard on that new home gave me hope that she at least partially believed in her future with David. Then suddenly, one day while we were working, we heard a loud commotion outside, with people shouting and drums beating. Before we could even get to the door in hopes of discovering what was going on, Jonathon came bursting in, out of breath. It was clear from the look on his face that he was not bringing news of David's death. Michal wrapped her arms around her brother and began to cry while she asked if David was truly coming home victorious. Jonathon then shocked even me when he told us of the message that had been received that day. Not only had David been successful in killing one hundred Philistines, but he had actually killed two hundred. Because of this extra one hundred, David stated in his correspondence that he expected to return to find all of the preparations completed so that he and Michal could be married the following day. In all of my years, I don't know if I have ever seen anybody quite as happy at the contents of a message as Michal was that day. I have to admit that I was filled with joy by the scene before me, combined with thoughts of David's success now and to come.

Much to my surprise, Saul fully agreed to this stipulation, and the day following David's return, he was married to Michal. It was not a fancy wedding by today's standards of a royal wedding, nor did it even compare to the wedding that was given to Merab and her husband. Still, it would have been against custom for the second daughter's wedding to be as large as the first, and David made it clear that he wanted a simple wedding. Just because the wedding was simple does not mean that there was not a rather impressive celebration following the ceremony, though. That was one thing that I made sure David and his new bride would not be denied for any reason. In addition to feeling that the bride and groom deserved a chance to celebrate, I had hoped that the festivities would help soften the jealousy-fed hatred growing within Saul toward David. I wanted Saul to see David as truly being family through not only the marriage to Michal, but by the rest of Saul's family so openly accepting David with open arms. Sadly, my plan did not work. In fact, it seemed to only anger Saul further. Rather than view David as part of the family, Saul came to see him even more as an outsider working to steal the throne away.

It was not long before the anger of Saul boiled over and every-thing changed for David. Following the wedding celebrations, David and Michal retired to their new home. For a few days, things seemed quiet. As with any newly married couple, David and Michal did not leave their home too often as they began their new life together. During this time I remained in my room in Saul's castle. With noth-ing else to do, I rededicated myself to prayer and meditation. At first this brought me a sense of peace and hope, but one day while I was praying for David, I got a feeling that something was about to go hor-ribly wrong. I did not know what this might be, and without any spe-cific information, I did not want to barge in and interrupt the newly married couple.

A sudden and loud knock on the door snapped me out of my state of concern, until I answered the door. As soon as I cracked the door the slightest bit, Jonathon came rushing in. Before I could even ask what was going on, he simply shoved a message into my hand and told me that I had to get it to David immediately. I asked him why he did not deliver the message himself or simply wait until David came out of the house. He told me that it would be less likely to raise suspicions if I was to go myself, given my long history with David and my quickly forged friendship with Michal. Sensing my hesitation, Jonathon stared deeply into my eyes and told me that if I did not de-liver this message, I would regret it for the rest of my life. Given how long I knew that was likely to be, I did not want to risk it at all.

Within a matter of minutes, I entered the home of David and his new bride, Michal. I was actually surprised that they were so wel-coming to me and not more upset at being disturbed. I told them of Jonathon's visit and insistence that I deliver the message immedi-ately. As David read the message, I could see the color drain from his face, and I knew that my bad feeling from earlier was indeed com-ing true. Jonathan warned David that Saul was sending some men that very night to kill David in his own home. Frantic for a solution, David began to dress in order to face Saul in person. I tried many times to convince him that such a plan would simply serve to make it easier for Saul to kill him, but he was determined to find a way to settle things. He was nearly out of the door when Michal threw herself at his feet and begged him to reconsider. She wrapped her arms around his legs and told him that her father would surely kill him if he did not run away to safety immediately. I was not sure what David was going to do, until Michal simply told him that she loved him too much to bear living herself if he simply allowed Saul to have his way. After hearing her declaration, David returned to the main room of the home and began gathering a few items of food, clothes, and weapons. He took a moment to look between his two swords: the one he took from Goliath and the one given to him by Jonathon. After a moment he handed me Goliath's sword, saying that he would trust his life to the sword of his brother in arms as well as his brother through marriage. He took Michal into his arms and gave her the kind of deep, passionate kiss that made me truly miss my Eve. As soon as the kiss broke, Michal urged us to leave quickly before it was too late. She told us that she would do her best to stall the men and buy us as much time to get away as she could. I thanked her and promised to look after David again to the best of my ability. With one final look back at his new wife, David promised that one day he would return and they would be together again. As the door shut to begin our escape, Michal could be heard weeping inside her briefly happy home.

Jonathon's warning had come in time. There was no sign of any movement toward the house yet, and we were able to make a quick path toward the edge of the city. It was hard to believe how quickly everything had changed for David. He had gone from a shepherd to a valued musician in the court of a great king, learned from the king's son, slayed a giant, won countless battles, and married into the royal family. Then with the delivery of one message, David had lost everything he thought he had gained. As we fled to the wilderness, I told David that I truly did not believe that his story was anywhere near finished and that I still saw greatness ahead for him. Hearing that he simply looked back toward the house that had briefly been his home, worried that his new wife was planning on risking her life to help protect him. After a moment of just staring, he told me that everything might have changed, but he still trusted in God. He would one day be able to return, and he vowed that when he did, he would make sure that the king of the Israelites would once again serve God and not human pride.

CHAPTER 26

ON THE RUN

Of all of the things that I have been involved with during my countless years of living among humanity, I can honestly say that the period of time spent with David after escaping that night from Saul's attempt to have David killed was probably filled with some of the most interesting experiences of my life. Well, I should say the most interesting among experiences related to humanity. Clearly nothing compares to having been in the presence of God during my years in the Garden. But still, those years with David spent on the run through the wilderness were truly filled with some of the most amazing stories and best memories imaginable. I would love to tell you all about everything that happened in those years, but there simply would never be enough time...well, at least not in your life. Instead I will simply try to focus on the important events as they happened. I fully understand that you could learn the basics of this time in David's life by reading a Bible, but you would only be learning the bare-bones basics. The story you have leaves quite a bit out for the same reason that I can't tell you everything here—there just simply is not that much time or space for it all. I know that I have told you similar things before and probably will again in the future, but if you had as many memories as I do, then you would understand what it is like to attempt to just hit the major points like I am doing for you here. Still, I shall press on to continue moving my story forward.

As our former home faded into the distance, David and I began to wonder where we should try to go for safety. David didn't believe that we would have any trouble simply blending in as travelers passing through any of the surrounding regions; at worst we would simply have to keep moving if we were recognized. David didn't believe that he was famous enough to be recognized travelling alone without the king's banners to identify him. Looking back from the present with an understanding of modern technology, I find it amusing how worried we were at the possibility of being recognized back then. It truly was much easier at that time to move around without being noticed. Still, at that point, as he talked about this plan, I had to work very hard to avoid laughing or making some comment about how I had been living that way for generations. The only thing that probably did save me from saying something like that was the gnawing fear in my mind that it would not be easy for David to slip into a region unnoticed like I had been doing all of my life. It wasn't my own pride in believing that I was particularly skilled at adapting nearly as much as it was my understanding that David was extremely well-known throughout all of the surrounding regions for his victories on the battlefield dating all of the way back to his slaying of the famous giant. Even though that time was well before Internet and TV coverage of heroes, one with the reputation that David had could still be recognized at times. In his years of service to Saul, David had proven himself to be an amazingly successful military leader, and Saul had never hesitated to use David's abilities to conquer land and expand the Israelite kingdom and dominion over the surrounding regions. I don't want to say that David had a bloodlust while in battle, but he was aggressive to the point of leaving absolutely no question as to his victory over the decimated lands. This drive, which had served him so well, and would come to benefit him in the future, only served at that point as an obstacle to finding a place to hide in the nearby cities.

It just so happened that the first place we happened upon was Gath. In later years I often joked with David about how fitting it was that the place where the second part of his life began just happened to be the same place where Goliath had lived. Even as we entered Gath, David believed that he would go unnoticed. Well, it was only a matter of hours before we found ourselves being questioned about his identity and legacy. While many of the regions had reason to hate the Israelites, especially David, the people of Gath took pride in having a deeper anger than the rest, as they remembered their fallen giant. Suddenly scared about our safety, David turned to me for help. I told him that the only way he would get out of there alive was if he acted in a way that nobody would ever expect of a great warrior. I was surprised by how quickly he took my advice and how well he sold it, which might actually be why it worked so well.

As soon as I explained my plan to David, he bought in and literally leapt into action. Before anybody else could question us about his real identity, David began to run around shouting and screaming random words at the top of his lungs. He jumped up on tables and danced all over the place, waving his arms and switching between nonsense words and animal noises. At one point he even began to have a conversation with one of the trees in the courtyard. While he was putting on his very entertaining, and quite effective show, I simply explained to the soldiers who had come to arrest the man who had killed so many of their own that they had to be mistaken. The man who they had been told was the great and mighty David was in fact a very sick individual who I was attempting to escort back to his family many miles away. Now, I have always had ability to talk my way through a tough spot, but in that case I have no problem admitting that David's performance really sold the story. In the end, the citizens of Gath were quite happy to escort us through the city and get us quickly back to our travels and away from them.

The experience in Gath left us both resigned to the fact that at least for a while we would need to resort to hiding away from populated areas. Even though this was not something new for either of us, given my travels and David's life as a shepherd, it was still not an overly pleasing prospect. After traveling for a while to ensure that we were a safe distance away from any towns, we came across some caves and decided to make that our home for the time being. Even as tired as we were, David insisted on building a fire and praising God for bringing us to safety in our new home. For David to be able to find such blessing from God in this cave gave me hope once again that he was going to be the one who would help me bring all of humanity back to a true home in paradise, where my Eve was waiting.

Even to this day I am not really sure how it happened. We had only been living at that place for a few days when a sound woke us both from our sleep early one morning. Instinctively we both reached for a weapon even before we were sure whether it was the soldiers from Gath or Saul's troops who had found us in the caves. Luckily before any blood was shed, the identity of the sound was discovered. Rather than being somebody coming to kill David, we were met at the mouth of the cave by members of David's family. After the initial shock of seeing the familiar faces had worn off and the greetings had been made, we discovered that they were not alone. Traveling with them, several hundred men had come, wishing to follow David on whatever path God set before us. Even if it was to a small degree and in hiding, David had finally come to have a nation of people to be responsible for and lead. This was not just an army of soldiers, but he now had families as well to consider. He no longer was simply a military leader alone; David was now finally a leader and king.

As that realization first hit David, I actually saw fear in his eyes. He quickly pulled me back away from the people, looking for advice and instructions. The very same David who at such an early age had taken it upon himself to face down a giant in open battle was white with fear at the prospect of looking after this small group of people in the wilderness. To some that might have been enough to lose faith in David's future, but for me his concern only strengthened my faith in him, because it showed me beyond question that he took his duty seriously. It is not the apprehensive ruler that needs to be doubted as much as it is the person who is eager and seemingly unconcerned about taking on the weight of such a responsibility. I explained to David that his being scared to lead these people to their doom and demise was all the proof anybody would need that he was indeed meant to lead. Still, I did not hesitate to be blunt with David and remind him that leaders make mistakes and that sometimes those mistakes hurt the people in any number of different ways, from annoyance to death. But that as long as he maintained his concern for his people and gave every decision the proper consideration, everything would work well.

I so desperately wanted give him examples about some of the other leaders from my past experiences and how his feelings were normal. Without being able to do that, I relied on the approach that I knew had always worked with David. I told him that I had faith in him and that God had chosen him for this path. As long as he kept his faith in God and based his decisions on that faith, I saw not only success and survival, but also greatness in his future. Adding a simple prayer asking God for guidance and thanking Him for placing such a noble leader as David in charge of these people in need was all that it took to help David find his strength in this new role.

With a newfound bounce in his step and smile on his face, David asked for some of the elders of the people to join us in the cave to discuss what would be needed to ensure the safety and protection of the people. Among the men to join us were some of David's brothers. Other than them taking the lead in making the introductions and keeping the discourse moving, his brothers seemed to show no expectation of special treatment or elevated status simply because of being related to David. I had not believed that this would be an issue, but was glad to see that my faith in the family was justified. In that meeting David and I learned how Saul had acted quickly in his anger against David for his perceived betrayal. In the short time since we had escaped, Saul had announced that Michal was no longer married to David and was to be given to another man. It was easy to see the hurt in David's eyes. Despite the fact that his first love had been Merab, he had come to truly cherish Michal as his wife.

The feeling of loss and hurt over his wife quickly turned to anger, though, when he was told that Saul had been looking for David in the surrounding areas. In his attempts to find information on David's location, Saul had resorted to burning down homes and even killing. That news bothered David deeply, and he retreated to the edge of the cave, claiming that he needed time to think. In reality, I knew that David mainly needed time to regain the composure that he always looked to maintain. I gave him a few brief moments before going to him, reminding him that as the leader he was going to be faced with these situations often. Drawing on my own personal experience, I began to give David my advice. With the larger goal being out of reach and inaccessible right now, smaller good deeds should be considered. As I explained that thinking to David, my mind was filled with all of those countless individuals I had met in the periods traveling between larger missions from God. In that cave, as I encouraged David to take pride in the small deeds that he could do now, I fully realized that to God my mission was not divided into the big important missions and the lesser good deeds. No, God had never used those labels; but rather, I had put them there myself, believing that the years I spent helping David were more important than helping the individual with the broken cart. God had only meant that some missions would be more complicated and take more time to fulfill, not that they were any more important. Just as all sin is equal to God, so too are all good deeds. Now clearly helping a king do the right thing also then translates to doing the right things for a lot more people at one time and is better for humanity on earth, but that does not mean that I should have any more pride in helping bring down a tyrant for the good of the people than I do in helping a stranger pick up their dropped belongings.

Taking my lesson to heart, David returned to the meeting and announced that to simply survive would not be the goal. David saw no way to stop Saul's actions at that point, but until that day presented itself, David believed that the goal should be to simply do as much good for the people of the region as possible. As I said, this is how I had come to see my overall mission from God. I was glad to see David mirror this belief in never losing sight of the value of doing good for the actual people while preparing to take on the bigger issues.

Over the next months in the wilderness, David was true to his promise, and countless good deeds were done while avoiding Saul's scouts. Looking back, I still find it amazing how David was able to motivate his men to so willingly take on all types of projects during that time. It was naturally easy to get many of the men to volunteer when it came to running off bandits. Even when it came to locating a lost sheep, he never needed to ask more than one time before somebody was taking care of the issue. Even with all of the other signs that had led me to believe David to be a good man, ready to be a king of God, seeing these men so eager to serve him showed David to be a true leader of the people.

That was how life was for us over the next while. Jobs were assigned and roles were defined. Some people were in charge of food and cooking while some others served as lookouts over the camp. Of the rest of the men, some were trained by David as soldiers and sent out to help those in need, while others were constantly scouting. Those scouts were looking for three different things. The first and probably most important task was to be aware of any sightings of Saul, as he continued his search to find and kill David as well as all of David's followers. If there was any hint that Saul was getting too close, those scouts had instructions to begin looking for new hideouts and regions that would be safe for all of us to move into quickly. On the other hand, if Saul was nowhere near, the work became finding people in the region who needed help of any kind. That system worked very well most of the time. We had a few occasions when we had to break camp quickly and make a fast escape, but in general we had enough warning to allow us to remain organized with our movements. There were only a couple of occasions in which Saul killed our scouts and we were left with no advanced warning. When that happened, David came to understand and was grateful for my insistence on maintaining lookouts around our camps in addition to the scouts. The lookouts were the only reason we survived our time in the wilderness. Without them, Saul would have been able to catch us completely unaware and kill us all.

In two of these instances, David decided to put himself in a face-to-face confrontation with Saul. Granted, he did listen to me enough to keep his distance during the conversation, even if he ignored my advice leading up to that point. The first time Saul found a way around our scouts, he came upon us when we were living around a system of caves. The camp for most of the people was actually out in the open, but David and a few others of us were actually living in the caves. When the lookout alerted us that Saul was closing in on our location, it was too late to pack up the two locations and remove the evidence of our encampment entirely. David ordered that the actual campsite of the people be taken care of first and sent them to a secondary location for their own safety. While they were working toward that goal, David and I went inside the cave to attempt to hide as much as possible and destroy any information Saul might be able to use to track the others or punish anybody for helping us along the way. Before we were able to finish that task and get out of the cave, Saul arrived with his troops, leaving us with no escape. Our only hope at that point was to simply hide and hope that Saul ignored the caves. It turned out that our hope was partially rewarded. Saul knew that we were traveling with a large number of people, so he must have assumed we could not all be hiding in the cave. He did not order his troops to actually search inside. He did, however, come into the cave himself. I could tell he was not looking for David in the cave, but rather simply a quiet space to contemplate his next move.

Of all of the times when I have been ignored, and trust me I have been ignored by many people through the centuries, that time in the cave with David always stands out. Not because it truly changed anything in the course of events, but simply because at the time I was so furious at David for being so reckless. Looking back now, it makes me laugh for how brazen he was at that time. While Saul was thinking and talking to himself in the cave, I encouraged David to remain as far back and quiet as possible. I honestly felt ridiculous telling him that at the time. After all, it seemed to be the most obvious advice possible. Still, David ignored the obvious advice, and before I could stop him, he was sneaking out closer and closer to Saul. Finally, David got so close to Saul that I wondered if David's plan was in fact to kill him from behind. Instead of killing Saul, David took out his knife and cut off a piece of Saul's robe before returning to our hiding place. Saul remained a few more minutes and then left the cave to continue his search for David.

After Saul had left, I was even more shocked at what David did next. Rather than simply taking the piece of robe as a war trophy to show his own followers that even in desperate times things would work out, David decided to use it to start a conversation with Saul. As I said, I did at least convince David to let Saul get far enough away from the cave that it was not a face-to-face conversation. I actually think that David liked that idea because it forced the two men to shout rather than simply talk to each other so Saul's men could hear the conversation as well. The exchange actually went quite differently from what I had expected. I figured that Saul would be furious at realizing just how close he had been to David in the cave, not to mention humiliated in front of his men. Instead Saul was moved by the fact that David had not killed him and swore to end the hostilities so that David could return home. Saul even went so far as to declare that David would indeed be the next and greatest king of Israel. Saul only asked that David spare the life of Saul's family and not destroy the legacy and accomplishments of his reign as king. Naturally David told Saul that nothing would be more pleasing to him.

Following that confrontation with Saul, David sat down in the cave for a brief moment of prayer. When we did emerge from the cave a few minutes later, Saul was already moving his troops back away from us and toward home. Upon catching up to the rest of our own followers, David declared that we should move farther away from Saul because it would only be a matter of days before Saul would launch a massive attack on the region, hoping to catch David off-guard and relaxed from Saul's promises. Sure enough, that is exactly what happened. I can only imagine that Saul must have really been furious to find David gone.

There was a similar occurrence a little while later when we realized Saul was camped out on the other side of a small mountain range. After sending the people all to safety, David snuck into Saul's tent and stole the very spear that Saul had once promised to use to kill David. After moving a safe distance away, David called out in order to wake up all of Saul's men. Saul quickly realized that David had his spear, and once again David had been close enough to kill Saul and had not done so. It was very strange to listen to the two men repeat almost the exact same conversation as the one following the incident at the cave. I am not sure if Saul thought that David would actually believe him or if it was all a show for the people. Still, at that point I don't think anybody believed a single word being said by either man. There was no way Saul could allow David to return and still hope to maintain control, and there was no way that David trusted Saul enough to remain in the region any longer. At the end of the conversation, David took the spear and slammed it into the ground, telling Saul that if he wanted the spear back, somebody would have to come and get it.

Those two confrontations with Saul, in addition to all of the good works David's men had been doing for all of the people, had softened the views of many who had previously lost battles to David while he was fighting for Saul. Because of other nations seeing David in a new light, he was able to lead his people to safety and settle in lands under Philistine control. We continued to keep an eye out for Saul, but he did not dare come straight at David, as it could not be done without being seen as an act of war against the Philistines, which was something Saul could not afford at the time. Between all of the resources wasted chasing David around the wilderness and some military losses incurred without David to lead the troops, the Israelites were in no position to risk a large war. Without having to worry about Saul, David increased his efforts to help out in any way possible in the region. For the most part, it was a time of relative peace for the followers of David, and many took the opportunity to enjoy the normalcy of family life. Even David could be seen taking time to relax with his wives, as well as playing with his sons. The Philistines were actually quite welcoming for the most part, especially considering how many of their family members David had defeated over the years. And we all enjoyed the time we had at the moment, unsure just how long it would last.

Finally the day came when that relative peace vanished. The Philistines and Israelites were going to go to war again over some random perceived offense. I would have considered it a possibility that the renewed hostilities were somehow related to David, had it not been for the long-standing history of war between the two nations. I tried to encourage David to stay out of it entirely, as I did not see any way that it could go well for him. My biggest fear was that he would find himself face-to-face with Saul or Jonathon. I knew that if he killed either one of them, he would hate himself for the rest of his life; but if he hesitated in battle, it would most likely mean his own death. Still, after hours of trying to convince him to keep his troops home, David told me that it was his duty to help the Philistines, as they had welcomed all of us and allowed us to live in peace for so long.

I had learned by that time that once David made up his mind, there was no way to simply talk him out of it. No, if I was going to make sure that David did not face Saul in battle, I knew that I had to find a different way. So, as we were marching out to yet another war, I began to talk to some of the advisors to the Philistine nobles. I knew that I had to be careful with what I said. It had to be enough to accomplish my goal, but not so much that it led to actual problems for David. I decided that it was best to simply rely on something that was actually truthful. I talked with them about how I was worried what would happen if and when David and Saul were together on the battlefield. Soon I could see my plan working. My concern for David having to kill Saul or Jonathon had been altered just a bit in the retelling so that some were now afraid that David would turn on the Philistines to regain favor with Saul. Now, clearly, anybody could realize that even if David had intended such an act, Saul was never going to forgive David. Still, fear and uncertainty going to war are not good things, and rather than risk it, David was told to take his troops back home and protect things there. It did not take David long to assume that I had something to do with the rumors, and he clearly was not happy with me. At that point I honestly didn't care, because I knew that it was best for him and hopefully in the long run all of us.

It turned out that this "betrayal" of David was a very good thing. Upon arriving back home, we discovered that all of our land had been attacked and pillaged. The men who had remained behind had been slaughtered, while the women and children had been taken. David retreated into his home and was destroyed by the loss of his wives and children. I had never seen him so withdrawn, and neither had any of his men. We had all been expecting the fiery leader to inspire hope and offer a plan to follow, but instead David was showing himself to truly be human. Even though I had not lost my family to attackers, I knew the pain that came from losing loved ones. The problem was that all of the men outside now knew that feeling as well, and they were looking for somebody to blame. Either from a lack of better options or because of his lack of action, that person to blame quickly became David, the man who had kept them safe for so many years was now seen as a failure who needed to be killed.

When I realized David's life was in danger from his own people, I did something that I had never before imagined doing. I simply walked up to David, holding his sword. I told him that at this point he had two options: take his sword and lead his men to recover any living family member and seek revenge against those who were responsible, or he could take his sword and fall on it himself. I explained how his inaction was going to lead to his own men killing him, and he needed to either take responsibility to lead them or accept their blame and die. When David stood up with his sword in hand, I could see rage in his eyes, and I knew that nothing was going to stop him. I held back to allow David the moment to inspire his men and to ensure that they knew it was coming from him and not from me, so I don't know exactly what was said. I do know that from all of the yelling and cheering, it was no surprise that David led his men to kill and destroy every single Amalekite, sparing none, not even the women or children.

With the return of their women and children, as well as the vengeance of having killed all of those responsible, David and the men were once again relaxing to enjoy the peace they believed they had earned. There were still some rumors and curious conversations about the war between the Philistine forces and the Israelites, but for the most part, everybody was simply happy to have their families back home. All of that changed when I was handed a message. The fighting was going well for the Philistines. So well, in fact, that they had overrun some of the more veteran troops of Saul's army. In doing so, they had killed all of Saul's sons, including Jonathon. When Saul had learned of this, he had taken his own life. While many would see the good news that Saul would no longer be trying to have David killed and that David could easily return home triumphantly, I did not see it that way. I knew David too well to believe that he would see it that way, either. Even though Saul had wanted to kill David, David had not wanted to kill Saul. David had actually on several occasions gone out of his way to avoid confrontation with Saul, and he had spared his life many times. Still, it was not Saul's death that would be hard for David. I had seen how hard David had taken it when his wives and children had been recently abducted, and I prepared myself for much worse at the loss of his beloved Jonathon.

I told a few of the more trusted men to keep watch over the others and to remember that despite all of the problems, David had grown up with Saul and Jonathon, even being brought into the family at one point. I asked them to respect the mourning process that I was sure David would need to endure before any plans regarding the future could be made. With that business taken care of, I went to deliver the message to David, something that to this day remains one of the most difficult things I have ever done. As he read the words, I could tell by his eyes which information he was learning. The joy of learning that the war had gone well and was ending came first and then I saw the combination of anger, pain, and sorrow at learning of the death of Jonathon. He let go of the message, ripped off his robe, and cut his flesh with his blade before dropping to his knees in a blood-chilling scream. At that point I did the only thing I knew to do for him. After taking the knife from his hands, I knelt with him. I took his bloody hands in my own and prayed.

I am not sure how long we remained there praying or how long David remained inside his home. I do know that by the time David was ready to move forward, the cut on his chest had already begun to heal, and the Philistines had returned from the battlefield. I was thankful that I had spoken with some of the others before going into David's home, as they were able to ensure that we were not disturbed. When we finally opened the doors, those men were still standing guard, and a group of people had gathered. Some were offering their prayers of strength for David while others had official business that was waiting to be handled. Mixed in with all of the familiar faces from the years on the run through the wilderness, David and I quickly recognized faces from Israel waiting to speak with David. I knew then that our days of hiding and living in exile were soon going to be over. David had passed another period of testing and had emerged stronger. I was filled with such joy at that moment as I again allowed myself to imagine David living up to all of my hopes for him and returning humanity to a level worthy of God's paradise. Coming out of that house, I once again believed that I would be holding my Eve very soon.

CHAPTER 27

THE RISE OF A KING; THE FALL OF A MAN

As I said, the time spent with David in the wilderness was some of the most rewarding time that I have spent on this earth. The joy and pride that I felt watching David refrain from exacting revenge on Saul in the cave or in his tent showed me just how noble and righteous this young man truly was as compared with most people who would have simply killed the one chasing and trying to kill them. Still, it was not just the fact that he had not killed Saul that impressed me. Even in the course of battle, David had found a way to place the greatest importance on the safety and well-being of the people who had entrusted him with their lives. Rather than chase greatness at every opportunity for military victory that presented itself, David chose to only press the issues when it did not risk the lives his noncombatants. He even went so far as to not risk his soldiers' lives at every instance, deciding often to retreat and reform until an advantage could be found. That concern for his people over his own glory found him great favor with God and an unquestioned loyalty from his people. It truly was an amazing time for me and fed a great deal to my hopes that all of my work would soon be rewarded with a return to paradise and my family. If only I had known what was about to follow.

With the death of Saul and Jonathon, it was clear that major changes were on the horizon for David and all of the people in the region. Many of the people believed that with Saul's death it was a clear choice that David would return to Jerusalem and become king of Israel. I think it is safe to say that this was actually what most of the people and even a large number of the nobility believed should happen for the good of the nation. Many remembered hearing Saul's words outside of the cave after David had showed restraint in not killing the king. While it was clearly nothing official, hundreds of men had heard Saul declare that David should be king.

I had some very deep conversations with David during this period of time about what it might mean for him to assume the throne and be entrusted with the needs of the entire nation of Israel. David often tried to change the subject or simply appease me by telling me that he would approach that responsibility in the same manner with which he had led his people in the wilderness. The fact that he saw it as simply being an extension of what he was already doing gave me great hope that he would continue to make the right choices, but it also gave me some growing concerns that he did not realize just how much larger the role would be if he were to become king of the whole nation. When I would press him further, I was always cut off by his argument that it was pointless, as he was not the king of Israel. David always ended the conversation by reminding me that even if many of the people wanted that to be the case, he simply could not declare himself king over all when the rightful heir to Saul's crown was his last remaining son, Ish-bosheth. I knew that there was some truth to what he said, but I also had a feeling that things were already in motion to get around that fact.

Just as I had believed, the fact that Saul had a living son was not of concern to most of the people, including many of the leading families of Israel. Soon after David and I had emerged from his period of mourning over Saul and Jonathon, we were approached by those familiar faces I had seen in the crowd. They had in fact come to anoint David as king of Judah and pledge their loyalty to serve and follow him. True to his word, David refused them and sent them away. I knew in my heart that David needed to take on this role and move forward if he was ever going to fulfill the potential he had for greatness. Even without my own selfish desires to return to the Garden, I knew that David had it in him to be a great king for the people. It turned out that changing his mind was not all that difficult. I simply took him out for a walk and showed him how the people responded to him as their king already. These were not simply the people he had led through the wilderness, either. In the time since we had settled in that region, our numbers had been increasing steadily as people flocked to his leadership. Even without him being declared a king, the people followed him as if he was one. To deny them the proper protection of real authority would be wrong. Keeping true to the same nature that he displayed in the wilderness, David agreed to be king of Judah only because it was best for the people.

Now, it goes without saying that it pleased me that David once again was putting the fate of the people first. On the other hand, as David had feared, Saul's remaining son was not about to relinquish his claim to the throne without a fight. Soon after David had become king of Judah, Ish-bosheth began to march against David. As the battles were fought, David began to get concerned about the loss of life the war was causing and contemplated a way to surrender to Ish-bosheth without placing any more people in danger. Even though I was opposed to the idea, I agreed to go and meet with a representative from the other side in order to discuss the possibilities. It was a strange feeling knowing that David was trying to protect the people through any way to end the war, but I firmly believed that the only true path toward actual peace and prosperity, not to mention the Garden, was for David to become the king over all of Israel. I figured that I could always tell David that there were no options truly available to him that would protect the people other than to win the war. I knew that it could be seen as dishonest to go into the meeting with that decision already made, but as I said, I knew in my heart that it was the right path.

Any guilt that I did feel over that dishonesty quickly vanished when I got to the meeting and met face-to-face with Abner, Saul's former general and one of the main driving forces behind Ish-bosheth's war effort. At the sight of Abner, I felt pretty safe in assuming that he was there to simply tell me that the only way to end the war was for either David or Ish-bosheth to be killed. I don't know what he expected of me, but he never even let me open my mouth to make an initial offer. He spoke quickly and to the point that he had seen the error of his ways, and he was ready and wanting to come serve David in order to help him become the full king of Israel. I must have had a very shocked look of disbelief on my face, because Abner quickly added that he would do anything to prove his loyalty to David. It only took me a moment to think of just the perfect way for Abner to prove himself. That is how David was able to regain his first wife, Michal. Upon Abner delivering her to David as proof of his desire to serve and aid David, the spirits of everybody began to lift to new heights with confidence that the war would soon be over.

The belief that the war would soon end did in fact come true, just not how anybody expected. I fully thought that with Abner joining David, the two of them would be able to destroy the forces of Ish-bosheth very quickly and easily. While the defection of Abner did lead to the death of Ish-bosheth, it was not related to a battle. In fact, Abner sadly was killed by some of David's own loyal men who were not aware of the defection. Abner's absence in Ish-bosheth's camp proved to be more destructive than any battlefield strategy could have ever been. With Abner gone, some of the men started to get out of hand and break with military discipline and structure. That quickly escalated and led to a couple of intoxicated bad decisions, which culminated in them sneaking into Ish-bosheth's bedchambers one night and killing him in his sleep. I still remember the night when they came drunkenly whooping and hollering into our camp, looking for David. They presented the head of Ish-bosheth and stated that they had just won the war for David. It was clear that they expected to be received as heroes and given great rewards and positions in David's kingdom. Before David was able to react, I grabbed him by his arm and pulled him back to a private room as if he was once again a little boy. I did not hesitate to tell him that if he accepted this behavior, he would forever be burdened by the stigma of a cowardly victory unworthy of a real king.

David couldn't help but laugh at me for thinking he would be so naïve as to accept his victory in such a way. After assuring me that he knew what he was doing, David left me to begin his preparations. That very night he had those men put to death for their actions, and he sent messengers to all of the troops and cities still loyal to Ish-bosheth, stating that he had nothing to do with this heinous action and completely renounced such behavior. He emphasized that he had executed the men responsible and would not simply take the vacated throne. David promised them all safe passage back to Jerusalem and urged them to assemble and make their own choices about how to move forward. It did not take very long at all before David received a response from Jerusalem. They had accepted his sincere and sympathetic apology for the death of Ish-bosheth and believed that David had nothing to do with the death. They also stated that they had no desire to continue fighting and were prepared to pledge their loyalty to David as the king of Israel. The message continued that they remembered the actions of David at the cave and the camp where he refrained from killing Saul. That man was one whom they would gladly serve as their king. With that settled, we broke camp the very next day and returned to Jerusalem once again. The first time I had traveled with David to the city, he was a small boy who I hoped would find a place. Years later I walked with a man who had won many great

battles, found wives, lost loves, and continued to show why he was des-
tined for greatness. The former scared child and now confident man
truly was a king capable of being all that I had hoped for and able to
help me return humanity to paradise.

It did not take long before David was firmly established as the
one true king of Israel. All accepted him, and his subjects truly were
grateful for the end of the internal fighting. The enemies of Israel,
assuming that there would be an awkward transition period with
David becoming king, attempted to take advantage of the situation
by grabbing land and attacking areas loyal to David. While that plan
made sense logically, it turned out to not be a very wise move, as
David's armies seemed to have only become more skilled since he
had become the ruler of all of Israel. Unfortunately, as the victories
kept becoming easier for David, I began to notice a change in his attitude. David no longer prayed as much, and he had almost entirely
abandoned his studies of the ancient texts, which he had loved so
much in his youth. In our time hiding in the wilderness, David would
often talk about how he missed the royal library and the collections of
ancient texts. After becoming King David, he had not made a single
visit to the library, as his focus was entirely on the battles to be fought
and won. The humble warrior of God had become convinced that he
could not be defeated. That worried me a great deal, as I knew that it
would not lead to his success at helping me finish my true mission on
earth. I tried talking to David about this change on many occasions,
but it always ended in me getting frustrated and leaving the room.
Then one evening we were having the same discussion as always, but
this time we were in my room. So instead of me leaving, I firmly suggested that he go take a walk in the fresh air on the walkways atop the
castle. I am sure that you have already figured out what he saw when
he was outside.

That fateful night, when I just happened to force David outside
because I was tired of the fighting, became one of the most famous
nights in the story of King David. In that moment, he happened

to look out across the other rooftops and see an amazingly beautiful woman bathing. Yes, it was because I lost my temper with him and sent him to the roof that he saw and completely fell in love with Bathsheba. From the moment he saw her, David was madly in love with this exotic beauty. Now, because of our fight that night, I had no idea that David had sent for Bathsheba to join him for the evening. This might seem shocking to many that David would do such a thing. But he was the king and well within his rights by the laws of the time. I know that much has been made over the years about her being married to Uriah, but that is not completely true. They had been married, and had Uriah not been sent to the front lines of the war to be killed, then they might have returned to being married after the war. This was the custom and law of the time, during periods of war, all marriages were dissolved so that life could continue to thrive and grow at home. The fact that David had gone out of his way to ensure Uriah did not return home alive was indeed a problem with God, which cost David the firstborn child with Bathsheba.

Still, in the end, there is no denying the love that they shared was pure and true. Of all of his wives, David was most relaxed and happy with Bathsheba. It is also important to note that Bathsheba was the mother of Solomon, who was in fact the chosen heir to David's kingdom, even though he was not the oldest son. Still, I sometimes wonder what might have happened if I had not sent him to the roof that night for fresh air. Perhaps he would have never seen Bathsheba, and things would have never followed that path. It is even possible that had path not been started, the rest of the events of David's life might have been different as well. Still, that is all just wild speculation and wishful thinking, because the story for David from that point on moved quickly and only got worse.

While the story of Bathsheba is one of the better-known stories related to the downfall of David, it really had nothing to do with the troubles David came to face moving forward. In fact, it is possible that had he met Bathsheba much earlier, before she had married Uriah and before David had some of his earlier wives, everything might have worked out better for David. As I said, that doesn't matter. David did have previous wives with whom he had children. Now, don't get me wrong, I have nothing against children, and David loved all of his kids as best he could. That being said, it was with these older children that his path was turned away from the greatness I had hoped to find in him. There are countless details and probably hours of content if I were to tell you the whole story from start to finish. I will do my best to summarize what happened so that you can understand how this mighty king who I had hoped would lead humanity back to paradise ended up dying an old man denied even the earthly goals that had been set before him.

To put it bluntly, Amnon, the son of David's second wife, Ahinoam, raped Tamar, who was David's daughter from his fourth wife, Maachah. This greatly angered one of David's other sons born to Maachah, Absalom. When others found out about what had happened, Tamar was ashamed and did not know what to do or whom to go to for help. Obviously, David was furious when he learned about the actions of Amnon. It wasn't like rape was uncommon at that time in history, but for Amnon to have raped his half-sister was not acceptable to David. I felt sorry for David, knowing firsthand what it was like to know that your own child had committed a horrible act against another of your children. The conflicting emotions clearly were battling inside of David. On the one hand, he wanted to protect his daughter and give her the peace that the crime against her had been punished; but on the other hand, he did not want to punish his oldest son. I talked with him at length about this issue, encouraging him that he must find some way to punish Amnon. Despite being the king's oldest son, he should not be allowed to escape unpunished. Still, in the end, David did nothing more than lecture Amnon about his actions and make him promise to do nothing like that again as well as to never show himself in the presence of Tamar again. Following that talk with his son, David considered the matter closed and put it from his mind. I tried a few more times to get David to do more, if not punish Amnon, than at least do something for Tamar. My pleas once again fell on deaf ears, pushing me even more to believe that all of my dreams for David had vanished.

Despite David feeling the matter to be closed, Absalom did not forget what had been done to his sister. Still, he was not a stupid man, and he did not act right away. Instead he waited, and as he waited for his opportunity, his level of hatred grew. Finally, one day Absalom found himself alone with Amnon and decided that it was time to avenge his sister. Absalom would later swear that he had only intended to greatly injure Amnon, but his anger got the best of him, and before he was finished, Amnon was lying dead in a pool of his own blood. Fearing what David might do to him for killing the oldest son, Absalom quickly fled Jerusalem. David was brokenhearted at the death of his oldest son. The pain was only made worse in knowing that Amnon's own brother had killed him in cold blood over a crime that David himself had let go mostly unpunished.

I had felt bad for David before, but now I clearly was beside myself with pain as so many memories came rushing back. While Cain and Abel often found their way into my thoughts, that experience of watching David agonize over his own sons was one of the few times that I allowed myself to think of the actual murder of Abel by his brother. I could look at David and imagine how I must have looked all of those years ago as I realized the truth of what had happened. I am sure that David was thinking about everything that he might have done differently to prevent things from spinning out of control. I tried to console him as best as I could, but he would have no part of it. I can't say that I blame him. I know the pain that he was feeling. To him my words were simply empty platitudes. There was no way that he could understand that I truly did know what he was experiencing at that moment. To him I was the trusted advisor and friend who had come into his life when he was a boy. I had no family other than his, so my sympathy was hollow and meaningless. As much as it pained me to do so, I had no choice but to leave David to his misery.

I spent the majority of my time over the next few days in my own room. I would go back and forth between remembering my two sons and praying to God for guidance. Part of me believed that it was time for me to leave and allow David to live out the rest of his life without me pushing him to be what I had hoped. I couldn't help but feel like maybe I had put too much pressure on him with my constant discussions of all that he would be as the king of Israel for God. I had just about convinced myself that the only humane thing I could do at that point was to sneak out in the middle of the night and not bother David again.

Just before I began to pack my meager belongings, I was summoned before David. I was not sure what to expect, but when I found David, he simply apologized for sending me away when I had only been trying to help. We talked for a bit about how to move forward. Something about the way in which he was talking to me reminded me of how I had come to see David as a surrogate son to the ones I had lost. In all honesty, at this point I had spent more time with David than I had actually gotten to spend with Cain or Abel. This thought brought about many conflicting emotions. I was proud of David, even with the recent mistakes and realization that he most likely was not going to bring about the return of paradise. I was also obviously sad at missing my own sons and wishing that I could have had more time with them.

I was also conflicted about my earlier thoughts regarding leaving David. While I felt again that he needed me and was open to my advice to help guide him toward greatness, I also knew I had been with him for a long time and feared he would soon be noticing that I had not truly aged. I did what I could to help give some of the illusion of aging. I walked slower and a bit more bent over. I pretended that my eyesight and hearing were starting to decline. I even cut some of my hair as close as I could to try to give the impression of balding. Still, these were all simple cosmetic disguises that could easily be seen through if I did not maintain them perfectly. In the end, I decided that I could not abandon David at that point and would find a way to stay longer.

I worked with David to help stabilize things in his kingdom following the shock felt by the death of Amnon. David began to regain his confidence, and he also returned to his faith in God, which had served him so well throughout his life. Just as I had started to feel confident that things were going to turn around, we were alerted of the next major crisis. While David had been trying to repair his kingdom and himself, Absalom had been hiding, scared of what was to become of him. Unfortunately, during that time, Absalom had fallen in with some enemies of David, and they had begun planning a way to take over the kingdom. I knew that David had been looking forward to the day when Absalom would return to Jerusalem, but clearly he had pictured it as a son seeking forgiveness and not as an enemy seeking the throne.

Being caught off-guard we were forced to once again flee the city to the safety of the wilderness. I won't bore you with the details of all the battles that were fought other than to mention that despite everything that had happened, David still issued a direct order that nobody was allowed to kill Absalom. Even as his son was trying to depose him from the throne, David refused to wish any harm upon him. With all of the brutal battles that took place between the two sides, I was amazed that all of David's soldiers held true to that order and nobody ever tried to kill Absalom. I know that David had hoped that one day he would be able to talk to his son and settle things through conversation, but Absalom rejected all of the invitations for a summit. Still, David did not give up hope, until one day he received the message that he had never wanted to get. While trying to escape from a lost battle, Absalom had been struck in the head by a low branch on a tree and had died from his head wound.

The death of Absalom was very difficult for David to endure. It was made worse by the fact that it immediately put an end to the efforts to take over the kingdom. This meant that in addition to grieving the loss of his son while coming to terms with the fact that Absalom had killed Amnon and tried to take over the kingdom, David also had to work to restore order all at once. It took some time, but eventually everything seemed to get back to normal. The people were happy. David was learning to cope with the loss of his sons while also making sure to spend more time being a father to his other children. It was a very common sight to see David and Bathsheba walking hand-in-hand through the hallways on their way to watch the children play.

As things began to normalize again, it also meant more fighting with outside enemies. Once again David's armies seemed to be invincible and found victories in all of their efforts. Sadly, things were going so well for David and the Israelites, I again began to let myself imagine that things would be set right for humanity to earn back the paradise I had lost all of those years ago. David had found his faith again and was doing his best to spread that belief throughout the land. I knew that there had been mistakes, but David was showing he had clearly learned from them and was doing everything he could possibly do to live according to what would be pleasing to God. I have to admit that I once again was daydreaming of sitting under a tree back in the Garden with my arm around Eve. I thought about Abel being there, sitting across from me, as we discussed any number of topics and laughed together as a family, not quite the full family, but as close as I could get.

Just as every other time in the past, when I started to get my hopes up about achieving my goal, everything came crashing down. David truly had been blessed to have come through so many obstacles and still be thriving as a king and a father. Sadly, he fell victim once again to the temptation of human arrogance. If it were not for human pride and arrogance, my mission to return humanity to the paradise of the Garden would have been simple. To be honest, humanity would have never lost the paradise of the Garden if it were not for my own pride and arrogance. In all of my years, I have seen so many lives destroyed by human pride and arrogance.

Through all of David's struggles, he had always been the one on the wrong side of the math. He was much smaller than Goliath, he had won victories for Saul by using smaller armies than his enemies, he evaded Saul in the wilderness, he fought other armies while in the lands of the Philistines, he took on Ish-bosheth, and his army was smaller even when he was opposed by Absalom. His faith in God had always given his armies strength to win against all odds. Still, even after all of those successes and near-failures that David had overcome, he began to be filled with pride in his human accomplishments.

In an attempt to prove just how great he was as a king and leader, David ordered a census to be taken so that all of his enemies might know the greatness of the entirety of his kingdom. As if that wasn't bad enough, David then took it one step further and decided that each region of his kingdom would be required to supply soldiers for his army in proportion to their population. By doing this, he would never again be facing a larger force on the battlefield. I had tried to talk him out of doing the census and again with the military increase, but David would not pay any attention to me. He had become obsessed with showing that he was the greatest leader Israel had ever known. I tried many times to get in to see David, but I was always told that he was too busy. It seemed I had once again been pushed aside so that he didn't have to hear what I had to say, which he knew would go against his actions. I knew that I was not the only person who advised David, but I did not like being denied access to him. Finally, one day as the census was finishing up, I found my way in to the throne room. As I entered, I saw a man leaving out the back exit. My mind immediately flashed back to entering Saul's throne room with David as a similar-looking man was escorted out the same exit. I could not say for sure, but in my gut I knew that this was not just my imagination. I suddenly was concerned that not only was David making a mistake with the census, but that he was about to make many other mistakes at the lead of this stranger.

A couple of days after my visit to the throne room, a prophet came to Jerusalem to talk to David. Suddenly I was called back to advise David about what to do. At that point I had nothing to tell him other than to listen and take heed to what the prophet had to tell him. Listening to the prophet talk broke my heart as he told David that God was very displeased with the census. God had forgiven other mistakes made by David, but the act of taking pride in the size of the kingdom and abandoning his faith in God in favor of increasing the number of soldiers in the army had to be punished. The prophet went on to offer David his choice from three possible fates from God in response to David's sin. The kingdom could be forced to endure three years of famine. Or David would have to spend three months running from his enemies before he would be able to turn the tide. Or Israel would be struck by three days of plague, which would spread through the population and many would suffer and die. With the choices delivered, the prophet turned to leave, telling David that when his choice was made, all he had to do was pray to God.

As the door closed, leaving me alone with David, I noticed that his face did not show any great remorse or even fear over what had to be done. To be honest, his face was actually quite natural as he weighed the options. I suggested that he choose the second option because it seemed to me that it would put the fewest people at risk. I thought for sure that this point would get through to David, given all of the times in the wilderness and since becoming king when he had based his decisions on that very principle. At the time I was not sure if he was listening to me or not, but I soon got my answer as he simply stated to God that his choice was option three. I was shocked that he had chosen the option guaranteed to result in death for people; I was also shocked that he had not even bothered to truly pray. He simply had declared his choice and moved on to other business. I knew then that all hope for David being the one to help me restore paradise was truly lost. He had chosen to let people suffer and die in order to avoid having to run from his enemies again. When I tried to tell him that he should beg God to forgive him and change his choice, I was told to stop wasting his time. David explained that his choice was based on the simple math that the plague would last only three days as opposed to three months of running like I had suggested. With no concern for those who would die from the plague, David defended his choice as being the quickest option, allowing everybody to move on with life.

After hearing that statement from David, I knew that it was indeed time for me to leave. I gave him a very proper bow and left his presence. It was the one and only time I had treated him as a king rather than as a son or a friend. I am not sure if he even noticed the very intentional change or if he was truly oblivious to anything but his own pride at that point. Either way, I left the throne room and went to pack my things and leave David behind.

CHAPTER 28

THE LOSS OF ANOTHER SON

As I began my walk back to my room, I ran into the prophet. At first I thought he had been waiting for me because he knew my true identity and was bringing me a message from God. That thought initially excited me, but quickly turned to fear given my failure with David. Once he spoke, I knew that he was there about David and not me. He told me that he knew David had made the wrong choice. Had David picked the second option and allowed his pride to be injured in order to protect his people from famine and plague, God would have forgiven everything and not punished David at all. The fact that David had chosen in such a selfish manner had left God no choice but to follow through with the plague. In addition, God would deny David the honor of building the true temple for the people and living out many years of his life as the unquestioned king of Israel for God.

It broke my heart to hear that news. I knew for certain then that David was not going to help me finish my mission no matter what I tried to do from that point forward. I had no lingering doubt about it being time to move on and leave. Still, more than my own selfish desires to bring back paradise, I was saddened by the fact that David could have been so much more than he had been. His life had been filled with amazing accomplishments, and those are the things that I feel he should be remembered for rather than his failures. I had known David better than anybody else in his life, including his beloved wife Bathsheba. I hurt when I admit that even with such knowledge of him, I had not been able to help guide him away from his own downfalls of pride. As I said, human pride and arrogance simply will not go away, and they continue to prevent so many people from actually achieving all that they could if they would simply humble themselves and focus on what is truly best rather than making it all about desire.

As much as I had wanted to simply grab my meager belongings and leave Jerusalem without any hesitation, I knew that I would regret not saying good-bye to David. I also knew that if I tried to talk to him in person at that moment, it would only lead to more hurt feelings and bad memories. I had even considered having one of the soldiers help me fake my death in some way. That sounded like a good idea at first, but I realized it was just me being a coward and avoiding the pain of good-bye. I owed David, as well as myself, more than a cowardly escape. I began to write a letter explaining that I needed to leave and that I hoped in time he would understand the errors of his pride and return to the faithful man who had been a true blessing to call a friend and son. The more I thought about the letter, though, the less I liked the idea. There was no way to be sure if and when he would get it, and I would have absolutely no control over that if I was gone. If he got it too soon, he might not even read it, or he might simply rush through it and toss it aside. I imagined him being furious at me for leaving with only a letter, which would destroy not only any good memories of our time together, but also push him even further away from the path I had tried to guide him toward. On the other hand, if I simply left it in my room for it to be found when I was gone, there would be no guarantee that anybody would find the letter for a long time, if ever. The letter might sit there in my room for days, months, or even years before anybody ever thought to do anything with that room again. By that time the letter would be covered with so much dirt they would most likely not even see it. Even if they did, David could have already died or even worse grown so angry with me that the letter meant nothing to him. Even though I did not like the idea at that moment, I knew that the only way to leave was to talk to David in person.

Not knowing what else to do, I put my trust in God to provide the right time to talk to David. I resigned myself to wait in my room until he came to realize his mistake and seek me out for advice. As angry as I was with him for everything that had happened, I knew in my heart that he would come to his senses soon and come to find me. With that thought in mind, I closed my eyes and began to pray. I prayed night and day, and I kept praying some more. I lost all track of time, but I do know that it was less time than David and I had spent in prayer following the death of Jonathon.

When David finally entered my room, he had tears running down his face and fell to his knees. He had seen the victims of the plague from his window, and even worse, he had heard them screaming from their pain and suffering, which had been caused by his selfish pride. Despite the fact that part of me still wanted to yell at him for all that he had given up for himself and what I had believed he could have achieved for humanity, I couldn't make myself do anything other than take him in my arms and comfort him. Before I knew it, he had begun to pray for forgiveness, for guidance, and for comfort for all those suffering for his mistakes. Hearing that prayer filled me with joy, and I believed that the true David was finally back for good. I realized that even if he wasn't going to be able to help me finish my mission, he was still a noble king who truly did love God.

After David ended his prayer, we both sat in that room in silence for a while. I kept going over and over in my mind how to tell him that it was time for me to leave, but nothing ever seemed good enough, so I sat there not saying anything. To be honest, I have no idea what

David was thinking of for most of that time or if he was even thinking at all. As exhausted as he was, it would have been perfectly natural for him to have completely blanked out his mind. When I finally looked in his direction, I could see in his eyes that he was in fact thinking about something. There was no denying that look that I had learned so long ago. Knowing that he was in fact deep in thought about something led me to simply sit quietly for a while longer. I knew that when he figured out what he was focused on, he would share his thoughts, and I would then have to find some way to transition the conversation so I could tell him it was time for me to leave.

When David did finally open his mouth to talk to me, I was completely shocked to hear what he had to say. He told me that he knew I was planning on leaving. Before I could ask how he knew that, he nodded his head at my packed bag. Then he laughed and said that actually the bag was just the final bit of proof. He had actually known that I was not planning on staying around much longer now that his kingdom had finally been stabilized. David wasn't sure how he knew it, but he said that he always knew that I would leave him at some point. He was just grateful that I hadn't actually left before we had been able to talk. I am not sure if he was joking or serious when he told me that had I left while we were not speaking he would have sent out all of his best scouts to find me and drag me back just so he could say good-bye to me properly. Whether he was kidding or not, his words moved me, and I could feel the tears streaming down my face. I truly had come to see David as another son, and I would miss him dearly. One would think a moment like that might lead to having second thoughts about leaving, but in fact it was the opposite. Through his words I knew that it truly was the right time for me to leave and allow David to flourish on his own. Besides, now that I was positive that David was not going to be my final mission, I needed to move on and find the next assignment.

Before I could leave, David managed to talk me into staying one more night so that we could have one last dinner. I had been afraid that he meant a full royal dinner, but in fact what he actually meant was filled with much more meaning than any royal send-off. Dinner that night was simply a family affair. With all of his wives and children present, there were so many stories and memories shared that it was hard to believe I had not actually been there longer than I had, and I thought that I had been there quite a long time. As it got later, the younger children had all been sent to bed, and one by one, the rest of David's sons and daughters excused themselves. After that the wives began to leave until the only ones left were Michal, Abigail, and Bathsheba, the three that I would miss the most. Finally, I began to give in to my exhaustion and said my good-byes. I made them all promise to not see me off in the morning. I wanted to simply walk out on my own, or else it would be too difficult.

As David walked me back to my room one last time, he apologized to me for letting me down so many times and failing to be a better person and king. I knew that he truly meant it, because I could see it in his eyes. Even with knowing how great he could have been and how much his errors had cost, I could not let him believe that he had failed me. I simply loved him too much as my son. Giving him one last fatherly hug, I told him that it was me who had failed him. I apologized to him for all that I had done and not done to prevent bad things from happening. I know that he believed me to be talking about events during his lifetime, but in my mind I was apologizing for my mistakes in the Garden as well, which had destroyed perfection. Finally, we broke the embrace and shook hands as men. David promised me that despite his previous mistakes, he would live out the remainder of his days as king of Israel working to be as Godly as he could and fighting his temptations, especially pride and arrogance, until his dying days. In my heart I knew that he meant it, and I had faith that the kingdom was in good hands and would be for generations to come.

The next morning, before the sun was up in the sky, I left Jerusalem. Unsure of where I was going, I knew that it was right. I had yet to get any feelings as to which direction I should be traveling, so I took a moment to stand on a distant hill and look back toward the city. Thinking of everything that had happened, it was easy for me to believe that I had been close to the greatness I was seeking, but in the end I could take solace in knowing that David and his family were devoted to God and that great things would come from them in the future.

SECTION 4, CHAPTER 29
DOUBTS

I still find myself conflicted over the result of my work with David. On the one hand I feel that I failed. I failed to help David become the king of Israel for God, which he was supposed to become. And because of that I failed God in my role as custodian of humanity again. I often wonder if it was my failure with David that led God to not allow me to work with Solomon, who was able to fulfill all of the things David was supposed to accomplish on earth. It would have been so amazing to be there as the temple was built. The beauty and wonder of it did reach me no matter where I was on earth from those who had seen it, but by the time I was ever sent back to the area, the temple was long gone and destroyed. Yes, I am sure that my failure with David was the reason why I was never allowed to see it. In that way I understand how Moses felt not getting to enter the promised land, or for that matter, how David felt knowing that he was not going to be allowed to go ahead with that work himself. At least Moses got to see it before he was denied entrance, and David knew that his son was tasked with building the temple in his place. I know that I deserved to be denied that gift, but it still would have been nice.

Then again, at other times I don't see my time with David to be such a failure. He may not have truly become the king he was supposed to be, but he still was a very good man who did amazing things for his people and for God. Yes, he had many faults, but that is a pretty steady constant of being a human. The story of David is still talked about today as one of inspiration, showing his faith helping to overcome great odds to succeed. He led his people well and brought them many great victories in battle and in peace. So I find myself torn in regard to how I feel about my level of success with David. He did not achieve the ultimate goal, but in other ways he has actually come to surpass that role to become an even greater messenger of God's love and greatness.

I wish that I could tell you that David was the only case I have had where I still wonder about my level of success. It isn't like God comes down and congratulates me or gives me a grade card after each mission. Obviously sometimes I simply knew without any doubt that I had accomplished exactly what God had wanted me to do. Then again, sadly, there have been times when I have known that I failed. Not to brag, but I do feel that it is safe to say that I have had more successes than failures. It is only natural that knowing of my successes has helped keep me going strong even through the failures. The desire to finish my missions for God, return humanity to the intended state, and for me to finally be reunited with my precious Eve is always the major driving force. It is just that the successes help keep that goal growing closer. Still, the knowledge that I have failed has at times given me pause to wonder if I was ever going to be able to do enough. Even after all of my conversations with God in the Garden and having seen my son and wife rewarded with a place in paradise following their deaths I, at times, doubted that there would ever be an end to this endeavor. I wondered if maybe I was being punished for leaving the Garden and forced to live for all of eternity chasing a futile attempt at making up for my sins. In fact, at one point I was very close to simply giving up. If I was going to be forced to live throughout all of humanity stuck on earth among all of the temptations, then why not partake and enjoy myself? If I was never going to find my true happiness by returning to the Garden, then why not find what I could here in this world?

Yes, there was one specific time when I was about to just give up and move on with my life. It had been so many years since my Eve had died and I had begun my mission. That also was the last time I had talked to God directly. Yes, I knew that He heard my prayers and that He guided me with my missions, but with it being so long since I had talked with God, doubts were starting to creep into my mind. Then everything changed. I was sent on a mission that forever guaranteed that my doubts concerning my role in this life were gone forever. I still doubt my successes at times, but following that assignment, I have never again doubted God or His desire to have me return all of humanity to the Garden and the perfection He had created.

CHAPTER 30

A VOICE FROM THE PAST

In the time between missions, I would make my way to areas with higher populations as I waited for my next calling. I figured that in those regions, I would be able to talk to the most people about God and His love. I won't deny that it was also a benefit that those areas also offered me the most comforts, relaxation, and entertainment. Now, that doesn't mean that I went overboard or lived in great extravagance during those times, but there is nothing wrong with preferring a roof and bed to the ground under a tree for sleeping. So, yes, I took full advantage of my time to rest when I could, but I still made sure to focus on helping others over my own desires and ego. It just so happened that a mission had taken me to Rome; so when I finished, I remained in the area. I actually found myself in Rome quite a bit early on, as it was the major power of the day.

I assume the name of Julius Caesar is familiar to you, so I won't go into a lot of detail explaining to you all of what happened or what my role was in settling the disputes created during those years. I will simply tell you that I was in the Senate on that fateful day when Caesar was killed. I will also tell you that, despite the fact that some versions of history try to pretend that everything became wonderful following that day, things were thrown into a spiral from that point, which nearly destroyed the entire Roman Empire. It is quite ironic that I worked so hard to help save Rome and bring strength and stability to the empire only to return later to help ensure the fall of Rome. I guess that only shows how much things can change, and what was at one time my mission to protect later became my job to bring down. Good Intentions and potential are dangerous things. While both are well worth protecting, they so often fail to reach expectations and become corrupted. This does not have to occur over a span of many years or decades. As I remember with David, many ups and downs led to his failure to become the king God had planned. Even with one such as Hitler, there were moments early on when I thought that the potential for good was the driving force behind me being there. I never was completely sure how things were going to turn out once I started. That clearly was the case with this significant mission, which would not only serve to comfort me in the role I was living, but also strengthen my resolve to complete my tasks and trust in God.

I was done with my assignment in Rome, and yet I was feeling that I was not supposed to leave the region. I knew that I had finished that mission, but for some reason I also knew that I needed to stay there. I wasn't sure what my next task was going to be or when it would start, but I couldn't risk straying too far from Rome. Until I was sure what I was supposed to do, I filled my time living in Rome working with everybody that I could find who might allow me to spread God's love. This was at times quite easy and at other times quite difficult. Many in Rome at the time held very strongly to their Pagan rituals and faiths, while others were very well-trained in the writings of God's story. It always amazed me to read through the ancient texts and see what details were included or left out. When I was talking with the scholars, I often found myself asking them questions where I knew the answer from firsthand experience simply to watch them struggle to form an answer. So much is left out of the texts that I often wondered who had decided what was put in or left out. In many ways, talking to the Pagans could be easier. They were always looking for signs and order in nature, which allowed me to talk about how God provided that structure and order in which their rituals functioned.

While I was living in Rome, I started to hear some rumors and rumblings disturbing the status quo of the religious world. Now, I was very used to hearing stories and accusations between the various religions during my time on this earth, but there was something different about it this time. Rather than the normal divisions between the existing sides, this time all of the standard religions actually agreed to oppose the new movement I was hearing about. By itself that was enough to get my attention, seeing as how those different religions would disagree simply for the principle of not agreeing with anybody else, a habit that has carried on to remain in practice today. Still, what really caught my ear was hearing some of the concepts being attributed to the new "heresy" growing among the people.

It seemed that this new teacher was spending less time focusing on the rules and restrictions of living a proper life. Instead of telling people what they were not allowed to do, the message was centered on what people should do to help others and show love toward each other. The more I heard these stories about what was being taught, the more I knew it was connected to my next assignment. In addition to the normal feelings within me, the lessons attributed to this growing movement sounded so right and pure that I simply wanted to learn all that I could. As much as I wanted to simply take off and trust my instincts to take me to the source of the new teaching, I needed to avoid attracting attention. With all of the religious scholars looking for the source of revolution, I needed to use caution to avoid finding myself in trouble with the authorities. Finally convinced that I had been able to avoid raising suspicion, I left Rome and headed toward the newer regions of the Empire.

Many new cults or religions had formed during my time on earth, but this one actually caught my attention. It was not the fact that it was new. It was not even the fact that it was drawing the ire of all of the established religions, although that was quite noteworthy. No, the thing that truly caught my attention was the familiar feel to what I had heard about the message. Unlike the religious scholars who found the message to be in opposition to their own teachings and labeled it as revolutionary, I actually found it to be the familiarity calling to me. I did not see the message as a new view on anything, but in fact the oldest possible. Everything that I heard about the new teachings brought back memories of walking in the Garden of Eden conversing with God. Even more than the times within the Garden, it was the few times after I left the Garden when I spoke with God about my role as the custodian of humanity that came to mind. I had always found it hard to allow human religions to develop unhindered. Seeing them stray more and more from the God I knew personally broke my heart, but I couldn't do anything to show them the errors of their views. Then, suddenly a new movement speaking the old truths seemed to have simply started from new rather than growing from any of the existing systems.

The timing of it was perfect. As I mentioned, I was suffering from a crisis of faith in my role and starting to have thoughts of giving up. As I left the city of Rome to investigate for myself, I still had not ruled out the possibility of quitting. I knew that I could have just stayed in Rome and had a very prosperous life. As I considered that possibility, I was bothered by the question of what would happen to my life if I were to quit on my missions. Would I still be immortal or would I die immediately? Still, before I could fully give that question any serious thought, I needed to look into that one last thing. Whether I would continue or quit I simply did not know, but I did know that I needed to investigate and understand that voice from the past.

CHAPTER 31
QUESTIONING THE TRUTH

As I was traveling to find this new teacher, I was discovering just how much controversy had been created by his teachings. The views tended to be quite polarized, with very few people lacking a strong opinion on the subject. Some saw these new concepts and teachings as long overdue and a start to a better era for all. Others simply saw a revolution designed to grab power and control. I admit that when I first started, I was already on the side of thinking that this man was trying to rise to power through the creation of a revolution using religion. This practice was not uncommon for the time, and it is something I have seen happen many times during my years on earth. I knew that before I left Rome, those in power were very fearful of what would happen if this revolution was allowed to grow. They fully understood that the control of their power was helped by military strength, but it was useless if they lost control over the faith of the people. Maybe it was because of my years of experience seeing these uprisings, or maybe it was the fact that I was tired and doubting my mission, but I felt certain that before this ended, I was going to help put an end to this new teacher.

The further I got away from Rome, the more I found the views to be shifting. The hatred of change and the feeling that everything good was being threatened by this new teacher began to be replaced more and more with a sense of longing toward these new ideas. I couldn't help notice that these people clinging to the new teachings over the old were the very same people who were most oppressed by the older beliefs. The poor and the desolate would spit on the establishments of Rome while sitting in reverent adoration at a mere anecdote of the new teacher. I was truly beginning to see why those in power were afraid. After only a short time with these people, I understood that they saw the end of their oppression in the new movement. They were convinced that this man would bring an end to all of the old teachings and practices that had kept them in poverty and slavery. It truly had the feel of a political revolution at its core, fueled by the cover of a new religious understanding condemning the old oppressors and lifting up the masses.

I was starting to become convinced that it was not truly a new religion being formed, but was actually nothing more than a war being prepared. Despite the problems I have had watching new religions form without being able to help them, it was much better for another religion to get in the way of God's truth than to see these people slaughtered by the Romans. With everything that I had put into motion in Rome recently, there was no way that anybody with any power would allow these subjects to even begin to start an uprising of this kind without meeting the harshest of endings. It was easy to see that all of the people were desperate for change and were willing to follow anybody who might promise them a better life than they had as slaves and peasants under the Empire. I have seen many revolutions in my time on this planet, but I have seen many more would-be uprisings fail. I simply do not understand how people can be so sure of their movement to believe that simply having more in numbers or passion can easily overcome better weapons and training. A group of starving, weakened farmers with wooden tools is not going to be a match for trained Roman soldiers carrying steel blades and shields. Throughout history this concept of right over might has been tested many times, and sadly it fails nearly every time. Might does not equate to being right, but it does make it easier to win a war. As bad as it would be to see the Roman Legions march over these peasants, it could not be as bad as the horrors that came to pass as the weapons have become more and more powerful. My only hope at that point was to find this teacher and stop him before he pushed too far and discovered the true strength of the Roman Empire.

At first everybody I came across was willing to tell me all that they could about this new teacher and his followers. It was almost as if they felt it was a source of pride and power to simply have any knowledge at all of the man. That changed as I began to get closer to finding this man who had caused such controversy. The people were no longer eager to brag about having experience with the new teaching, but rather seemed intent on hiding his identity and protecting him from outsiders. Despite all of my efforts to blend in with the masses, it seemed that I was easy to spot as having spent the last many years living in a position of power with a life of comfort and means. I was accused of being a Roman soldier sent to kill their teacher, a spy looking for information, and much worse. When it became clear that I was never going to be able to blend in as a common peasant, I gave in and embraced that I seemed to be a Roman citizen. I began to let it slip that yes I was Roman, and that I had heard many powerful people in Rome talking about this new teacher. Once I was open about being from Rome, people actually asked me why I was looking rather than assuming that I had evil intentions. Despite my initial feeling that I would have to put an end to this man, I had not decided for sure that I would follow that path. When I was asked I was able to answer honestly that I was seeking to learn of his teaching for my own needs.

As with all other assignments, I needed to be sure and have as much information as possible before deciding upon a course of action. With that said, I already had several plans forming in my mind, trying to cover all possible scenarios. I knew that I might not have many good chances to act against him, so I was trying to think of ways to discredit him and his teachings. I would sometimes let myself think of ways in which to help him, just in case that was the path I was supposed to follow, but that seemed very unlikely to me, so I didn't waste a lot of time on that train of thought. My mind kept coming back to the notion that maybe if I did the opposite of what God wanted me to do, maybe I could end this curse of mission after mission being put in front of me without end. Maybe I would find where he was and simply go back to Rome with the information to trade for a nice retirement on the edge of the city to live in peace, until I was forced to leave due to my lack of aging. These thoughts were on my mind one day as I was sitting under a tree in the middle of nowhere. Then everything began to change for me—again.

CHAPTER 32

FINDING ANSWERS

My search had finally led me to a small village outside of Jerusalem named Bethany. I was quite familiar with that area, having travelled through the region often on my missions. For that reason, I had actually purchased land in the area years earlier. Its proximity to Jerusalem was a huge benefit, giving me the access to the people and markets of the city while also offering the peace of life outside of the commotion inside the walls. With all of my wanderings, it was also nice to simply have the ability to sleep on land that truly was mine, and not just part of a current mission. The land that I had purchased had a beautiful garden on it, not quite as amazing as my Garden, but very nice. In an ironic twist there was also a tomb on the property. I would often spend time just staring into that tomb, contemplating my life and wondering about the death that I could not experience.

There, in that region, I knew that I was indeed getting close to finding this teacher, as everybody I tried to question about him was extremely suspicious of my intentions in seeking him. In the past people would almost brag about any small bit of information that they could offer me, but here things were different. While it was obvious that they were very fond of this man, they were also extremely protective and seemingly afraid of a stranger seeking to find him. I was getting very frustrated, knowing that I was obviously close but finding no answers to help me start the mission. That frustration was making me more and more certain that it indeed would be my final mission. I was simply tired and wanted to stop the crazy never-ending quest.

I remember sitting under a simple fig tree having a drink while I wondered what my next step was going to be in my search. I also entertained the idea that possibly I should just go ahead and quit right away. When I thought about stopping, I decided that I was ready to, but my pride required me to finish the current mission first. With that decision made, I refocused my mind on how to find the teacher I was seeking. With no answers coming to mind on that topic, I let my mind consider what approach I was going to take when I did get close enough. What signs would I look for in order to decide if he was to be merely discredited, silenced for good, or any number of other options? I did force myself to at least consider the possibility that my mission might not be to put an end to the uprising, but to actually help him rise to power. I knew that it was highly unlikely that this teacher was legitimate and had the best interests at heart, but then again I had been working to sabotage aspects of the Roman Empire recently. Maybe this new sect was intended to help fill the void and lead the people in a new direction.

As I was exploring my thoughts and trying to figure out my next move, a stranger sat down next to me under the tree. I admit that I didn't really notice anything about him, and to be honest, I didn't want to be disturbed at all. It was only when he nudged me and offered me a fig from the tree as a snack that I began to take notice of him. There was nothing physically special about him, but for some reason I felt that he was not there simply by chance. As I thanked him for the fig, he simply smiled and told me that accepting the fig might be easier than the answers he had to offer my troubled mind. My first thought was that this man was going to try and sell me something, perhaps some miracle tonic to cure all my ills. While sometimes I admit that it is fun to mess with such characters and leave them in total frustration, at that moment I had no patience for anybody looking to waste my time and swindle my money. Just as I was about to get up and walk away to avoid a confrontation, the stranger grabbed my arm, insisting that I must be tired after wandering the earth for all of creation. Now, you might think that this would have set me on edge regarding how this stranger knew who I was, but the notion that anybody would know my identity was so foreign to me that I simply assumed he was speaking in hyperbole in reference to my worn clothes and look of exhaustion. Sensing my concern, the stranger quickly changed topics to the most mundane conversation in all of humanity. He asked me how I was enjoying the recent weather.

I fought back my initial impulse to simply walk away from this stranger. After all, I was truly exhausted and wanted to rest awhile. If that meant putting up with some weird man wanting to talk about the weather, then so be it. Besides, he had given me a fig to eat. I sat back and relaxed, happy to take the time to not only rest my body, but to allow my mind to shut off for a while. Truth be told, I had been spending so much time fighting with my crisis of faith, looking to solve the latest mission, and of course trying to decide if I should continue these tasks, that my mind was as much in need of a break as my aching feet were. So, I sat under a tree in Bethany talking to a stranger about the weather.

The relaxation was almost addictive. There was something about the man that put me totally at ease, and I felt comfortable talking with him despite my earlier thought of trying to get away as fast as possible. In all of my years on earth, that was truly a rare quality for me to find in another. I know many had said that of me, but I always attributed that to my history and connection with God giving me the skills to accomplish His missions. When it dawned on me that this stranger had this same attribute, my mind quickly jumped from relaxing to trying to figure out if it was possible that he too had some connection to God or if maybe I was just not as special as I thought. That notion played right into my doubts and the crisis of faith I was going through.

I began to worry that all of the times on my missions when I felt comforted that God was looking out for me were simply lies I told myself. Perhaps the skills that I thought made me special were simply natural human characteristics that everybody possessed. How did I accomplish so much if I had not been blessed with any special gifts from God? With that revelation I became very certain that this indeed would be last mission. Clearly I had been fooling myself into thinking that I was ever going to accomplish what was needed in order to be reunited with my beloved Eve. If my skills were truly nothing special, then I truly had no chance of ever finishing. In that instant I knew that when I found this new teacher who was creating such problems, I was going to find some way to quickly put an end to him. With the decision made, I turned my attention back to this stranger, looking to once again relax for a while before my last effort.

The conversation at that point quickly turned from the weather to hearing more about the man's life. He shared that his name was Andrew and that until recently he had been making a very good living as a fisherman. His father had partnered with another wealthy fisherman to form a rather successful fishing company, which had been passed on to the next generation of Andrew and his brother, Peter, as well as their friends James and John. I again considered just blowing him off and walking away. I simply did not really care to sit here and listen to Andrew talk in depth about fishing. Just when I had heard about all that I could handle, he said something that changed everything. He told me that he had recently walked away from his fishing business in order to follow his faith. It turned out that while I thought I was just talking to a random stranger being polite, he was actually a follower of the teacher I was here to stop.

Now that I knew that Andrew would be able to lead me to this new teacher, I had to be sure to play my cards right. If I let him know that I planned on stopping his teacher, then obviously he would not help me arrange a meeting. On the other hand, if I did not show enough interest, then I would also destroy my chances. I needed to find the perfect balance in order to ensure that I could use Andrew to help me, whether he wanted to or not. Before I could implement any plans of my own, Andrew interrupted my thinking. He could see that I was suddenly on edge again and looked to help me relax. The real shock came when he put his arm around me and told me that his teacher was looking forward to talking with me. I was so taken by this statement that I almost missed the most shocking aspect of Andrew's statement. He had not just said that his teacher wanted to talk to me as a generic comment, but he had actually called me by my real name, Adam. I hadn't used that name in centuries. I didn't know what was going on, but I had to find out. My whole plan on destroying this new teacher suddenly was not nearly as important as finding out exactly how my true name was known. So, as Andrew got up and began walking, I simply had no choice but to follow.

CHAPTER 33

MY PATH

I followed Andrew in silence. I had no idea what I could have asked or said at that moment, so I just kept silent. My brain was going crazy trying to catch up to the fact that this man who had been a complete stranger when he sat down next to me under that tree had actually been sent to find me by the target of my current mission. Even more troubling was the fact that he knew my real name. I had no possible idea at that point to even guess at how much this teacher knew about my true story, and if he did know, how much he had shared with Andrew. If Andrew did know more of the story than just my name, he wasn't giving me any sign that he was aware of who I actually was.

Whether he knew everything or had just been given my name to use in order to ensure that I followed him really was not important to me at that moment. What was important was that it did mean that this teacher I was looking for and planning on stopping did know about me, the real me. In all of my years on earth, I had never had anybody come even remotely close to discovering the truth, or at least that was what I thought. Maybe I hadn't been as careful as I believed, and he had been able to piece together the truth from a close study of history. Was it possible that I had made mistakes and been careless? I tried to think through everything to see how it could have been pieced together, but I couldn't be sure of anything until I met this teacher and could test him on his knowledge of me.

The man I was following to meet the teacher did not seem to be anything but genuine and concerned for me. The ways in which he had spoken of his teacher had seemed devoted and vaguely familiar to me. There was some part of me that hoped it was a sign that this teacher might be real and actually sent from God to find me. That would explain a lot. My feelings toward this place and teacher being slightly different could be because there was a mutual connection to God through this path. It would also explain how he had known my name to send with Andrew on his quest to find me. Of course, it was also possible that this teacher was an agent of Satan sent to stop me. I had heard rumors for years of a man travelling through the world claiming to be cursed to live forever, something I could clearly relate to. The difference was that as he walked the earth for eternity, he was tasked with causing conflict and destruction instead of helping humanity. While considering that thought, my mind flashed back to my time with David. There had been that strange man with Saul a few times before Saul turned against David as well as with David before his own failings. Thinking back through my life, I seemed to have vague memories of similar figures on a few of my missions. If this teacher was indeed that man, an agent of Satan, then it would make sense that he would know about me. No matter what was true, I needed to know for sure before I could fix the problem.

Still, even with all of the possibilities running through my mind, I kept hoping that this teacher Andrew was so devoted to might somehow be here to help me and allow to me to finish with this world. Maybe he was an angel there to tell me that I had completed my tasks and that he was there to take me home to Eve and Abel in the Garden. I would have been happy with just another person cursed to take my place, allowing me to rest and live in peace. The whole time while my mind was racing through all of those thoughts, Andrew simply kept walking in silence. I got the feeling that he knew my mind was struggling with difficult issues and that I was not in the mood for any further small talk. I considered breaking the silence and demanding to know everything, but that would have been a waste of time, as clearly Andrew was not going to tell me anything more than he had already. Realizing that also put an end to my thoughts of trying to trick him into letting something slip. No, there was something about Andrew that made it quite clear he was there to do his part for his teacher and nothing would get him to change his mind. I decided to simply continue on in silence and not risk making any mistakes myself. I didn't want to show my hand and give away any information that might not already be known about who I was. With that decided, I just settled in and walked along with Andrew, having no idea where we were going, but knowing that it was the right path. A few moments later, Andrew suddenly stopped and told me that his teacher was staying at the house up ahead of us. I was to wait outside while Andrew went inside to talk with his teacher. Not knowing how long Andrew was going to be, I sat down and rested, trying to stay calm despite my emotions going all over the place from fear to hope and even to a strange sense of familiarity.

I'm not sure how long I waited, but it was long enough that I fell asleep. I dreamt that I was back with my family, all of my family, including Cain. I often would dream of Eve and sometimes of Abel, but rarely together and never with Cain as well. Still, that day while I was waiting for Andrew and his teacher, I was happy with my whole family, even it if was just a dream. As always the image of my precious Eve filled me with joy. As I said, I often would dream of Eve and her smiling face looking back at me, but it was never as clear and beautiful as it was that day. As joyous as it was to see Eve in my dream, it was the sight of Abel and Cain walking side by side with their arms around each other that brought me a true sense of peace and happiness.

Obviously that day when Cain killed Abel was one of the worst days any man can imagine. Still, as the years have gone on, I have realized that it wasn't just that day. It had been years before that day since I had seen them as happy in life as they were in my dream outside of that house. As a father I had often imagined seeing Cain and Abel growing old together as brothers. I pictured them having families of their own and still remaining as close as two humans could be. I had imagined taking them all back into the Garden with me and all of us living together in paradise for eternity, but then that fateful day that cost me both of my sons put an end to those thoughts. I had not allowed myself to think about it for years, as it was just too painful. Then suddenly I saw them in that dream. It truly was the best dream of my life to that point, but in a flash it was all over.

I could feel the hard ground under me and the rough wall of the house I was leaning against. I wanted to be back in my dream: happy with my family in the Garden, sitting on soft grass, and surrounded by love. I kept my eyes closed, fighting for any last chance of reclaiming the dream. Finally I gave up and opened my eyes. I was so shocked that I leapt to my feet. Suddenly I was not sure of anything. There standing in front of me was none other than God Himself. It had been thousands of years, but trust me, you don't forget standing in the presence of God. Andrew introduced Him as his teacher, Jesus, but I knew the truth. God was once again walking on earth. Before I could say anything, God suggested that we take a walk so that we could speak in private.

Just as with Andrew, I followed in silence. This time it was not because I was trying to plan any strategy, but simply because I was once again in the presence of God. On the other hand, exactly like when I followed Andrew, my mind was working overtime, thinking about all that could possibly be meant by God being here on earth again. I immediately hoped that it meant that it was all going to end soon. I held images in my mind from my dream of my happy family all together again. Yes, I knew that my dream couldn't truly come to be real. I knew that Cain was lost to that world, but Abel and especially my Eve were in the Garden, waiting. As I let myself think about what a joyous reunion it would be, I suddenly was struck with a sense of fear. Surely God knew that I had been having doubts. Had I ruined everything through my selfish thoughts and desires to quit doing as I had promised? I began to feel cold as I became more and more convinced that God was here to replace me, or worse. My dream would be all that I had left of my family as they spent eternity in paradise, and I had tossed away any chance of joining them simply because I got upset. I was convinced that all hope was lost. I knew that in the past I had begged and humbled myself before God in order to put things right, but I feared that I had gone too far this time.

I had been so focused on my thoughts and fears that I had not paid any attention to where we were walking. We had left the town of Bethany and were actually on my own property now. After all of my conversations with God in the Garden, it was fitting that we went to my garden to have what I assumed would be one final conversation. God suggested that we take a moment to rest from our walk. I figured that this was solely for my benefit, yet I was quite thankful. Despite my recent nap, I was a bit tired from the walk. God had offered to rest with me during our talks after I had first left the Garden, but it was different. This time as I stretched out, I saw that God was doing the same. Not only was he stretching, but to my total shock, He was drinking from the pool of water. In all of my previous experiences with God, I had never seen Him act this way. He was acting human.

It took a while for me to be sure of what I was seeing, but yes, without question, God was behaving exactly as would be expected of any human being. All I could do was sit and stare in wonder. I had talked with God so many times while living in the Garden and after leaving the Garden. In all of those conversations, I could say without any doubt that He had not once displayed any of these human behaviors. It did not take long before God noticed me staring at His actions. Seeing my confusion, God set to telling me how He came to be in that place with me. The first thing that He wanted to clarify was that yes, indeed He was human. It truly was quite an amazing story hearing of His birth in the small town without a proper room to be found. He also made sure to tell me that yes, He was the one and only God that I had known in the Garden, but that in this human form His name was indeed Jesus, just as Andrew had introduced Him. Now, it was quite a change to think of Him with an actual human name, but I also knew that it would lead to problems with His followers, as well as the rest of the people around, to not use His human name. At that point I was sure that I didn't know anywhere close to the whole story, but being in the presence of my Creator again, I was already starting to feel my spirit being filled up once again. I couldn't wait to continue the conversation and learn the whole story of how the God I had known before became the Jesus I was meeting now, again.

CHAPTER 34

REUNION

As I listened to Jesus, I found myself feeling quite stupid for the lack of faith I had been experiencing recently. How could I have doubted anything? Hearing how God had indeed been watching over me all of these centuries, I felt sick to my stomach to know just how close I had been to throwing it all away. Jesus was able to tell me about all of my missions and my life dating all of the way back to my creation. I could clearly see that I was not just some part-time interest to Him. What really got to me was when He told me just how proud He was of me for all of my efforts. Hearing that pushed me over the edge, and I collapsed in tears of shame. The shame kept building as I thought about my recent days and how I had planned on stopping this teacher, who turned out to be the very God who had created the entire world, and that I had been looking forward to a nice, long life of luxury and retirement here on earth. Those thoughts were nearly too much for me to bear.

As my shame continued to grow, I realized something else was happening: my faith had fully returned and was actually becoming much stronger than ever before. The thought of quitting made me physically ill at that point. I wanted nothing more than to continue to do all that God wanted of me in order to finally earn humanity's true return to the Garden. I knew that Eve, Abel, and all of the other human believers who had died already had been rewarded with their place in the Garden, but here with God, I was once again determined to earn that place for all and restore the paradise He had created. I fell to my knees, begging for forgiveness. I understood that I had been wrong to doubt my place, and I pledged to never again consider quitting. Jesus simply touched my head and told me that He understood. He understood the temptations of being human and that my faith through the thousands of years truly was amazing. He offered me the forgiveness I sought and encouraged me to remember this feeling, as my journey was far from over.

This statement, that my path was to continue for a long time, could have been discouraging. A few days earlier, the realization that I was nowhere near finished would have been more than enough to finalize my decision to simply quit and never look back. That was before I was kneeling before Jesus as God on earth. In that place I was peaceful and optimistic about my future. Once again I believed beyond question that I would succeed in the end, only I had no idea what that end would be. Quickly my thoughts turned back to that moment and how I had been drawn to this place on a mission. I had believed that I was searching for just another human teacher, with the assumption that my goal would be to stop him in some way. Only with the discovery that this teacher was actually God, I had no idea what the correct path could possibly be, but I had a feeling that it would be of great importance.

Sensing that I was growing uneasy kneeling before Him, Jesus asked me for a tour of my property. I was a little bit shocked by that request. I had assumed that Jesus would tell me more about His life or what I had been brought there to do. I also remember wondering what I could possibly be able to do that He couldn't just do easier on His own. Still, a tour of my land was what had been requested, and who was I to deny any desire of God? In all honesty, my land wasn't all that impressive, but I was more than happy to show it off. The trees and water made for a nice, peaceful escape. Of all of the property I owned at the time, I had always felt a pull to that location. I had always attributed that to the garden feel reminding me of my Garden. I had often considered building myself a small home on the land so that I could always have that one place to still call home throughout all of my missions. Then as I was considering quitting, I had felt that pull toward that land grow even stronger. Then as I was giving Jesus the tour, I began to wonder if He had actually been the cause of my feelings about this location. If not from the beginning, then surely it was meeting with Him that made the pull feel so strong. I just had no idea why until we reached the tomb on the property. At that point we sat down to enjoy a meal as Jesus explained more of His plan to me.

CHAPTER 35

A SECOND FLOOD

I had a hard time believing what Jesus had told me. God had come to earth as a human with the intention of allowing Himself to be captured, tortured, and executed. This act, this sacrifice of Himself for humanity, would serve to purify humankind and essentially give humankind a clean slate once again. My initial thought was a selfish one. I hoped that this sacrifice would mean that I was truly done on earth and that humanity would be welcomed back into the paradise I remembered of the Garden. The sense of relief that I had reached the finish of my time here began to come over me, but then I remembered my own past. I thought back to when I had first started these missions. God had told me then that He was cleansing the world to grant humanity a fresh start outside of the Garden. I began to understand that it was not an end to the suffering of humanity, but merely an action similar to that of the flood I had experienced with Noah, his family, and the animals aboard that boat. Rather than flooding the whole world with water, destroying life on the planet, God had chosen to flood the souls of humankind with His love and grace. Understanding that, I knew it was not a sign of my success, but rather my failure. It was my fault that Jesus had to come to earth, preparing to suffer and die for humanity. My guilt started back in the Garden when I made the mistake of not protecting Eve from Satan. Through that failure, sin had entered the world, allowing paradise to be destroyed. I failed again when I could not protect my sons from human sinful nature and pride. My failure continued through the years, as I did not find a way to finish my missions or bring enough people to know the love of God. I had failed at every step of my life, and because of me, Jesus came to earth, forced to sacrifice Himself to make up for my shortcomings.

Jesus knew my turmoil as He came over to embrace me. He told me how He understood that the conversations between us always caused such extremes of emotion within me. I never left a conversation with God without feeling emotionally drained from the experience. Ignoring the fact that I was talking with God, not something that can actually be ignored, He was right that I always found myself experiencing the extremes of emotion. Already in this conversation, which I knew to be nowhere near complete, I had been filled with great happiness and joy at the thought of being able to see Eve again and then quickly had been overcome with guilt and failure at not being able to prevent the need for Jesus to die for humanity. I understood that because I had been created in perfection, my emotions were heightened to reach levels above what others are capable of feeling, but these limits were never pushed as far as when talking to God. He wanted me to experience peace of mind as well as a calm soul. He did not want me to feel that I had failed, but He reminded me that I had been created in perfection in His own design.

His sacrifice had always been part of the plan for returning humankind to that very design and life in the Garden. My efforts had not been a failure and had served the purpose well. In fact, my success in the end would bring back paradise on earth. His sacrifice on earth would be brutal for Him and painful for others to watch, but through it many more would come to find His love and be saved. Still, the end would be the same, and peace would be victorious as long as I was able to complete the missions before me, especially the one true goal that had always been set for me. I began searching my memories to figure out what true goal He could be talking about. As far as I could remember, the goal was general overall: protect humanity and bring as many people as possible to God's love. Jesus told me to relax and not worry about it right now. He would discuss it with me in a few days when we talked in that very place again.

Assuming that our time at that place was over, at least for now, I began to pack up our things, preparing to leave. Jesus simply told me to sit and clear my heart and soul of guilt. He then took a piece of bread, broke some off, and gave it to me to eat. After that He filled a cup with water for me to drink. He told me that through that act, He was symbolically acting out the sacrifice of His body and blood for all of humanity. I had no idea at the time what I had just experienced. Later when I realized that this had been a truly special moment, I broke down in tears at the immense honor I had never known was being granted to me. Even now when I think about that gift, I wonder how I ever could have doubted my faith or my mission.

Following my first of thousands of communions, Jesus said that we needed to get back to His disciples. This time while we were walking, we continued to talk. The conversation was generally light and friendly, a nice change from the serious topics we had been covering previously. During that time, He actually spoke about His disciples. It quickly became evident that He felt a deep connection and trust toward each and every one of the twelve. It was more than Godly love, but the human qualities of friendship and camaraderie. Naturally, I was especially interested in hearing about Andrew, who had found me and taken me to meet Jesus. Andrew had told me some about his life as a fisherman and then as he had become a follower of John the Baptist. One day Jesus had come to John, leading Andrew to understand Jesus to be the Messiah that the world had been waiting for. I had to admit that I had never known what to think of those Messiah rumors. Of course I had heard the stories and promises during my many years on earth, among many other supposed promises from God that had never seemed even remotely believable. I had quickly come to learn that humans would often use the notions of "God's will" or other empty promises of God's plan in order to gain money, power, or a position of control. With my personal experience talking to God and the feelings God used to guide me on the path of my missions, I saw through many of those stories as being human in origin. Still, once in a while, I would come across a story that seemed possible and I believed to be true. Now, with Jesus on earth, I obviously knew that the promise of the Messiah was in fact true.

I was moved to comment to Jesus about how amazing it was to me that Andrew had been able to have such faith from the very beginning. I was even more impressed that he did it without the personal experiences I had been able to hold close to my heart. Jesus truly had a special place for all of His disciples, but Andrew as the first was quite important. That was why Andrew had been sent to find me and talk with me before bringing me to Jesus. That was the strength of his role. While others were good at working large crowds or making other preparations, Andrew was exceptionally skilled at dealing with individuals and looking out for that personal connection needed for true faith to grow.

Hearing how special Andrew was, I felt honored that he had been chosen to seek me out. While I had been searching for the teacher, He had sent Andrew to find me. I could not believe that I had ever doubted anything, knowing just how blessed and important I truly was. Then Jesus shocked me again by asking me to do some favors for Him. Of course I would have done anything for Jesus. I simply had no idea what He could have needed me for at that point. I had heard His whole plan and I saw no place for me to add anything or to help Him. It turned out that He was not specifically asking for me to help Him, but instead to help look out for others. The next few days were going to be quite difficult for everybody, but especially for three of His disciples. I promised that no matter what else happened, I would look out for all of them, paying special attention to those needing it most. He told me that Jesus and His disciples would share a final meal, after which things would begin to happen quickly. During that time there would be many chances and temptations for them to lose their faith. Jesus knew eventually they would all be fine, but He asked that I help them in the short term in hopes of keeping them safe physically, as well as spiritually. As we neared the location for His dinner with His disciples, He left me with the promise that not only would He see me in a few days to answer my question, but also reassured me that everything was and would remain as it should be. He promised me that this second flood would offer all of humanity a cleansed soul, allowing for the path to the eternal Garden for humankind to be easier for all.

CHAPTER 36

SURVIVING THE DARKNESS

I am sure that you are well aware of the events that followed that dinner between Jesus and His disciples. If you are expecting a long description of those horrible scenes, then you will be greatly disappointed, because that will not be something I talk about here. I see no reason in going into a description of the extreme pain and suffering of anybody just to do so. Besides, it isn't like I actually was there watching Jesus be tortured and executed anyway. Instead I was busy taking care of the favor that He had asked me to do for Him during our conversation on my property. That doesn't mean that I don't know exactly how the Romans handled prisoners in those days. Having spent much time in the Empire, I became quite familiar with the Romans' extreme practices. Seeing as how many saw Jesus to be one of the biggest threats to the Empire in ages, I could tell you without being there that anything you think you can imagine in regard to His suffering falls well short of reality. To think about those practices makes me sick to this day to know how close I had been to giving up on my true path and walking away from a God who was so willing to endure such atrocities for the likes of me and all of humanity. Beyond that I sometimes struggle with the fact that I did so much to try to save that very Roman Empire. I know that the good I saw and hoped to save was not the powers that executed Jesus, but ever since then I have never been able to travel through the region with the same appreciation as I once had for the achievements of the Roman Empire.

Now, the story of the passion of Jesus is clearly more important than my changing views of the Empire, but as I said, I cannot really add to the details of that story to increase your understanding. On the other hand, I am sure that you haven't heard the story of my life during those days. After my earlier confusion and fear that somebody had figured out who I truly was, I made special effort to ensure that my presence was always kept as quiet as possible. Even though my fear was unwarranted given that it was God who had known my true identity, I decided to learn from that momentary scare and protect myself, and more importantly my mission, through secrecy. So, while Jesus was suffering in ways that nobody should ever be treated, I did my best to fulfill my promise to Him to help His disciples through that difficult time. Most of them were simply too scared to allow themselves to be seen in public. They found a safe home and were hiding from the soldiers there. To be honest, with the capture of Jesus, there was not a lot of searching going on for the disciples. Don't get me wrong; if one of them happened to find himself in the presence of a Roman soldier, then the soldier would most likely have captured him, but there was no extensive search going on to hunt anybody down at that point. As far as the soldiers were concerned, they had captured the head of the threatening group, and the followers would lose heart, especially after seeing what was to be done to Jesus. Still, I can't really blame the disciples for hiding out during that time. It must have been incredibly scary for them. So, with most of them staying out of sight together, it made it easy for me to talk to all of them at one time. Knowing how scared they were, I didn't do much more than simply encourage them to stay together in that home where they were safe. I knew that if they stayed out of sight for a couple of days and stuck together, it would make it easier for the future plans to begin to unfold in a few days. I offered them some words of comfort and faith in God, encouraging them to remember what they had learned from Jesus. If they shared in their memories and strengthened each other, everything would be just as God had planned and they would be rewarded soon.

While the majority of the disciples were safely hidden away, there were three that I had to seek out in order to help. Jesus had known that this would be the case and had prepared me for what help the three would need from me. The first one who I would find was the easiest to help find his way. He was also one whose story has endured somewhat through the years as well: Peter. It is true that Jesus told Peter that he would deny any knowledge of Jesus three times. Now, Peter of course did not believe that he could possibly betray his faith. Arrogance and pride are often to blame for the falling of seemingly strong men all through history, as I have discussed many times. That fact made it even more important to find Peter and keep him from falling too far following his denials. A man of lesser faith denying Jesus would find it much easier to recover what little faith he had quickly, but a man such as Peter was a different story. Jesus told me that without any help at all Peter would eventually return to his faith, but it would take a long time, and that should not be allowed to happen. I was to find Peter and keep him strong in his faith despite his prideful fall of denial.

After Peter had denied Jesus for the third time, I found him cowering and crying in a dark corner, huddled in the shadows. He was clearly ashamed at his failure, something I could very easily relate to, given all of the massive failures in my own life. Still, it only took me a few moments to help him see things in a better way. As Jesus had said, Peter would return to his faith, but I have no idea how long it would have taken him to see the points I had prepared to help guide him back on path. I simply pointed out a few facts for him. Jesus had said that three times Peter would deny knowing anything about or following the teachings of Jesus. Even after knowing that he was going to be tempted to do so and swearing his faith to Jesus, Peter still made the denials. After assuring Peter that I wasn't trying to make him feel worse, he calmed down enough to allow me to make my next point. Jesus had also told Peter that he would be a great man of faith and love for God moving forward in building the church and continuing to teach the lessons of Jesus. So, if Jesus was right about the denials, it would only be natural to assume that He was also right about the other things He had told Peter of what was to come. Hearing this laid out in that manner allowed Peter to fight through his anger and self-loathing so that he could see the bigger picture of his life. He regained his stoic control and strengthened his faith in God. With his heart and mind set at ease, Peter rose from the shadows and embraced me as a brother in faith before seeking out some quiet privacy to pray, reflect, and consider his future.

The second of the disciples that Jesus asked me to look out for might surprise you. He was by far the most complicated of the three to figure out and handle, but he was also the one that Jesus was most adamant that I find and help. So, when I finished talking to Peter, I set off to find Judas. I know that the common thinking for most, even surviving to modern times, is that Judas betrayed Jesus out of selfish greed and then killed himself when he realized what he had done. Yes, Judas was the one who led the soldiers to find Jesus that night, but the story never was that simple—you should know that by now. I won't bore you by going into great extremes to tell you all of the details about how everything came to play out as the story you know, but instead I will simply appeal to your common sense. God was intending to come to earth in the human form of Jesus for the sole purpose of sacrificing Himself. In order for this to work out according to His plan, the soldiers needed to come to Him. Turning Himself in to the soldiers would have caused an extreme commotion and most likely cost many more people their lives. To help facilitate His peaceful capture, Jesus needed somebody to lead the soldiers to where He was that night. Plus, although he was human, Jesus was also still God and could not have been deceived by any human. Nearly every version of the story recounts how following dinner, Jesus made a comment to Judas about doing what needed to be done. This was not merely an acknowledgement of what was going to happen, but was actually Jesus giving instructions to Judas. This was not an act of betrayal but a loyal disciple following the orders of his God in order to help fulfill the most important mission any man had ever been given, my own missions included.

Understanding that to be the case, I wasn't sure what to expect when I found Judas. Part of me hoped that he would simply need a few words of comfort to be reminded of his vital role in God's plan. On the other hand, because Judas did what he was instructed to do, Jesus was being tortured and was going to be executed. That is a knowledge that no man should ever have to bear. I knew how crushing it was when I had been told of what was to happen; I couldn't imagine how Judas must have been feeling. When I found Judas huddled under a tree, I realized just how easy and calm Peter had been. Maybe if I had been able to find him sooner, I could have done more to help Judas.

If I had it to do over again, I would have ignored Peter at first, at least until after I took care of Judas. It was a mistake on my part. I thought that Peter would be more upset because he had such pride, which as you saw actually made it easier to help bring him back to his faith. With Judas having actually been given an active role in God's plan, I assumed that he would be more at peace with what he had done. Of all of the many mistakes I have made in my life, this one is among the few that still haunt me at times.

By the time I got to Judas, he was extremely distraught and no longer able to fully comprehend reality. I tried talking with him to show him just how vital he had been in helping all of humanity, but my words did little to comfort him. He began shaking with tears as he just kept saying that he had killed God. I know that part of him understood that he had done what was needed and what he had been instructed to do, as occasionally through his whimpering he would reference talking to Jesus about it ahead of time. Somewhere in his mind, he knew that he had been chosen to play a specific part in God's plan. But that was pushed aside by the guilt he felt, and nothing I said seemed to help him. Finally, he stopped shaking and looked to the sky. He started praying for forgiveness, but his words were choked off by the tears still streaming down his face.

Wanting to help him in any way that I could, I picked up the prayer for him. I honestly am not sure what I said, but I know that by the time I was done praying for Judas, I was emotionally drained and exhausted myself. When I noticed that I no longer heard Judas weeping, I looked down to see that he was completely silent. At first I thought that he had fallen asleep from the strain, but I quickly realized that he was not sleeping. Even before I checked to see if he was still breathing, I knew the answer; Judas had died in my arms while I had been praying for him to find peace. In the end, the heartbreak of what he had done was too much for him, and he had found the only peace he could. I like to think that when he entered the Garden, he was greeted by Eve with a big, comforting hug and led to a very special place to relax and enjoy eternity in peace. While this was not what I had originally hoped for or intended, I saw that it was what was needed for Judas to find the true peace that he needed and deserved.

The third and final disciple that Jesus asked me to help out was the most personal of the three, so I had saved him for last on my list. He also was the one I felt would be most able to hold out until I found him. Maybe that was because even though I had only recently met him, I did feel a very strong connection to Andrew. While it could have simply been because he had been the one sent to find me and bring me to Jesus, I honestly think that it had more to do with being the first. I was the first human, period, and that was something I took to be a serious responsibility, especially after beginning my missions. Andrew was the first to follow Jesus, and from what I could pick up, he took that as a great honor that he did not want to tarnish in any way. The position of being first also carried with it the burden of feeling responsible for protecting Jesus. For that reason Andrew was experiencing a very personal struggle, knowing what was going on with Jesus. The inner turmoil was clearly visible on his face and in his body language, even from a distance. Andrew was clearly hurting, knowing that nothing could be done to save his Teacher, but even more so that he could not save his friend. To me, Jesus was God. Yes, He was in human form, and I felt sick knowing the degrees of torture that He was enduring, but He was still God, and I knew that everything was working how He had planned. Then again, I had not spent years traveling, living, and learning from Him in this human form, as Andrew had done. For him, being the first carried a very heavy extra burden. I know that the other disciples were hurting as well, but none other than Judas came close to the true pain that Andrew felt.

With no clear options in mind, I decided to simply tell Andrew my true story. I figured that Jesus had already trusted him to send him to me with my real name, so I should trust him with my tale. I guess that I should not have been too surprised at discovering that Andrew was not shocked at all when I started to tell him about my life. I quickly became curious to know if the others knew about me as well. Andrew explained that he was the only one that knew the truth. He had been told in a private conversation with Jesus before being sent out to find me. If using my name hadn't gotten my attention enough to follow him, Jesus had given him the rest of the story to convince me to follow.

When I expressed surprise about how easy it was for him to simply accept my story as true, Andrew actually laughed. While that was not my intention, it was kind of nice to know that at least for a moment he found humor in the world again. When he regained his composure, he explained to me why he had laughed. To hear him tell me his thinking truly made me sit back in amazement at how silly it really was of me to be surprised. For years Andrew had been following

God in human form sent to be a sacrifice for humanity. In that time he had witnessed many miracles, including the healing of horrible diseases and even the raising of the dead, so from his perspective, nothing could truly be seen as shocking. At that point I felt a bit like the naïve beginner taught an obvious lesson by a more experienced person, but then Andrew added one more thought that bothered me.

One reason why my story was not entirely shocking to Andrew was that he had heard many other tales of a man cursed to live forever on earth. At first I thought that he meant me, but it seems that the one he was familiar with was tasked with leading humanity toward evil and sin. As soon as he told me this, Andrew got very quiet and tried to change the subject, as if he had just made a mistake and let something slip that I was not supposed to know. I wanted to ask more and push him to tell me everything about the other man. As hard as it was, I held back and didn't ask. I knew that Andrew was suffering over not being able to help Jesus, and it was obvious from his reaction that mentioning this other man to me only made things worse.

Naturally, I had heard many people claim that a stranger had led them to sin. It would have been impossible to live this long, completing my missions, without hearing this mentioned. I simply had always assumed that they were making excuses for their mistakes or that they were referring to Satan. Just thinking that name always gave me chills, as my mind flashed to an image God had once shown me of Satan leading my precious Eve to taste the fruit—no longer in the form of a snake, but in the form of a human of indescribable beauty and stature. Knowing that Satan was capable of taking on human form like this had always led me to believe that the man leading those people to sin was indeed that snake once again. Still, the way Andrew had talked about him did not make me think of Satan. Instead, I got the impression that he truly meant another human like me. My mind again flashed back to the stranger that had been talking to Saul and David so many years ago.

Before I could think about that any deeper, Andrew and I locked eyes. We knew everything at that moment. We could see the sky turn black, and our feelings shifted to match the dark color outside. We knew at that very moment Jesus had died. A cold chill growing from deep within our souls consumed us. There really is no way to describe it other than feeling that everything good in the world had simply vanished at once. I curled up in the corner and closed my eyes, seeing only blackness. No matter how hard I tried, I could see nothing but darkness: no Eve, no Garden, and no family. There was just a blank, black, empty void filling my world. I have no idea how long I kept my eyes closed, staring into the nothingness. I could hear my breathing, and I could hear Andrew breathing as well, but no words were spoken. There was nothing to say. Jesus was dead.

Then suddenly the black void I was staring into flashed a brilliant white. As the flash faded, I was no longer staring into nothing, but instead I was looking at the Garden. It was the dream from earlier, as I waited outside the house for Jesus. I was no longer sitting in a corner of a dark room with my arms wrapped around myself. Instead I was in an open area of the Garden, leaning against a tree with my arms wrapped around Eve as we watched our two sons, Cain and Abel, walk toward us. The cold that had been filling me was replaced by the warmth of perfect love. Just as quickly as it had appeared, it was taken from me when Andrew shook me back to reality. The sky had returned to normal, and we were both feeling more like usual, or at least as close as possible, given the circumstances.

Andrew began to panic over what would be done with the body. He was worried because the common practices of the Romans were not what one would consider respectful toward the remains of those executed. The best treatment one could generally hope for was to simply be tossed into a mass grave. I assured him that I had made special arrangements for the body of Jesus and that it was being taken to the tomb on my nearby property. With that crisis solved, Andrew began to ask what I knew of the other disciples, especially Peter. I explained about my conversation with Peter and promised Andrew that his brother was going to be stronger than ever. At that point I was finally able to get Andrew to sit down and relax enough to take a drink of water. I knew that he was simply looking for anything to keep him distracted and busy to avoid thinking about things related to what we both knew had happened. I tried talking to him about fishing and things from his life, but he was much more interested in my experiences. Hearing from me about how I learned in the Garden what and how to eat, use for shelter, and so much more, Andrew was able to relax and be taken away to other places in his mind. He started out just listening in order to let his mind drift, but after a while he began to ask questions about places I had been and people I had known. He took a particularly strong interest in learning about Byzantium and my experiences with the Greek regions. I talked for hours about those topics while Andrew seemed to absorb everything I said. I thought that he was asking questions to simply keep me talking, but later I learned that he put all of my information to good use in his own travels and teachings. With Peter I had used logic to show him his strength, and Judas had needed a peaceful and understanding soul to help him let go of his human guilt. But for Andrew I had simply needed to be a friend who was there during a hard period of time.

CHAPTER 37

TO LIGHT THE WAY

W hile Andrew and I continued to talk about anything and everything that either of us could think of, time seemed to have no meaning. We simply talked, oblivious to anything going on outside of the room we were in. There was no sense of fatigue, hunger, or thirst, as we seemed to just float through the hours, fully absorbed in our conversations as a protective shield from the pain of the outside world. After what we learned to be days, not hours, that all changed. As I finished up one of my stories, I felt a very strong pull to leave the house and go to the tomb on my property. Knowing that I needed to go alone, I encouraged Andrew to eat and rest, as his life was about to get much more hectic and interesting. I thanked Andrew for all he had done for me, even if he didn't understand how much he had helped me. With that said, I took off running for my property, knowing that something amazing was about to happen.

When I got to my property, I saw some Roman soldiers standing guard in front of a huge stone that had been placed to block the entrance to the tomb. I quickly hid behind a tree, not wanting to be seen. I knew that it was my property and I therefore had every right to be there, but for some reason I felt that I should stay hidden so that I could observe all that was going to happen. It did not take long for me to be rewarded for my decision. Suddenly a flash of light blinded the soldiers. For some reason I had seen the flash but was not blinded, so I could continue watching. Then I saw two angels standing next to the soldiers. They were whispering to the Romans and gently guiding them away from the tomb. With the guards gone, I began walking toward the stone. I wasn't sure how I was going to move that huge rock, but I had faith. When I reached the stone, I simply placed one hand upon it and found that it rolled away as if it was nothing more than a tiny pebble on a smooth surface. With the stone out of the way, I slowly bent down to look into the depths of the tomb. There, sitting on the stone platform, was Jesus. He was just sitting there as if He had been relaxing and waiting for me to get there. I immediately fell to His feet, struggling to find the fitting words to express my feelings at that moment, but nothing came out. Even though I had known what was going to happen, I found myself speechless at the honor of being able to witness the resurrection of Jesus following His sacrifice, which was needed because of my failures. Jesus simply placed His hands on my head and told me that no words were needed. Instead, I needed to listen, as our time alone would be short.

With His hands still on my head, He blessed me as a loyal and faithful servant of God. He continued to tell me that my path would become much more difficult from this point forward until the end. I knew that things up until now had not exactly been easy for me; so hearing that it was going to get even more difficult made me quite nervous. Still, following my conversation with Jesus just a few days ago outside of this very tomb, and only hours before his capture, my faith had been fully restored and strengthened to a point where it would never again be in question. God's sacrifice to die for humankind was something that I would never forget or allow to have been done for nothing. Hearing me express my now unbreakable faith, Jesus smiled and continued to tell me more of what was to come. Humanity had been cleansed by the literal flood thousands of years ago and now again by the flood of His mercy through His death and resurrection. There would not be a third flood of any kind to cleanse humanity again before the end. I felt confident that people would be told the story and would clearly accept God's love into their hearts. Jesus simply grinned and said that He wished it truly was that easy. He told me that many would still deny Him and in the end would perish. So, yes, I was still greatly needed to help guide as many as I could to find and to accept Him. The difference would be that now I would have much more help from the disciples as they spread the word and built churches all over the world. That, in turn, would leave me more time to work through my larger missions that would arise throughout the rest of humanity's time on earth.

I took that opening to ask Jesus about Andrew's comments regarding another human living through all of human history. I admit that I was still partly expecting and largely hoping to have Jesus tell me that it was just another false story spread through ignorance and deceit. Yet at the same time I can't honestly say that I was shocked when Jesus told me that the other man did indeed exist and had been working against me for thousands of years. Without knowing it, I had many times been fixing and correcting problems this stranger had created through his lies and deceptions. My mind quickly connected the thoughts and I jumped to the conclusion that when I stopped this other man, I would find the end of my missions and achieve my goal. In order to return to the arms of my Eve in the Garden and return humanity to a state of perfection, I had to find and put an end to this evil counterpart that I had never known existed. I asked Jesus why I had not been told this sooner. If I had known about him earlier, I might have been able to stop him one of those times when I had been close to him in the past. Jesus explained that my recent crisis of faith needed to be resolved before I would be able to find the proper strength and understanding to do what needed to be done. Even more importantly, humanity needed to be given this gift of God's grace in order for all to be cleansed this one last time. Being bathed in God's love would allow all of humanity to truly be able to accept God and return to the Garden in perfection for all eternity. I knew that He was right. Of course He was right; He was God. I also knew that had I known about this other man I would have simply become focused on finding him and not paid attention to the bigger picture. Jesus confirmed that only through working to care for all of humanity would I be able to find a way to complete the final true mission. That was the second time that Jesus had referred to a true outcome. I remembered that He had promised to explain it to me during this conversation. My first thought was that it was somehow hidden within the information that I had just learned, but I also sensed that there was something more.

Jesus told me that, yes, my last and true mission involved the other man, but it was not simply a case of stopping him. As with all of my other missions, I could not simply kill him. But this time I would also not be able to arrange for his death at the hands of another. It seems that just as I could not die a human death, the other man could not be killed, not even by me. In the same manner, he could not kill me. I could stop his plans, and he would continue in his attempts to tip the scales toward Satan and sin. The only way that I could succeed was to bring this man back to God's fold. Meanwhile, he would continue leading mankind to sin in hopes of convincing people to deny God. If this were to happen, there would be no chance for any souls still lacking in faith to be saved. I realized then what Jesus had meant when He told me that my faith needed to be secured and strengthened through this experience. Now that I knew this information, I felt quite overwhelmed. On the other hand, I now knew what needed to be done as well as the consequences of my failure.

I could hear some women a short ways from the tomb. They were no doubt coming to mourn the death of Jesus. I knew that once they got to the tomb, I would not have another chance to talk with Jesus, so I needed to make the best use of what little time I had left for this conversation. I simply asked Jesus how I would know this man when I found him. I had met many men that I believed to be evil and yet none of them had been this man, so I wondered what would be different. The times that I had seen him with Saul and David had been so fast and at such a distance that I doubted that I could recognize him again, even if he wasn't altering his appearance as I had learned to do. Jesus took my hands and looked straight into my eyes to tell me that yes it was that same man that I was thinking about, but that I would never have trouble recognizing him once I stopped looking with my eyes and learned to look with my heart. The man that I sought and the man I needed to return to God's loving embrace in order to succeed in my true mission and bring me back to my family in the Garden and restore perfection was none other than my eldest son, Cain.

David L. Bishop devoted most of his life to the study of politics, philosophy, and history before making a course change to pursue writing. Years of academic study, a childhood in a Lutheran household, and a deep-seated desire to understand the "why" questions of life provided a natural environment for the development of his novel, *The Gospel of Adam.*

He currently resides in Cape Girardeau, Missouri.

16404191R00161

Made in the USA
Middletown, DE
14 December 2014